About the author

Ian Callinan is a former Hi   e
nation's highest civil honour   )
'for service to the judiciary and the practice of law, to the arts and to the community'. He has served on the boards of numerous publicly-funded organisations – including the ABC and the Australian Defence Force Academy – and, most recently, was the commissioner for the inquiry into the outbreak of equine influenza in Australia. Besides being a successful novelist and playwright, he has written reviews, short stories, and occasional pieces – as well as a vast amount of legal material. One of his great interests over many years has been art, and he has been a member of the boards of several high-profile art galleries – his most recent appointment being to the council of the National Gallery of Australia.

Ian Callinan lives in Brisbane with his wife and two cattle dogs.

Other works by Ian Callinan include:

Novels

The Lawyer and the Libertine
The Coroner's Conscience
The Missing Masterpiece
Appointment at Amalfi

Plays

Brazilian Blue
The Cellophane Ceiling
The Acquisition

The Russian Master

A novel

by

Ian Callinan

Central Queensland
UNIVERSITY
PRESS

First published in 2008 by CQU Press

PO Box 1615
Rockhampton
Queensland 4700

Ph: (07) 4923 2520
Fax: (07) 4923 2525
Email: cqupress@cqu.edu.au
www.outbackbooks.com

Copyright © 2008 Ian Callinan

Ian Callinan asserts his moral right to be identified as the author of this book.
All rights reserved. Apart from any fair dealing for the purpose of private study, research, criticism or review, as permitted under the *Copyright Act of 1968*, no part may be reproduced by any process without written permission from the publisher.

This is a work of fiction. Names, places, characters and incidents are either the product of the author's imagination or are used fictitiously. Any resemblance to real persons, living or dead, or to real organisations, businesses or establishments, is purely coincidental.

National Library of Australia
Cataloguing-in-Publication entry:

Callinan, Ian
The Russian master

ISBN: 978 1 921274 09 1 (pbk)

I. Title

A823.3

Cover painting by Michelle Thornton
Cover design by Leslie Robinson
Typeset by Designs To Print
Printed and Bound by Griffin Press

I dedicate this book to the memory of my good friend, the late David Myers.

Acknowledgements

For some time before he was suddenly afflicted with a devastating terminal illness, Professor David Myers – the late editor and publisher of CQU Press – and I discussed the possibility of a sequel to *The Missing Masterpiece*. As always, he was encouraging. This book owes much to that encouragement. I miss it now as I miss his patience, scholarliness, and friendship.

I also wish to express my appreciation of Mrs Kaye de Jersey's advice and proofreading of the manuscript for this book.

Ian Callinan, February 2008.

Contents

1	Opportunity Knocks ...	1
2	An Eccentric Dealer ...	13
3	Gloria Reflective ...	23
4	A Career Move ...	39
5	The Lure of Russia ...	53
6	Gloria by the Ganges ...	61
7	At the Swinging Gate ...	75
8	Solutions Required ...	92
9	A Violent Encounter ...	105
10	The Return of Gloria ...	120
11	Londys on the Move ...	154
12	A Violent and a Gentle Confrontation ...	168
13	Davenport Takes Off ...	182
14	A Day in the Country ...	203
15	A Secret Visit ...	220
16	Rendezvous in St Petersburg ...	238
17	The Rivals Meet ...	253

1

Opportunity Knocks

There it was, on page three of *Jove*:

> The chief executive of Londys, Gerald de Pyne, has announced that he has appointed the Australian expert on the Spanish artist Divera, Davenport Jones, manager of the firm's topographical section. The appointment is seen as a move by Londys to strengthen their expertise in a field in which their competitors have dominated in recent years.

An account of Davenport's curatorial career in Australia followed, emphasizing his role in the Divera affair, and extolling his experience as the leading expert with Jeffrey's, the premier art auctioneering firm in the country.

There was a photograph of Davenport above the article. It showed him in profile, emerging from the Antipodean Museum in Australia where he had scored his great triumph. He was wearing his determined expression, the one he always adopted when he was overcome by shyness. The image was selected from many that photographers and video-camera operators had lined up to take as the story of the fake Divera reverberated around the art world.

Davenport rubbed his finger across the page. How could a piece of paper be so glossy? Who would have imagined that he, Davenport, would be the subject of a whole column in the finest art magazine in the world? The likelihood that money had changed hands between Gerald and the editor didn't distress Davenport. He was becoming a realist about the art world.

He turned the page. Overleaf there was an illustration of an eight-sided Chinese Imperial yellow baluster vase, guan glazed, forty centimeters high, six character seal and mark of Yongz Leng, and of the period 1723 to 1735. The only other words on the page were 'Stanleys, Mayfair'. If you didn't know where Stanleys carried on their craft, 'business' was too coarse a word for what they conducted, you weren't the sort of person with whom they cared to deal. He could only wonder at the price of the vase. Gerald had told him that a full page of *Jove* cost three thousand pounds.

He flipped back to the previous page, not because of vanity, but modesty. He had tried to explain to one of the journalists how the debacle of the Divera would never have occurred but for his initial gullibility, but no one was interested. The papers had cast Manning as the culprit and Davenport the hero, and once they had done that, no revisionism was allowed.

Davenport studied the photograph of himself. In it he was still wearing the thick, horn-rimmed spectacles he had put on to examine a Heysen drawing that his colleague Beverley Leer had asked him to verify. He looked scholarly as well as determined. It never would have occurred to him that his open, friendly face and thick hair – overdue for a cut, gave him a vulnerable look that some women found attractive. Had he been more intuitive sexually, he would have noticed the look of admiration in Beverley's eyes.

He heard a knock on his door. Before he could open it, Gerald de Pyne entered. The CEO was perhaps five years older than Davenport but the chronology was misleading. In cunning, he could have been a hundred years older. He wore a shirt with wide stripes under his pin-striped suit. It was, in the current fashion, unbuttoned at the neck. Only the young but senior executives, the partners in the big legal firms, and barristers, travelled to and from work tieless in summer.

Opportunity Knocks

It was more than mere fashion slumming. The whole world did that nowadays. It was also to demonstrate that despite their diligence and application, they had some time for – and understood – leisure.

De Pyne sat in the reproduction Empire chair on the other side of Davenport's desk. He buttoned his collar and took a yellow tie out of his suit coat. He tied it as he spoke to Davenport. "Settling in all right old man?" he asked.

Davenport suspected that this was the formula Gerald's housemaster at Brenton had used with generations of unhappy boys when first severed from their homes and families. Sometimes Gerald was avuncular, but sometimes he was uncommunicative – as if suppressing a justified anger for a great grievance. Today, plainly, was a day for avuncularity.

"Just a few words old chap." he continued, "That suit you're wearing, you don't think it's a little on the shiny side?"

Davenport had bought the suit in Regent Street the day after he had arrived in London. "It's a Rintori; fine wool, a leading Italian maker they told me."

"Bespoke tailors to the Mafia. I think you'd better keep it for holidays in Palermo. I'll give you the name of a good outfitter. You don't have to go to Saville Row these days. Even the Arab oil millionaires don't buy there now. Room satisfactory?"

Davenport looked around, taking in the peacock-blue walls painted in the same tone as the auction galleries, the white cornices and joinery, the cochineal rug from Isphahan, the partner's desk, and the matching Empire chairs only about fifty years out of period. It was a little on the grand side for Davenport, but he agreed with de Pyne that it was satisfactory.

"By the way what's your telephone number?" de Pyne asked.

"I wasn't aware it had changed."

"Your new flat, I mean?"

"I haven't got a new flat. I'm still in the one you gave me."

"Yes, but that was just to allow you to relocate. You have to be out by Saturday, you know."

"Nobody told me that."

"Bloody human resources department – never been any good since they changed their name from personnel. Still, we can't make exceptions, not even for our brilliant imports. Saturday's the deadline I'm afraid."

"But I haven't any idea where to go, what to look for, what I should pay."

"The last won't be an issue. Pay what you can afford and not a penny more."

"But today's Tuesday. How can I find somewhere to move into by Saturday?"

"I'll get Elena to help you. Time's not the only thing that little woman's got on her hands."

Elena, a compact, self-assured redhead of thirty years was an accountant, and nominally second in charge of the accounts section. She was far more competent than Ewan McKey, the middle-aged Scotsman who had been its manager for fifteen years and was an occasional drinking companion of de Pyne.

"You'd better set aside tomorrow for house hunting. I'll alert Elena, and McKey. It won't hurt him to do a solid eight hours for once." After a momentary pause, he added, "You Australians invented the eight-hour day didn't you?"

"So some politicians claim. But I haven't seen too many eight-hour days worked here."

"Not necessary when you're efficient old boy. Glad everything's going smoothly." De Pyne stood up, preparatory to leaving. "We'll have to have a talk soon. New blood, that's what we want. That's why we went to the colonies...the new world," he corrected himself, "to get some of that Australian vigour – aggression even. Like your fast bowlers, knock your bloody head off if they can. Ever play cricket Davenport?"

"A little, at school. By the way, Gerald, England invented bodyline."

"That's as may be." He turned before he closed the door behind him. "Saturday's the deadline. That apartment you're in is twelve hundred quid a week, you know. I'll tell Elena."

This was not the first time in the last month that Davenport asked himself what he was doing here. He had visited the United Kingdom twice before, but living and working in London was very different from taking in the museums and browsing in the British Library. Several of his friends in other professions had lived and worked for some years in this city and had warned him of the horrendous prices, the cold wet weather, and the inescapable congestion of the sprawling metropolis. He had thought that he was prepared for all of it. But the reality was harsher than he had imagined. He hoped that in time things would improve but, for the present, the urgent need to find an affordable place to live was just another, almost intolerable burden to carry.

The knock on the door startled him into calling out 'come in' louder than he had intended.

"It's all right," Elena said as she put her head around the door. "I'm not a deckhand. Is it safe to enter?"

Davenport stood up, confused. "Sorry. I got a fright when you knocked. Please sit down." He pulled out the chair that de Pyne has just vacated.

"I've been seconded to house hunting duties. I don't envy you, having three days to find somewhere bearable to live in this city."

"Where do you live?" Davenport asked.

"Nowhere fashionable; not somewhere that would suit you. Anyway, I want to move myself."

"I wouldn't even know what *was* fashionable here. Where I lived in Australia certainly wasn't."

"Well, some of the people in here laugh at me when I tell them I live at Wimbledon. The usual response is, 'Parking must be difficult when the tournament's on'. If what they claimed about where they lived was true, Notting Hill Gate must occupy half the Home Counties. I don't know what they're paying you - quite a lot I expect - but you'll need all of it. Everything's a compromise in a big city like this. Roomy flat, long way out, not near a tube, rent a lot cheaper, but taxi fare's more than a terrorist's ransom. There is

Canary Wharf I suppose. All mod cons. Wouldn't recommend it myself. Full of people in finance, as they'll tell you. My bet is one in five will end up doing time."

"It's good of you to help me."

"Superiors' orders, that's what I am acting under. And no Nuremberg defence either. You'd better make no other arrangements for the rest of the week. I'll pick you up at the front door at 9 am. In the meantime, start reading the property pages of the papers."

The traffic in Piccadilly four hundred yards away was no more than a muffled drone, but Davenport knew that if he were to make his way down there now he would be edged off the kerb by the endless stream of tourists, and commuters, already late, dashing out of Green Park Station to their workplaces in St James and Bond Street. How brave Elena was, and generous too, to offer to drive him, paying the Lord Mayor's congestion tax, and joining the taxis and the grand English and European touring cars that made the roads of this district their own.

Just before he had left Australia, one of Gloria's, his former wife's friends had told him that his erstwhile spouse had written that she had laughed aloud at the news that Davenport seemed to be doing well in private enterprise. "He's such a provincial," she had pronounced with all the authority of her travels to the Ashrams of India and Nepal, and after she had climbed the first twelve thousand feet of Everest.

Davenport had the impression then that she had been mentally stalking him, trying to make sure that she was not only always aware of his whereabouts, but also – and worse – that she was seeking to know precisely what he was doing, and where he was doing it. Her friend, with whom she had attended teachers training college, had made a point of telling Davenport that Gloria was talking about going to Beijing to conduct a course in English at the University of Engineering there. He wondered what had happened to Walter – the man Gloria had run off with. But despite the pause and the expectant look on his informant's face, Davenport's only response was, "I understand it gets very cold in Beijing in winter."

Opportunity Knocks

Gerald's visit had unsettled him. He stood in front of the small mirror that the previous occupant of the room had fixed to the back of the door. Except that his suit didn't have the chalk stripes of de Pyne's, he couldn't see anything wrong with it. Its defects would remain a mystery, like so many other mysteries in this country: words, the pronunciation of which bore no resemblance to the phonetics of their letters; the date upon which the shooting season started; when, or even whether, it was permissible to wear brown shoes in London; the occasions upon which you could adopt an estuarine accent, and those when southern educated English only was obligatory. So much to know. Davenport suspected that outsiders were never allowed to know it all. One acquaintance who had won a scholarship to Oxford and lived in England for a few years afterwards had advised him to act exactly as the English expected most Australians to act. "Always demand beer rather than wine; don't hesitate to get pissed at every opportunity. Don't on any account try to speak with an English accent. Mock all English sportsmen and sporting teams. And, depending on the company, point out that the English are still water, soap and deodorant shy. The last can be a bit risky but sometimes it goes over well. When I woke up to what was expected, I had more invitations on my mantelpiece than Santa gets cards in December."

That might have been the form at Oxford fifteen years before, but Davenport doubted that it would have been acceptable in Mayfair now. At one point, Gerald had suggested that Davenport would have to do his share of conducting the auctions after he had settled in. But Davenport couldn't imagine himself hectoring and mocking the clients as Tom Jeffery did when he was auctioning paintings in Australia.

"Not yet," he had said. He didn't explain that Jefferey had banned him from doing any more auctions after his first two.

"Not aggressive enough," his old boss had said. "The way you go on you couldn't sell a beer to a sunstruck shearer on the Barcoo. This isn't the perfume department at David Jones's. You might think we're selling paintings, but we're not. We're selling prestige. The *nouveaux riches* don't know what they have to have on their walls to gain it. We've got to tell them. And we've got to do it clearly, aggressively. That's how they've made their money, by being aggressive. They don't understand any other way of doing business." Jefferey had been quick to see – and to accept – that Davenport shouldn't conduct any auctions. He had come to realise Davenport's courtesy, quiet voice and scholarly understanding provided a good foil for his own forceful behaviour in dealing with clients.

Gerald had flown out from London to recruit Davenport. He had telephoned first, merely to ask him whether he would be prepared to talk to him face to face. Davenport knew, of course, who he was. It did not occur to him, however, that de Pyne might wish to employ him. Davenport assumed that he was coming to Australia anyway, and that he probably wanted him to verify a Divera sketch.

They had met at Gerald's hotel. He had a suite with a sitting room that overlooked the park. He began to explain the purpose of his visit immediately after Davenport had refused a glass of champagne from the bottle upon which he was well advanced.

"Hybrid vigour. That's what Londys need." Davenport had no idea what he was talking about. "There's not a lot of that in England these days I can tell you."

Davenport thought it prudent to nod knowingly.

"I went to Londys to be truly multi-dimensional. The days of debs and debs' delights at the front counter and in the back room are over."

Davenport nodded.

"Remember that scene in 'The Verdict' when they tell James Mason that Paul Newman's expert is a black man. He instructs his underlings that he wants a black lawyer at the bar table beside him for the trial. Well, that's the sort of thing I want."

"Well Africa's your place then," Davenport offered.

"I was speaking metaphorically."

"Of course."

"We've got a lot of clients in the col…Australia, that is. In America too, North America mainly. In the past, we also had a lot of clients – buyers mainly – in the Argentine. That was before the war: one of the richest countries in the world then. It's a good source for product these days, but not buyers."

Davenport, who had more than a suspicion that the famous fake Divera had originated there, shook his head this time. "I'd be a bit careful about what I found in Buenos Aires."

"Nonsense. The great ranchers of the Pampas visited Madrid, Paris, and London all the time. Anything could turn up there. Last year there was a rumour about a Goya. Nothing came of it, but there will be finds, big ones. Sure you won't join me?" He asked as he poured the last of the champagne into his glass. "Best cure of all for jet-lag." His eyes were closing and opening.

"You wanted to see me...?" Davenport left the question unfinished.

"What do you think I've been talking about?"

"Well, Goya, hybrid vigour, and so on."

"Wrong. I've been talking about the rejuvenation of Londys."

"Yes, of course."

"For decades we were the most famous auction house in the world. I want to put us up there again."

"It's very competitive out here," Davenport, anxious to deter any increase in local competition, warned.

"There must be some very good opportunities here. The country's full of gold and gold miners, entrepreneurs with vastly more money than class. Exactly the clientele we want. That's another string to your bow. You'll know who they are."

"Look, I can't divulge my employer's secrets. Don't forget I'm also a director at Jeffrey's."

"I don't want client lists old boy, just your retentive memory."

Davenport frowned. "I'm afraid I don't understand." For a moment he thought that Gerald had fallen asleep, but then the Englishman's eyes re-opened suddenly.

"If I were to order a half-bottle, would you take a glass?"

"Thank you no. I'm driving."

"Driving to work. Those were the days. Wish I could. The firm puts on a car and driver, but it's not the same. Bloody congestion charge! Soon it'll cost more to enter the city than to buy the petrol for the ride. Now, where was I?"

"You were about to tell me why you wanted to talk to me."

"I want you to work for me?"

"In Australia?"

"Certainly not. London, the UK, Blighty – and wherever the hell else we can winkle out arts and objects from ignorant widows and failing tycoons."

"Is that the reason why you flew twelve thousand miles; to offer me a job?"

"Principally. It was also an opportune time to give the Singapore branch a kick in the arse."

"Well, I'm quite comfortable here thank you."

"With Jefferey? Wouldn't know a Pollock from a Vemeer. You deserve better than that."

"I told you, I'm a director. I've got an interest in the firm."

"I bet he made you sign a restraint of trade clause as a condition of giving you some shares."

"He didn't actually *give* me my shares."

"Really? Anyway, what's the point of having a share in a Ford when you could be driving a Rolls? In a manner of speaking that is. Any restraint he's got on you wouldn't operate outside Australia. Probably wouldn't even in Australia. They're usually not worth the paper they're written on."

"Look, I appreciate the offer, and you coming all this way to make it, but I've no wish to go work in England."

"London, not England. You know what Dr Johnson said about London. A man who's tired of London is tired of life. Something like that. What's your package worth here?"

Startled by the bluntness of the question, Davenport answered it. "Two hundred thousand a year. That includes the car of course, and the dividends which I'm using to pay off the shares."

"How does two hundred thousand pounds a year strike you,

Opportunity Knocks

no car, no repayments, no strings, just the money? There could be bonuses on top of that for special finds."

Davenport still looked unimpressed. De Pyne was unused to indifference to money. He decided to switch to aesthetics. "Do you have any idea of the range of works that pass through our hands. In the season, our salesrooms are more exciting than most of the great museums in the world. You will be part of that, feasting your eyes on and handling Guardis, Rembrandts, Picassos, Rothkos - weekly. No person of culture could pass that up."

"If you want, what did you call it, hybrid vigour, why don't you go to the United States? There's been a lot of mixed marrying there. Anyway you've got a local branch here. Why not transfer someone from it?"

"Two reasons: it's not really a branch; it's a kind of a franchise. That's commercial in confidence. Secondly, none of them are any bloody good. Like that cricketer you had, can't field, can't bowl, can't throw, can't bat. Couldn't recognise a Munnings at five paces. No, I want someone with new ideas and an international reputation. That coup of yours with the fake Divera was front page news throughout the art world."

"I do appreciate the offer but I'm settled here thank you."

The more unreceptive Davenport was, the more determined Gerald became. "I like your bargaining style too. You've got a real knack for talking a price up. What about I go back to the board to see if I can get another fifty?"

"Thank you, no. Now I really had better be going." Davenport stood up. He was uncertain whether he should shake hands. Gerald jumped up from his chair.

"Think it over. I do have to talk to the locals so I'll be here for another forty-eight hours. I'll ring you before I leave. Think about it some more." He walked with Davenport to the door and paused. "Give me some advice. Is there anything special I should look at out here?"

"I don't suppose you're interested in Australian artists?"

"We get them in the salerooms. That would be something else

we'd get you to work on. But no, not this trip."

"I suppose the Jackson Pollock is our most famous acquisition but you'd have to go to Canberra to see that."

"Yes, of course, the Pollock. Now that was a brilliant piece of marketing. What was it, two, three million dollars, 1970s dollars, for an acre of drips?"

"It's worth a lot more now."

"Naturally, you made the market. If a national museum pays the price, that becomes the value, rather like a self-fulfilling prophecy. No, I don't think I'll make the detour. I'll call you." He sleepily ushered Davenport out the door.

2

An Eccentric Dealer

Just off the Kings Road near Worlds End, there is an enclave of fashionable dress shops, prohibitively expensive restaurants, and dealers in *objets* and antiques. The dress shops have been fitted out by London's leading shop fitters, and the furnishing of the restaurants is so minimalist that anything more nouvelle than an artfully arranged lettuce leaf would seem a glutton's feast. The *objets* in the dealers' shops are of old ormolu, and there is no piece of furniture, apart from the odd concealed replacement leg or two, younger than two hundred years.

Nestled between two of the dress shops there is a smaller shop front. It belongs to an art dealer named Rupert Collinridge, another old boy of Brenton. His neighbours would prefer that he were somewhere else. But he owns the freehold and will go, if he is offered sufficient money and is not in a contrary mood, in his own good time. In the meantime, he happily deals in paintings, selling mainly to the decorating trade – especially decorators who work in Palm Springs, San Francisco, New York, and Las Vegas.

Once, he made a spectacular sale to the designer of a new casino in Vegas. The subjects of the sale were six huge backdrops painted on canvas for a play that had been scheduled to open at the Strand Playhouse on the fifteenth of August 1940. The sets had never been used as the theatre was destroyed by a German bomb on the first of August, the day before they were to be delivered. They had languished in a disused warehouse in Earls Court until someone had found them and placed them in an auction sale at Olympia.

The style of the paintings had looked familiar to Rupert. He came to believe that they were the work of Bellario, an Italian who had lived in London from 1930 until he was interned in 1941. It was only after the war that he became famous throughout Europe as a portrait painter. Rupert knew that he could never prove that the sets were by Bellario, but then, as he said to himself, no one could prove they weren't.

Rupert was not a liar. He had told the designer that although he couldn't prove that the sets were by Bellario, in his judgement they were. The designer wasn't looking for proof. "The Italian connection will appeal to the owner", the designer had said. "His parents were from Naples."

Rupert was a man of somewhat eccentric tastes. He had handled many unusual pieces since he had opened his gallery in 1982. It had taken him eleven years to sell three billboards, each ten by fifteen feet, that another artist, later to be hung on the line regularly at the summer exhibition of the Royal Academy, had painted in 1955 for a manufacturer of tinned soups. "He was ahead of the game," Rupert used to tell prospective buyers. "Moreton painted soup cans years before it occurred to Warhol to do it."

Eventually, Rupert had sold them for two thousand pounds to a budding pop star. It hurt him to part with them but he knew they had to go when the café latte set began to move into the area. Dressed fashionably down in jeans with strategic tears, and big labels on the back, they would stop and laugh uproariously at the woman in the pictures in her ballerina-style dress holding a can of soup in front of her as if it were a priceless jewel.

Rupert was not a tall man. He wore his hair long, the same length as he had worn it in the mid-seventies. Sometimes he wore a suit of the same vintage, with flared trousers. His father, who was a doctor, had spent most of his working life as the director of medical services

An Eccentric Dealer

for the then colony of Kenya. Rupert had been conceived a few months before his father died. From his birth his mother treated him as if he were a prodigy. Despite that he was so spoiled, he grew into an engaging young man but not one known for his reliability. As with most eccentrics, characteristics deliberately cultivated had become spontaneous. He had a quick smile, regular features, moved adroitly, and women thought him amusing.

Moving adroitly had become a necessary trait. His tiny gallery was stacked and restacked with dozens of pictures. It had an upper level raised a few steps, like a stage, above the floor at the front. There was also a basement in which he kept odd frames and pictures which, even for him, had been so impulsively bought that he was unwilling to expose them to sight. The narrow wooden stairs, splintered and creaking, were a challenge to even the sleek Abyssinian cat he kept on the premises as a mouser, although no one had even seen it consuming anything other than some of the clotted cream Rupert's mother brought up from Devon for him, and a carefully selected cooked chicken breast from the streamlined delicatessen around the corner.

Rupert moved about the gallery on points like a ballerina. The spaces between the stacks of pictures were only just big enough for his small feet: not for him a few paintings in gessoed frames on a stark white wall, their colours reflected in a highly polished parquetry floor that bespoke money and minimalism. His pictures were stacked according to subject matter: still lifes, European landscapes, portraits, seascapes, pictures of ornithological interest, pictures of botanic interest, stage material, orientalist pictures – he was trying to cultivate the rich Arab trade – female nudes, and male nudes. The last he did trouble to display out of their stack when two of his best clients, Derek and Dwayne – interior decorators from San Francisco, made their annual buying trip to London.

No one except Rupert had any idea how successful the business was. He always maintained that he was a meticulous book-keeper and knew exactly what he had in stock and the state of his trading at any given moment. It was true that he did keep a series of large ring-back, leather folders which he consulted whenever anyone inquired about the price of a picture. "It's all here," he'd say, pause, and then give his quote. He never bargained and he never let anyone see the contents of the folders. Whether these were the only set of books he kept was impossible to say. There had been an occasion in 1989 when an inspector from the Inland Revenue had called and told Rupert that he was to be investigated. The inspector had explained that he was entitled to full access: all the books and all the stock. Furthermore, Rupert would be obliged to provide him with a desk and chair on the premises. "I could be here for some months," he had said.

Rupert was headed for a sale of house contents in Oxfordshire when the inspector arrived. "No trouble," he had said. "Make yourself comfortable. There's no space for another desk, as you can see, so share mine. You can also use my chair for today. I won't be back until late. I'll fix the leg on that stool tomorrow so you can sit on it when I'm using the chair."

Rupert's desk, which was about four feet by two, would have made a kindergarten student ashamed. It was covered in sales catalogues, pages torn from editions of *Jove*, receipts, bills, ripped theatre tickets, loose family photographs and photographs of paintings, expired telephone books, diaries back to 1986, a shopping list to be filled that afternoon, two coffee cups with the congealed remains of two ancient cappuccinos, various other anonymous papers, a long forgotten apple with several bites out of it, and Selassie the Abyssinian cat lovingly licking its already sleek fur.

"Make yourself comfortable." Rupert had repeated as he headed to the door. A minute afterwards he returned. "I forgot; Julie, the girl who helps out, phoned in sick this morning. If any clients come in just get their names and telephone numbers, and note anything they seem interested in. Sorry, got to run."

At about twelve the next day, the inspector had put his pen and the exercise book, which was still in its virginal state, into his brief case. He had taken off his glasses, and inserted them into their case. As he stood up, the stool with its still unstable third leg, had fallen

An Eccentric Dealer

to the floor against the stack of female nudes from which he had been averting his eyes all morning. Concerned that he might have damaged the canvas in one of them, and embarrassed by having to look at the extraordinarily lush nude directly facing him, he had mumbled an apology. Rupert, who was on his mobile telephone, had graciously waved it away.

By the time the inspector had replaced the stool and made sure that the picture was undamaged, Rupert had finished his conversation. "I've made a start. I'll be back," the inspector had said, sounding as unthreatening as Chamberlain at Munich.

"Any time," Rupert had replied. "Any time. We're always here."

Rupert never saw the inspector again.

Only his closest friends and family knew how he came to be in the art business. He said himself that it was a business that attracted some odd people, although it wasn't as bad as interior decorating which was the refuge, he asserted, of failed dress designers and hairdressers. His reticence about his earlier career was due to its mundanity. He had trained as a pharmacist but the careful measurement of medicinal ingredients, and the mortar and pestle were not for him for very long.

Next door to the pharmacy in which he'd worked was an auction house that had some valuable connections with most of the solicitors in the prosperous surrounding residential district. The house handled many deceased estates whose families' affairs had flourished in less taxing times. At lunchtimes, and in quiet periods, Rupert would escape into auction rooms and, over time, the chief auctioneer took him under his wing. Many pictures by painters of high and lesser Victorian art passed through the room, paintings by followers of the Pre-Raphaelites, narrative painters, illustrators of long forgotten books, painters of pictures designed to improve morals, allegorical painters, and occasional painters as yet unrecognised but still with the possibility of a future.

The auctioneer had quickly seen that Rupert had a good eye but, even better for a person in the business of art, a retentive one. He practically never failed to recall a picture he had seen before, or a picture in the style that had earlier, even momentarily, passed in front of his eyes. "Have you ever thought of becoming an art auctioneer?" the auctioneer had asked.

"My mother wanted me to do medicine. I couldn't bear the sight of blood and cadavers. Pharmacy was the compromise."

"Judging by the time you spend in here, it doesn't seem to interest you very much."

"It's the only thing I'm trained for."

"There's no course in auctioneering. You learn on the job. It's obvious you've got a first class eye for a painting; so if you're bored maybe you should think about art auctioneering. I'd willingly give you a job here but I think you'd be better suited to a dealer's gallery, or a department of one of the large auction houses that specializes in paintings."

"But I don't know the market and I don't have an art scholarship."

"You think that makes you unique in the business? It's almost a qualification. You've got the right public school accent, the eye, and a feel for the price of a good picture. That's an impressive combination. I know one of the senior executives in Ballastys. I could give him a call."

"I doubt whether I'd fit in. I like my independence. I'm saving up to buy my own pharmacy."

"You know there are lots of trade journals and art sale indices which tell you what the market is doing. Six months of studying them, visiting commercial galleries and attending auctions are worth more than three years at the Courtauld, or three of those expensive courses Ballastys and Londys run. You should think about it."

Rupert took the advice. He began to read the journals and indices, and when he could find the time, go to the viewing days for the major art sales. It was then that he started to keep the folders that he consulted before quoting prices.

The impetus to enter the business had come from a legacy from his mother's childless sister. He received it at a time before the locality of his gallery became fashionable. Even so, he had to include

An Eccentric Dealer

most of his own savings to purchase the premises, leaving him with only eleven hundred pounds to buy his first stock.

Rupert's wife, Cecelia, like his mother, had boundless faith in his intelligence but an unspoken suspicion of his penchant for attractive young women. His friends used to say that it was just as well that he had a son rather than a daughter because he needed at least one person in his family who didn't idolise him. His mother had wanted to put up some money for him to buy stock but he wouldn't let her. On the other hand, he had made no objection to his wife's taking a job as a shop assistant in one of the nearby dress shops. "It'll be handy for you to be close by. You might be able to keep an eye on the gallery when I'm out."

Rupert was out a great deal, usually at sales in the country, in provincial auction houses, and in houses and tents set up in grounds for the day. He claimed that he had seen more lustre ware and vaseline glass than anyone else in the whole of the country.

After five years he was certified as a valuer of art works, a qualification essential for the business. People were always after valuations, for estate purposes, for gifts and donations, and for insurance policies both before and after the catastrophes in their lives. Valuers got into people's houses. They saw what the people owned. It was surprising how many were willing to sell paintings that had been in their families for generations.

Rupert may have been eccentric, and financially ambitious, but he didn't mislead anyone who engaged him to make a valuation.

"That's a Stamard," he'd say. "Do you know who she was?"

Sometimes the client would, more often not.

"She worked late last century and early this one. In her day she had quite a reputation as a flower painter. This is not a standard type for her, a portrait almost, although that vase of flowers on the table is typical. The last of hers I saw in an auction brought fifteen hundred less selling commission; nett about thirteen hundred. This is a little smaller. Portraits are not nearly as saleable. I'm prepared to offer seven fifty. If you're in any doubt, get another valuation."

Sellers rarely did. They tended to take Rupert's word on price.

The Russian Master

Every five years or so he held a clearance sale. But it was never a comprehensive one. There always remained a number of paintings in the basement that he was either too ashamed to reveal that he had bought, or which he believed would eventually have their day. There were a few, as happens to the most astute dealer, that had been sold to him by artists who, it turned out, had never laid a brush on the canvasses. These with one exception, he burnt, in the public interest, he said, when he discovered the truth. The exception was a group of Keating watercolours indistinguishable from the original works of Flint. They were so exquisitely done that few could tell that they were forgeries. Rupert had noticed that a market was developing for the forger's work. Young stockbrokers and fund managers thought it chic to have Keatings on their walls. They made, as their interior decorators said, a good conversation piece.

He had also had his share of good luck. Once, he had backed his judgement in buying at a house sale in the Lake District an oil study on paper of a landscape - catalogued as by a follower of Constable - for one hundred and fifty pounds. After much difficulty he had asked Martensen, one of the three current experts on Constable, to give his opinion on the picture. The expert had pronounced it a genuine Constable, one of a series done in the Lake District in 1832. Rupert chose to have Londys sell it at a major British Picture Sale with a full page illustration, and a note of authenticity providing a likely provenance by Martensen whom Rupert had been obliged, in consequence, to pay a thousand pounds. That hadn't mattered because the picture had sold for twenty thousand pounds.

As Rupert became more expert, and the business grew, he became bored. He began to consider risky schemes for making quick fortunes in exotic places. Cecelia had only just been able to dissuade him from investing a hundred thousand pounds in a joint venture for the conversion of a Transylvanian castle into a vampire theme park and shooting lodge to be called "The Last Stop Silver Bullet".

By 1991 Rupert had reached a state of profound boredom. He had said to Cecelia. "I'm on the verge of clinical depression."

An Eccentric Dealer

"Don't be ridiculous. You're just bored. You've got a very low boredom threshold."

"I've done everything in the art business that could be of any possible interest."

"It wouldn't matter what you'd done you'd still be bored."

"It's easy for you to say. You can please yourself, apart from looking after the boy. That must be a lot better than serving in a dress shop."

"Sometimes I miss the dress shop. Perhaps I should have opened one myself."

Rupert had been immediately enthusiastic. "Good idea. A lot of fashionistas go into the art business. Let's do the reverse."

"On reflection no." The idea of trying to conduct a business of which Rupert knew nothing, but in which he would insist on interfering, had not seemed appealing.

"Well, what can I do?" he had sighed. At times Rupert acted like a child denied a promised treat.

"Use your imagination. You're in a rut. The same old round of sales, the same cronies, the same customers. Think expansively, laterally. Build up a new clientele. I don't know. I only help out here occasionally. You're the ideas man."

"What about a trip; a long one? To China, somewhere in the East. We can afford it."

"Who'd mind the store? And what about Michael, who'd mind him?"

"That's a very negative response. We could start him early at Brenton."

"We could, but I won't. And there's no one else we know who's reliable enough to run this place."

"I could sell out."

That suggestion, made as it was, without reference to any proposal as to what he might do after he sold out, had really alarmed Cecelia. "Out of the question. Wrong time to sell. The art market is very quiet. You said it yourself."

"I could get Lawrence to look after it."

Then as now, Lawrence Burns worked irregularly – in every sense of that word – for Rupert. He was an actor, latterly spending much more time 'resting' than on the stage. There had been a time when he was thought to have had a future on the stage. At sixteen he had played a child of thirteen in an English film that had become an unexpected success. Afterwards, he was accepted at the Royal Academy of Dramatic Art, but spent only a year there. He had always been unwilling to discuss the circumstances of the parting of the way. In 1980 he had played the drums in a group that managed to sell eighty thousand records before it disbanded in a haze of marijuana smoke and an unannounced visit by the drug squad. His past and his face were still vaguely familiar to a generation of parents with children old enough to enjoy pantomimes. Most years he managed to get a part in a Christmas pantomime in one of the lesser provincial cities. Sometimes he worked as a stage manager. Very occasionally he was given a minor role in a real play. His membership of the Groucho Club was his most precious possession. Lawrence's personal life remained as irregular as his professional life.

"No, I don't think Lawrence is the answer," Cecelia had said.

"I'll give it some thought."

They had turned to other matters. When she left, Cecelia had been concerned. It was impossible to imagine Rupert in a genuinely depressed state but the current attack of boredom she'd observed had lasted for longer than any other. She still recalled how, as she drove away, she had seen Rupert standing disconsolately at the door of the premises with his arms folded.

Five minutes later Olga had come into the shop.

3

Gloria Reflective

Gloria sat at a table on the footpath outside Deux Magots on the Left Bank. The years, and particularly the two that she spent at the Ashram and travelling across India and into Nepal had matured her. But as with many women who enjoyed the sort of beauty that Hollywood favoured in the fifties when they were young and playing wholesome college co-eds, maturity agreed with her. She looked the sort of woman now to whom a rich, middle-aged man, tired of night clubbing with models as thin as spiders, might gratefully turn.

Her dark hair had kept its lustre. These days she wore it straight and short, not short and cropped the way old women trying to conceal its thinning, or predatory lesbians advertising their availability do, but for simplicity, to just below her ears. As the waiter leaned close to put down her cup of coffee, she could tell he detected the faint smell of her Chanel No. 5. She rarely used cosmetics. But this was by choice, not because her money was running out. Her clothing remained as simple as her hair: flat shoes of supple tan leather and a straight, sleeveless fawn dress. Since leaving India she had renounced trousers, for life she said, and saris. She blushed at the thought of how indiscriminately she had embraced everything that was Indian. How polite the women there had been in not laughing aloud at

The Russian Master

another superficial westerner trying to be as they were, and thinking that by wearing a sari she could be.

Gloria's face wore an unsettled, disbelieving expression. Unnoticed, her coffee was beginning to cool as she became increasingly preoccupied with the magazine in front of her. She had noticed it in a newspaper kiosk in the Rue de Rivoli. It had been the only magazine in English for sale. That was not, she was bound to admit to herself, the only reason why she had bought it. On this warm afternoon when all of the Parisians who could afford it were on holidays in their cottages or chateaux in the country, or taking the waters at the spas, or on the beaches, she was now gripped by a wave of loneliness, a nostalgia for the time when she had been married to Davenport and art was the topic to which he always returned. She assured herself that it was the English language and the art, rather than a nostalgia for Davenport that had made her buy *Jove*. She had not been aware of the magazine before but its glossy pages, its high intellectual tone, the apparent scholarship of its writers, and the beauty of the paintings and objects so professionally photographed and reproduced in it testified to its importance. She had been stunned by the article about Davenport on page 3 which she had not noticed even before buying the magazine. She read it again. She was at first incredulous and then suddenly sad. She tried vainly to push aside a deep regretfulness.

Who could have foreseen that Davenport – mild mannered Davenport – would not only expose a great fraud and become, as the children she used to teach would say, a 'legend', but also would become sought after overseas.

Gloria had certainly heard of Londys. Who hadn't? They were, with Ballastys and Shaws, world famous. She had seen scenes from films set in their auction rooms. Occasionally, Davenport had brought their catalogues home to study. Londys was a place of old masters, venerable pieces of delicate porcelain, signed gilded clocks, and famous impressionist canvasses. Others came and went. But Londys remained, brokers in fine things to the titled, rich, and famous as they had been for more than two hundred years.

Gloria Reflective

She wondered what Davenport's salary would now be. He had never been much of a traveller, so it would have taken a lot to lure him away from Australia.

Gloria closed the magazine. She glanced at l'*addition* that the waiter had put beside the saucer, but she postponed examining it. She tried the coffee. It was bitter as coffee is when it is cold. She looked into her handbag to check her money before picking up the piece of paper with the numbers on it. All of the money she had left in the world was in that handbag. She counted seven, one-hundred Euro notes. She looked at the bill, nine Euros plus a tip for an espresso. Well, it was her own fault for coming to such a landmark.

She rolled the magazine up, put down one of the notes and waited for her change. A light breeze had risen. The remaining leaves of the plane trees moved gently in harmony with it. It could have been summer. There was, in the air, the heady Parisian mix of diesel fumes together with the aromas of bitumen softening in the unseasonal heat, coffee, and Turkish tobacco – with occasional wafts of perfume as women passed by. Young couples walked hand in hand. Not even a procession of Japanese tourists following a guide holding a stick with a red pennant attached to it could impair the Gallic perfection of the day and place. There could be no doubt of it now. Gloria was lonely and regretful.

Of all the contrasts between France and India, the subtlety of the scents here was the greatest. It was a relief not to have to purse her nostrils as soon as she woke in the morning until she reaccustomed herself to the smells of curry, manure, hot cooking oil, human and bovine excreta, marigolds, body odours, and other undetectable alien essences.

At the Ashram the going had been even heavier. She had never become used to the food or the heat. Why was it, she had asked herself a hundred times, that thirty degrees in India felt like forty in Australia. Everything was excessive. It never seemed merely to shower. Instead, when it rained, the flashing lightning flickered through the huge drops so that they looked like violet and silver light bulbs falling from the sky. In the dry season the slightest contact with the ground caused a cloud of dust to eddy around toes in open sandals, and to cake bare legs in an orange powder.

They had travelled first to Nepal. The towering mountains had awed her as they did everyone, but they were not enough to lift the disquiet that began to settle upon her. It would be better, she and Walter agreed, when they reached the Ashram.

Apart from the food, the first four months were bearable, at times exciting. She thought now that the exoticism of it all had numbed her. It had taken a lot less time for Walter to begin to complain.

"What are we doing here, why did you bring us to this country?" He had developed an itch on his arms, and a suppurating boil on the left cheek of his bottom. Their teacher had prescribed a foul smelling black potion for both. Gloria told him that he had better sleep in the dormitory until he was cured and not the hut that she had rented.

"The man's no less a charlatan than my GP in Australia," he had said.

"You're too impatient. You have to meditate, will yourself to get better. You were told the potion alone won't work. You were the one who introduced me to holistic medicine."

"Like all converts you've become a zealot," Walter had grumbled.

The days had turned into months, and the occasional disagreements into constant bickering. His money ran out. The more he became her pensioner the more disagreeable he became.

It had taken quite a long time, though, for Gloria to realise how impulsive and unwise her behaviour had been. Her realisation had been heightened by a conversation she'd overheard between the Master and his treasurer – although the latter was never called that.

"The Australian couple, they're two weeks behind in their rent and tuition fees."

"Are they on the high rate?" the Master had asked.

"Of course: four hundred and ten dollars a week each." (The treasurer always insisted on payment in United States dollars.)

"They'll pay, or at least the woman will."

Gloria Reflective

"In kind, like so many of the other western women?" the treasurer had leered.

"No. Her image of me is of a true ascetic."

"She'd see it differently if she were hanging around your back door at ten o'clock most nights."

"They come because their mothers and their aunts boasted to them about the sixties. Remember those absurd, electric guitar players and their followers, coming here for hemp, free love, and sitar lessons. I don't think they got much of any of them. But they told one another what a wonderful time they were having. I think they believed it. Those who didn't come, thought they'd missed out. Their daughters weren't going to make that mistake."

"I don't think Gloria's much of a fornicator."

"Nor I fear, does Walter."

They had both laughed as they went off to the treasurer's room to check the accounts.

After a time, Gloria would disappear for a night or two, and Walter's financial dependence made him reluctant to ask where she went. But it was to the Blenheim - one of the few modern hotels in the western style in the city; about two and a half stars Gloria would have said. The linen was clean and fresh each day, the air conditioner was seventy to eighty percent efficient, and the kitchen was free of most of the worst germs to which foreigners were particularly vulnerable. But best of all were the fresh tablets of perfumed soap wrapped in fine paper, and the unlimited hot water.

Immediately after overhearing the conversation between the Master and the treasurer, Gloria had taken herself off to the hotel. The day manager had told her that her usual room was taken. She had not telephoned ahead, he had said. He would have kept it had he known.

"So long as it's got a big bath and plenty of hot water it doesn't matter."

"He's a businessman, American I think."

"Who is?"

"The man who's got your room. He has not stayed here before."

Gloria hadn't been interested, but Mr Keynon, the day manager had. He had come around the counter to walk with Gloria to the lift. She'd noticed that he was wearing a new black coat and striped trousers. He'd seen that she was looking at them.

"I had these made. The material for the trousers was not easy to find. I thought I would have to send to London for it. All of the senior staff at the best hotels dress like this. Do you not think it gives tone to this establishment?"

"Yes."

He had continued walking beside her. "I think he is in fabrics too."

"Fabrics, who...?"

"The businessman in your room."

Gloria had pressed the lift button and resigned herself to wait. The lift tended to be less reliable than the hot water.

"Would you like me to ask him to change with you?"

"That isn't necessary."

"He looked a gentlemanly person. He would probably be agreeable."

"No, don't ask him. I'm sure the room you've given me is all right."

"He is a man in early middle age I think. I would say this is his first trip to India."

"Why do you think that?"

"He asked me where he could buy Lomotil."

"Mr Keynon, I have been in this country for some time now but I still need Lomotil from time to time."

"You should eat strong curries."

The lift had juddered to a stop and after two trials and errors the doors had opened and stayed open.

Gloria stepped out. She heard Mr Keynon's last words as the doors closed.

"And garlic and chilli: These too need to be taken strong."

Gloria came down to the dining room two hours later. She

Gloria Reflective

chose to eat there not only because of the stiff white tablecloths and napkins, but also because she thought, she admitted probably optimistically, that she could make a better assessment of the purity of the food if she were closer to the kitchen.

There were no other guests at the tables. The manager of the dining room, another Mr Keynon a cousin of the day manager, had turned half of the lights off. Nevertheless, the menu that he presented to Gloria was long and elaborate enough for an imperial banquet.

"The Mulligatawny soup is very good tonight Madam."

She understood from this that the soup was the only first course that could be counted on. However, it was still necessary to play the game. "I see there is a duck pate with Tuscan olives and Syma figs."

"That rascal duck farmer sent three ducks that would give a vulture indigestion. I would insult you by serving you any part of them."

"I will accept your recommendation for the first course. Now..." Gloria studied the menu as if it were the emergency instruction card of a suspect airline. She pointed to item Number 27.

"The Dover Sole with a reduced tomato and cream sauce and new potatoes. What a good choice that would have been. Alas, when the Sole was in, all the way from the famous white cliffs, only yesterday, it was found that the ice in which it was packed for its long flight had melted. Instead of its normal, buttery colour and sweet smell, it was as grey as a Kaiser's greatcoat, and as high as an abandoned fish market. No, I am not recommending the Dover Sole to madam today."

"A pity. Perhaps I should have the chicken curry again."

"One of madam's favourites. A very wise choice."

"The chicken farmer is more reliable than the duck man then?"

"Very reliable, he is a cousin. Now, to drink?"

"Mineral water, a bottle."

He began to write as if the order were a detailed despatch from a corps commander to one of his battlefield generals.

"The bottle unopened and with a sealed cap."

The Russian Master

The manager's expression turned to one of disappointment. But he soon recovered. "You will be wanting ice?"

"No ice thank you."

He flicked his fingers and one of the three waiters who had been standing against the back wall hurried over.

"Madam will have the Mulligatawny soup and the curried chicken. She will be taking the very hot curry. And, waiter, mineral water, in a bottle sealed as tight as a submarine." He said the last as if he were ending a long and fiery argument. "It is all written here. Check that all is observed." The waiter moved towards the kitchen. Mr Keynon barked, as he did, "Every detail, every particular." He bowed to Gloria and moved magisterially towards the doorway where he stood poised and ready like an impresario about to be acclaimed by a grateful audience.

The soup arrived within five minutes. The waiter, under the critical eye of Mr Keynon, ladled it into Gloria's plate from a heavy bowl that had been copied in Benares in 1911 from a catalogue of that year from the Army and Navy store.

Gloria tentatively tasted the soup. That its taste was indeterminate was not important. That it was hot was, as was the western ritual by which it was served. Both of these were satisfactory.

On her last stay here, Gloria had taken her first alcohol for more than three years. Despite its rough taste it had settled her stomach. She waved to Mr Keynon who was beside her in an instant.

"The soup, there is some problem?"

"No, the soup is no problem."

"It's that boy then, that bothersome boy who served it, his dirty thumb as deep in it as a sea diver. I will change it immediately and admonish, yes I will admonish him with great severity later."

"I don't want the soup changed. I want a drink."

"An orange juice, a lemonade perhaps?"

"No. Last time you found me some whisky. That's what I want."

"We have many varieties of Scotch. Which one did you have?"

"I can't remember."

This was exactly the sort of conversation that all of the Keynons enjoyed.

"I will bring a sample of all of the varieties. That way your memory will be jogged."

"I'm not going to taste a dozen different whiskies."

"To tell you the truth, the difference may be less than you think. I will take you into my confidence. I believe that some of the varieties are made by the one house."

"Just bring the bottles."

Gloria finished her soup. It had a suspicious aftertaste. As she put down her spoon she noticed Mr Keynon pushing an ornate trolley towards her. When he was close she saw that there were various bottles standing upright on it.

He had arranged the bottles to present a dazzling array of labels: Gushing Burn Finest Whisky; Robby Burns Mellow; Harvested Dew Whisky; Antler Nightrap; Tamo'shanter Tipple; and Glen and Heather Purple Label.

"Are you sure they're all genuine Scotch?"

Mr Keynon was deeply offended by the question, and at first pretended not to have heard it.

"They may be by the same maker. But look at the labels: 'Guaranteed Product of the Burns of Scotland and Lock Lomand.' Import controls in India are very strict."

"Assuming the goods came from outside India."

"Madam, what can I add to the verification by the label on each bottle?" Inconsolably hurt, he reversed the trolley and began to push it as if it were a conveyance for a funeral.

"Come back, Mr Keynon. I think I may have had the Gushing Burn before. I will have that."

He poured her a generous portion. "Soda?"

Gloria examined the small bottle to make sure its seal was unbroken. "Yes."

"Whisky soda. The nectar of the Raj. A fine drink I believe. I do not take it myself of course. Alas, my religion forbids it."

Twice Gloria had seen Mr Keynon seriously the worse for wear. Once he had been singing 'Glasgow Belongs To Me', in an Indian imitation of Harry Lauder. On the other occasion, he had been attempting to play a form of hopscotch with a group of children on the footpath opposite the hotel. "You deny yourself a great deal. You must be very devout."

Mr Keynon nodded gravely as he pushed the trolley back against the wall. As he did, another westerner appeared at the door.

"Ah, Mr Pickford. You have decided to join us after all."

Mr Pickford was a tall, wide man, perhaps forty or forty-five years old. He was wearing a pale blue seersucker suit, a white shirt and a black tie. Perspiration was dripping from his anxious face. His obvious discomfort could not completely mask his usual expression of good nature and intention.

Mr Keynon showed him to the table furthest from Gloria's. She had overheard Keynon one day discussing in disapproving tones the hijinks between the occupants of rooms twenty-two and twenty-nine on the second floor during the previous evening.

The dining room was not large. Its emptiness and the absence of other conversation lent itself to eavesdropping.

Mr Pickford waved the long menu away. "I'm a little poorly. I would like two boiled eggs, hard boiled, nothing less than seven minutes, and tea, black tea. As black and hot as possible. Boil the tea water for six minutes too."

"What brand of tea, sir? India is the home of tea."

"I thought China was."

"Once perhaps. We have many types, many brands, more than that fellow who makes the baked beans, many times more."

Mr Pickford cringed at the mention of baked beans.

"You select one, just make sure it's strong and black."

"Why have the eggs when you can have the chicken that they come from?"

"Because, because ... Look would you just bring me the eggs please?"

"A whisky, a cognac perhaps, a tummy tightener as they say?"

"No thank you."

"I'm sure madam will vouch for our spirits." He glanced in the

Gloria Reflective

direction of Gloria.

"No, just the tea," Mr Pickford groaned. "Do you have an orange by any chance? That might help."

Mr Keynon closed his order book with finality. "There will be no need for this. I will check for oranges."

He returned almost instantly. "We have oranges, small pitted, bitter ones. I told the chef to send them back. But all is not lost. There is a street vendor around the corner who sells oranges as big as footballs with skins as smooth, as, as ... There is a lady present," he whispered as he winked. "I will say no more. In the meantime, I will dart around the corner for a gem of an orange." The manager left the dining room as if he were late for an important appointment.

Gloria coughed lightly. Mr Pickford nodded cordially. Gloria looked around to ensure that Mr Keynon had not made one of his swift, silent re-entrances.

"I don't wish to intrude but I wouldn't have one of those oranges if I were you."

"Thank you for the warning. But surely it will be all right if I skin it myself. I was warned never to eat unskinned fruit here."

"That street vendor has a set of scales. He sells the oranges by weight."

"Naturally."

"He has a long syringe. He injects them with water to increase their weight, with whatever water comes to hand."

"You're sure?"

"Yes. I've seen him do it: with water from the gutter."

Mr Pickford winced. "Thank you, I'll take your advice."

Mr Keynon returned a few minutes later carrying a bowl of gleaming oranges and a sharp knife.

"You make your selection," he said to Mr Pickford, "and I will peel it before your eyes. I do that not because it is necessary but for the reassurance of the suspicious occidental mind." With a flourish he presented the bowl.

"Look, if you don't mind, I'm afraid I've gone off the idea of an orange."

"Off the idea? There is suddenly something repellent about a sweet orange?"

"No, not at all. It was the flight, yes the flight. It seems to have unsettled my stomach."

"But that is the purpose of fresh fruit, the settlement of an unruly stomach. Look, I will peel it and quarter it to expose its delicious heart."

"No. It's very kind of you. I'm sorry to put you to the trouble. On second thoughts I have decided to have nothing at all."

A long discussion ensued which culminated in a compromise. Mr Pickford would have his black tea and one boiled egg. After these were served, Mr Keynon left the dining room in disgust announcing that the boy would clear the tables.

Mr Pickford asked Gloria whether he might join her. She said he could.

"He's thin-skinned isn't he?"

"Perhaps three hundred or so years of colonial oppression would make you that way."

"Are you British?"

"No, Australian."

"They oppressed you too?"

"Some Australians think so."

"How?"

"More the indigenous people than the colonials."

"I read that it was the colonials who did the oppressing."

"There isn't time to give you a history lesson of Australia." Gloria could have been speaking to her last class of ten-year-olds. "What brings you here?"

"Business, I'm in fabrics." He produced a card.

'Harry M. Pickford Jnr. Fine Fabrics and Textiles, 11 Garrison Street, Indianapolis.' There were two telephone numbers and an email address on the card.

"You're a long way from Indiana."

"And you too, you're a long way from home. Why are you here?"

"For the getting of wisdom and peace."

For a moment Mr Pickford thought that she was mocking him. "How's it going then, getting there?"

"No one gets there. Not in this incarnation anyway."

"How do you know what incarnation you're in?"

"You don't unless it's the last one. And because I don't know, then it can't be my last one."

"I see. No idea at all then how many you've got ahead of you?"

"No."

"What about the past? Is that the same?"

"Yes."

"But you are becoming wiser, feeling more peaceful?"

"The master says so."

"Peacefulness though, isn't that something only you can know about yourself?"

"The Master knows everything."

"I suppose it's a long journey."

"Ideally yes, but I'll have to move on soon. The Master says we have to go out into the world sometime."

"To be tested, is that the idea?"

"The Master makes us renounce conflict."

"I see. Been here long?"

"We tend not to count time here."

"Will you go back to Australia?"

Gloria was labouring under a great sense of injustice. Although she had taken practically all of Davenport's and her own property in the divorce settlement, that he was prospering in Australia in the private art business rankled. It had never occurred to her that he would work in anything other than a public museum. Here she was, beside the Ganges, Walter dependent on her, the Master's fees increasing, and her money diminishing daily, while Davenport was lounging around in fine woollen suits, appraising and selling paintings, hobnobbing with the rich and famous, and no doubt earning huge, easy commissions.

Mr Pickford asked his question again.

"I don't know." She wanted to return to Australia but to do so would be to acknowledge failure. She had talked a great deal about her plans before she left, but none had included going back to school teaching. "I'm minded to go to Paris."

"Fine city Paris, France."

"You've been there?"

"In fabrics you've got to travel."

"Indiana's a Midwestern state isn't it?"

"Some might say so. It's northern too. Not far from the Great Lakes and Chicago. Now that's a city."

Mr Pickford was becoming a person of some interest. She studied him as he bent his head over his black tea: he could be as young as forty-two, a good head of dark curly hair, clean shaven, regular features except for a prominent nose, well groomed, polite, and he sounded educated.

"How did you get into the fabric business?"

"Always been in it, family business, third generation."

"You went into it after school?"

"After university, Indiana State, at Bloomington. I studied economics."

"Where's Bloomington?"

"Fifty miles from Indianapolis. It's a campus town, a good place to be a student. What university did you go to?"

She told him. He looked perplexed. She could hardly have expected him to have heard of it. Gloria looked to see where Mr Keynon was. It was Mr Pickford's turn to study her.

The mature, thin look suited Gloria. It made her appear reflective and grave.

"You must know this area pretty well," Mr Pickford said.

"I wouldn't say well. We don't leave the Ashram often."

"You're here with someone else?"

"A travelling companion, just a friend," Gloria lied.

"Well in that case would you be prepared to show me around, go to the factory with me perhaps, that is if you've got the time, tomorrow? I've arranged a car and driver through that man at the desk."

"Did you stipulate the sort of car?"

"No."

"It'll be his brother's, a 1969 Rover."

"What's a Rover?"

"British. It's tied together with wire. I'd sooner ride on one of those cows in the street."

"That's why I'd like you to come with me. You know the ropes here." He was reminded of something. "Ropes. Say, do they do the Indian Rope Trick here?"

Mr Pickford's naivety made Gloria feel knowledgeable and wise, wiser than the Master made her feel, but older too, older than she had felt at any time since the judge had pronounced her divorce from Davenport.

"Would you?" Mr Pickford pleaded. "I don't even understand the English these people speak half the time."

"The educated people speak very good English."

"Sounds like something out of the nineteenth century to me. Look, I don't mean this to be offensive but I'd pay." Realising the implication that his suggestion might carry, he tried to explain. "As a guide, kind of, translator, at whatever the going rate is."

"I don't speak Hindi."

"To translate their English."

"What time do you start?"

"You will, then? I'm very grateful. About ten o'clock, would that suit?"

"I'll talk to Mr Keynon in the morning. I'll tell him he'll have to arrange for a better car. There's nothing I can do about the driver I'm afraid. He'd just produce another relative, probably a worse driver. You should be aware, however, that I know nothing about business."

"Mr Lehru, the owner of the factory where we'll be going has never talked on the phone about business. He called it 'commerce'."

"How will you introduce me?"

Mr Pickford thought about this for a moment. "Would it be all right if I said you were my part-time local assistant?"

The Russian Master

"Commercial assistant."

Flustered, Mr Pickford agreed.

Gloria finished the last of her whisky, grimaced at the after taste, and stood up. She put out her hand. Mr Pickford held it for a second more than she, and he, for that matter, thought appropriate for a slight and recent acquaintance.

In her room, as she prepared for bed, Gloria wondered what she would tell Walter about Mr Pickford. Increasingly she was becoming indifferent to what he thought about anything she did. But what about the Master? The truth was that there were things about him that she was questioning more and more these days.

Now, on the Rive Gauche two months later, so much of what she had done and seen in India, seemed to have been a waste of time, and, she reminded herself, of money as well. Her thoughts returned to Davenport. At least he had always been decent. She corrected herself, biddable.

4

A Career Move

Although Davenport and Beverley Leer – former senior curator with him at the Antipodean Museum, and now its director after Silas Morning was sacked following the Divera debacle – had had their disagreements, they still used to meet for coffee occasionally. She had confirmed that he would be unwise to go to Londys. In truth, she had always been more than a little fond of Davenport. "Come back to the museum," she had said. "You're not a man of commerce."

Having rejected Londys's offer, Davenport had nonetheless thought he should tell Tom Jeffrey about it. He knew his boss would also be interested to learn that the managing director of Londys intended to shake up the local franchise. Jeffrey had been at his desk when Davenport entered his room. He had looked preoccupied, and then sheepish when he saw that it was Davenport.

"Ah, Davenport, there was something I wanted to talk to you about. Take a seat."

"There's something you should know too."

"Yes, in a minute. Have you seen the last set of management accounts?"

All accounts were a mystery to Davenport. The only figure he had looked at was the one in the bottom right corner of the last page. If

The Russian Master

it had no square brackets he understood that they had not made a loss. The last such account, so far as he could recall, had been free of the dreaded brackets.

"I had a glance at them."

"Not too good are they?"

"We seemed to be," he had searched for the right businesslike words, "in profit".

"Down on the last quarter, seriously down."

"But isn't that to be expected? We have only the one sale in this quarter."

"Davenport, the competition's heating up. Everyone's going to have to make sacrifices. Do you think you're cut out for the business side of art?"

"I didn't think so at first. But I'm beginning to get the hang of it now. Accounts aren't my thing of course but that's why we employ bookkeepers and auditors."

Tom Jefferey had looked uncomfortable at the mention of auditors.

"It doesn't give me any pleasure to have to say this. The fact is..."

Davenport had been intent on telling Jefferey about Londys's Australian operations. "You're right about the competition. Londys..."

Jefferey had interrupted him. "Londys don't worry me. It's the minors that are the problem. Low overheads, reduced commissions. Some of them are not even charging buyers' premiums."

"I've often wondered about those premiums."

"You think we could increase them to twenty percent?"

"No. I wondered whether we should charge them at all. It's not as if we do anything for the buyers. I was talking to a barrister I know the other day. He asked me how we could, discharge...I think that's what he said, our duty to the vendor to get the highest price while at the same time do whatever we do for the buyer to earn the premium he has to pay. He said something about a conflict of interests. Not that he said he was an expert on breach of duty. His field is torts; I think that's what he said."

Jefferey, incredulous, had taken a moment to reply. "Ambulance chaser. Don't ever let me hear you say anything like that again. It does make my point though, you're not a businessman, Davenport."

"I thought you engaged me for my art knowledge."

"That's the problem: not much call for art expertise these days. We all know the big names. That's what people want, the big signatures, and acreage. Anyone can sell those. Look, this isn't easy to say but..."

Davenport had tried to interrupt him. "Well I just want to tell you..."

"I'm going to have to rationalise, downsize. As I say, sacrifices have to be made."

"Just listen to me for a moment." There had been a rare note of asperity in Davenport's voice.

"I'll come to the point. I'm afraid there's no room for you here anymore, Davenport."

Davenport had tried to absorb what Jeffrey had said. "Do you mean to say...?"

Again, Jefferey had cut him off. "I can understand that you're upset. Still, with your reputation you'll have no trouble getting back into the public sector."

"I've lost touch with that. Besides, I doubt whether I'd be persona grata with too many museum directors any more." He had omitted to mention his friendship with Beverley. "They'd consider me a threat to them after what happened to Silas Morning. One day museum director, next picture framer. I could talk to my friend the barrister I suppose. He'd be able to advise me what I should do."

"No, don't do that. We can sort this out. I'll buy your shares and options and make you a decent severance payment."

"Well Tom, I don't know what to say."

"Don't say anything. There's no point in it. The best I can do is one hundred and fifty for your shares and options, and one hundred severance payment."

"If you say so."

The Russian Master

Those were the circumstances in which Davenport left Jeffrey's and agreed to accept Gerald de Pyne's offer to work for Londys in London. Now, as he sat at his desk and waited for Elena, he asked himself whether he should have tried to obtain a position as a curator in a museum after all. London was so big and competitive. The sums about which people talked intimidated him. He had not even bought a car because he was too scared to drive one yet. Even though estuarine and dominion accents were no longer unacceptable, he continued to be unsettled by the debutante accents of the smartly dressed young women who, despite Gerald's assertions to the contrary, still guarded the reception desks at the front of the house.

Elena did not, however, worry him. Her mother was born and raised in San Francisco before she married an English doctor. Elena's accent was a transatlantic blend derived from her parents. She came into Davenport's room without knocking. "Ready for house hunting?" She asked as she sat down. "Have you any idea where you'd like to live?"

"Somewhere I can afford."

"Bad choice. No one of your age in your sort of position lives within his means in London."

"I'll break that rule."

"You should really be at Holland Park or South Ken. You'd meet a lot of potential clients there."

"I certainly couldn't afford anywhere that any of the clients of this firm live."

"It will have to be a compromise then. But definitely not Canary Wharf or Bloomsbury, nothing in that direction. Too predictable, too utterly banal for words. The west is still the best. You couldn't compete with the Arab money at Knightsbridge. We'll compromise on Chelsea, or somewhere near Worlds End."

"Worlds End. That doesn't sound too optimistic."

Elena smiled. When she did, she became a different person from the humourless martinet who calculated the accounts. It crossed Davenport's mind that she might perform a better service on the front counter than the condescending client repellants who served there now.

"You know how the English are about place names. It's quite a good area, actually. There are still several small dealers out there, although boutiques and minimalist restaurants are taking over. I brought my car in. It's in the garage around the corner. Ready?"

"It's good of you to help me. You don't have to you know."

"A day out of here's a bonus. Anyway orders are orders."

Elena pointed out places of interest as she drove down the Kings Road. As she did, she was careful to keep her eyes ahead of her. She drove competently and just within the speed limit.

"I've never been to Australia," she said. "I've a cousin who emigrated there. He's living in Adelaide. All the capital cities seem to be named after English aristocrats or politicians. How do Australians feel about that?"

"I doubt whether they even think about it."

"Our tabloids say Australians don't think about anything except beer, surfing, and cricket. Is there any truth in that?"

"Some, I suppose."

They were both quiet for a few minutes. There was an unspoken curiosity between them. Elena broke the silence. "It can't be easy to uproot yourself and come to another country."

"No, but WE1 is hardly outer Mongolia."

"I sometimes wonder about that."

"You've always lived in England?"

"I spent six months with a family at La Rochelle learning French when I was nineteen."

"The Huguenot part."

"How did you know that?"

"I learnt it between surfing and cricket."

"Touché. You've probably travelled a great deal more than I have too."

"To a few countries, just the capitals. If a museum wants to borrow a painting, the deal is that the borrower has to pay the fare of a curator from the lender's gallery to accompany it. It helps to keep curators as well as works of art in circulation."

"I read that article in *Jove*."

"Just PR by Gerald. Pay no attention to it."

"Did you really rumble a fake Divera?"

"It's a complicated story."

"Nothing's ever simple in the Byzantine world of art."

She stopped the car in front of a real estate agent's office. "There's a yellow line here. I'll have to drive around to find a park. You get out and start looking at the cards in the window."

"I'll help you find a park."

"No offence, but as a stranger I don't think you'd be much help. Out you get."

Davenport got out and wandered across the footpath to the real estate agent's window. Reflected in it was what looked like a large portrait of Lenin. He turned around and looked across the road. In a small shop window there was a portrait of Lenin that dwarfed everything around it. The great Soviet helmsman was wearing a cloak and casting an imperious eye over a team of peasant women industriously tilling a vast field of wheat.

Davenport crossed the road for a closer look. The painting was well executed. It did not have the appearance of a copy. Its composition, with the lordly Lenin and the poor peasants below him, conveyed more than a hint of cynicism. There was a signature in the top right hand corner. It was in Cyrillic and Davenport couldn't read it. He peered deeper into the shop through the window. Its griminess prevented him from seeing anything. He tentatively tried the door. It was locked. Just as he was about to turn away it was loudly opened.

"Yes?" A young woman demanded. She could have been no more than twenty-four or -five and was beautiful in a far northern way; hair the colour of faded gold, blue eyes, a large mouth and high cheek bones. "Yes?" she demanded again.

"I was just looking in the window."

"At that monster. One day I slash it to ribbons." Her eyes glowed with a fierce anger. Her accent was foreign.

"Well, er, why, why have you put it in the window if that's the way you feel about it?"

A Career Move

"I did not put it there. Rupert did."

"I must say I wouldn't have thought there'd be much of a demand for life size portraits of Lenin around here."

"You'd be surprised. The world is full of crypto-bolsheviks."

"Not here, in London, now, surely."

"Everywhere. What is it you say, Krug communists?"

"Bollinger socialists, actually."

"All the same."

"It seems to be well painted."

"*Academie* style. Trained monkey could do it."

"I don't quite think so."

"From 1920, art stood still in Russia when not going backwards. Everything done in semi-impressionist style of forty years before. Not just subject bad, execution worse."

"In its way it's at least a reasonable piece of craftsmanship."

"Five hundred and fifty pounds if you want."

"Thank you, but no, I'm not in the market for a portrait of Lenin at present."

"You just tyre-kicker then?"

"No, I do have a genuine interest in art."

"There is much more inside, mainly Russian but some English, some from God knows where. Rupert put Lenin in window because he say it make people curious. He say Lenin portrait is bait. I wish shark would take it and swallow it up. You like to look inside?"

Davenport was about to say yes when he felt a light touch on his arm. He turned around to see Elena sizing the girl up.

"Some other time thank you."

Elena took his arm and drew him away.

"Did you see anything interesting in the window?"

"Only that Lenin portrait."

"In the agent's, didn't you look there?"

Davenport apologised. "I'm sorry, I was distracted by the portrait."

'More likely the girl,' Elena thought to herself. "Well we can't dawdle; we may have to cover a lot of territory today."

They recrossed the road and went straight into the agent's shop. "We're..." Elena blushed, "Mr Jones that is, is looking for a flat in this area: two bedrooms, small but modern kitchen, bathroom, small separate cloak room with amenities, and a big reception room, big enough for a couple of large couches and a dining table to seat six. That sound about right Davenport?"

"Do I need all of that?"

"Definitely."

"I can't imagine I'd ever have five people to a meal."

"You might need to entertain: better to err on the safe side."

"It sounds expensive."

The agent, a short, rotund man who had been attempting to speak, intervened. "You're right about that."

"I don't want to buy, just rent," Davenport said.

"Still expensive. Landlords have to get a proper return on capital as well as pay their rates, taxes and bear their opportunity costs."

The last offended Elena's intelligence. "Nonsense, getting a return on capital and opportunity cost would be double dipping. What have you got?"

"Very little of the kind of thing you're talking about. I'll show you some photographs."

Three agents later, Elena looked at a series of photographs of a flat fifty yards around the corner from where she had just left Davenport. After an inspection and an hour of relentless haggling by Elena, Davenport found himself the tenant under a lease for two years of a flat in a Victorian building that had undergone its last renovation in the final days of post-war austerity.

They had gone back to Mayfair after Elena had arranged for a solicitor to check the documents. It was just after one when she parked the car.

"Well that was quick," she said. "Relatively painless."

"It seems a lot of money for such an old building."

"You sound like a colonial now. This is the centre of the world."

"And the dearest real estate in the world."

"Tokyo's dearer," Elena contradicted him.

"I don't know about dearer, but it's certainly cleaner."

"That's only because it's not as old. This would be dearer too if the Huns had destroyed as much of it as a few hundred daily B-29s had Tokyo."

"I didn't mean to sound ungrateful. I do what everyone says you shouldn't, translate whatever I pay here into Australian dollars. Anyway, it's time for lunch – my shout. You tell me, where should we eat?"

"You should be economising after committing to the flat. There's a trattoria around the corner."

"Definitely not. I'm celebrating finding a home." Davenport tried not to sound dubious.

"You're sure?"

"Yes."

"Well, Stuarts then, the best fish restaurant in London. It's just up the road."

After they had ordered, Davenport asked her whether she liked art. "At least as much as anyone else does in that place," she said. "I like money too but not as much as anyone else there."

"Just because you're a chef you don't have to like food."

"Chefs are creative, some are artists. People who sell art aren't artists. You don't strike me as an art salesman."

"I sold quite a lot in Australia. My former boss said it was because my honesty shocked the clients." He didn't mention that Tom Jefferey had added that if only Davenport could temper his honesty with a touch of guile he would double his sales.

"I thought I would have liked to work at the front," Elena said. "Gerald told me that my accountancy degree made me overqualified for that. But it wasn't my degree that disqualified me, it was having at least a modicum of brains. Absolute vacuousness, an air of condescension, and a cut glass voice are the qualifications for a job there. I said I'd like to be a porter then."

"One of those people who wear the yellow aprons with a discreet Londys logo on it? Wouldn't that involve heavy lifting?"

"You don't think I do most of the heavy lifting in that place now?"

"Metaphorically speaking I suppose you do."

"There are quite a few women working as porters at our rivals. Gerald's going to be in serious trouble with the Equal Opportunity Tribunal one of these days. No, the auction room floor is the place to learn the trade and about art. A porter sees a lot of pictures and objects in a year. I look as much as I can. I don't buy at Londys though. House rule, observed more in the breach though by the others. Do you collect?"

"Drawings occasionally. Not many curators do. The salary doesn't allow it. Most curators say, why would they collect what must inevitably be inferior to what they see and handle daily? It's only partly true. I don't think they approve of private collectors. And they practically never admit that any collector has any sort of eye. At my old museum, one of my colleagues made a practice of depressing anyone unwise enough to ask her opinion about a work. 'Not even a good forgery', she'd say. Or if it was signed and genuine, but not dated, 'an early student work, very clumsy'."

"Do you miss working in a public museum?"

"Only when it hurts."

"I know what you mean. I worked as an auditor in a big accountancy firm before I came here. Any place that has a staff manual is to be avoided. Are you married?" she suddenly asked.

"Not at present."

"You were once then? So was I. Mine was a futures commodities trader. What was yours?"

"A school teacher."

Elena was unperturbed by Davenport's reluctance to discuss his former wife. Davenport had thought that the English were stoics, unwilling to discuss their personal affairs. He was coming to believe that the opposite was the case. Most of those he had met seemed as anxious to discuss their affairs as the characters in a late-night television series on American television.

"The bastard!"

Davenport was startled by Elena's vehemence. He thought she

was speaking to someone behind him. He turned around to see their waiter backing away. "What did he do?" Davenport asked.

"Not him, my former, I wish I could say late, husband. Was yours a bitch?"

"I wouldn't quite say that."

"Davenport, you strike me as a fairly inoffensive sort of man. I couldn't imagine you out tomcatting."

"No."

"Perhaps that was the problem," Elena had drunk two glasses of the Sancerre and signalled for the waiter to pour her another. As he warily did, she continued to speak. That was another thing about the English that Davenport had noticed: they were prepared to speak frankly and loudly about their affairs in front of waiters and taxi drivers as if neither were present. "You were probably too unadventurous for her." Elena drank a couple of mouthfuls of the wine. "I think you need to live a little, Davenport. Branch out." A look of deep concern crossed her face. "You don't like boys by any chance do you?"

"No, not in that way."

"Well, that's something. I suppose it's because the Guards regiments have been downsized. Your Sydney seems to have taken over. That's where they have that Mardi Gras isn't it?"

"Yes."

"Worse than Rio by the look." She finished her glass of wine and held her finger up for another. "You don't seem to be drinking. You've got to loosen up." She told the waiter to top up Davenport's glass before he could cover it with his hand.

"Do people at Londys lunch very often?" he asked.

"Not bloody often enough. Except for Gerald that is. He's on a huge expense account. I wouldn't divulge it of course." She put a finger to her lips. "Chinese walls. No one except the chairman's supposed to know about that."

"Speaking of the chairman," Davenport asked, "Have you met him?"

"Once."

"What's he like?"

"Buxom blondes mainly."

"I mean, what sort of a person is he?"

"He's originally American as you must know. He tries to be very British. He's got a croquet lawn on his estate – he calls it his estate – in Buckinghamshire. He's become a British subject, wants to get on the Honours List, get a K, but can't pick political winners. He's always donated to the wrong party or at the wrong time. Sir Kenneth Swain, he'll probably get there one day."

"He's said to have put a lot of money into Londys."

"He's got a lot. He's supposed to have made near enough to three billion dollars when he sold his pharmaceutical business in Pittsburg. Owning Londys is better than owning a newspaper or a film studio. If he were an American woman he'd have married a duke, or at least an earl. He doesn't interfere in the day-to-day management so far as I'm aware. Perhaps he should, shake Gerald up a bit."

"Gerald seems to be very business-like."

"Well he can do long division and almost read a balance sheet. That's a lot more than his opposite numbers in the other houses."

"I must say that it's a lot easier here than in Australia. There are so many paintings and objects floating around the country, and people send good things here from all over the world."

"Overheads are much higher. You were complaining about the rent on your flat. Imagine what it costs to rent the firm's premises in Mayfair. And that's only a start: salaries, repairs, advertising, taxes. Only a wealthy dilettante or a social climber would touch our business." Elena was looking around to order another bottle.

"Do you think we should be going?"

She closed an eye and looked at her watch as if she were sighting a rifle. "Three-thirty, you're a piker aren't you?"

"I thought we ought to be heading off."

"Gerald said take the day to find something," Elena had a disconcerting habit of jumping from topic to topic. "Speaking of blondes, that Nordic looking woman you were talking to at that broken down gallery, who was she?"

A Career Move

"I don't know. I'd never seen her before. I've never been in the area until today."

"It seemed a pretty animated conversation you were having."

"Not on my part."

"Australians are supposed to be uncomplicated, not like English men. Did you go to a boys' boarding school?"

"I went as a day boy to a school that had a boarding house."

"Well, that's something. English men, what they say about them, or a certain class of them is true." She rose unsteadily to her feet. Davenport clasped her shoulder. "Just getting my sea-legs," she said. "Back in a minute." She headed for the lavatory as Davenport paid the bill. When she returned, Davenport hailed a taxi and put her in it.

He had only been in his office for ten minutes when Gerald came in and sat down. "I take it you're a London householder by now?"

"If that's what being a tenant in a decrepit flat in London at an exorbitant rent is, yes."

"Good. Where's Elena?"

"We had lunch. She seemed tired so I suggested she go home."

"Tired, you mean drunk."

"That's going a bit far, Gerald."

"I'll give you a tip Davenport, that woman's a tigress when she's aroused. And it only takes a few drinks to get her fur up."

"She was very helpful."

"You'd better be aware, the firm strongly discourages in-house liaisons."

"We have not liaised, Gerald."

"Actually I didn't come here to speak to you about that. I've been thinking since we last talked. We really do need some new ideas, big projects, around here."

"You seem to have tried everything already: old master sales, modernist, deco, art nouveau, abstract, post impressionist, surrealist, Tibetan, Indonesian, anything that anybody could come up with."

"There's always something no one's thought of yet. You're the whiz kid. Surely you've got some ideas."

Davenport had broken a vow he had long ago made to himself, not to drink any alcohol at lunch. The whole of his brain was vibrating like a soundless cymbal. The pain made it difficult for him to focus on Gerald who was waiting expectantly for the big idea.

"Have you thought about a Russian sale, proletarian art for example? I saw an exhibition in New York once. It was called the 'New Utopia' I think." He embellished the story a little. "They were turning people away in droves."

"Some of the West End dealers have had Russian shows, none of it very proletarian that I can recollect: still lifes and landscapes, undistinguished stuff, very derivative. They must have had norms for the artists as well as the workers. What was in this exhibition in New York?"

"Industrial designs, theatre designs, hand painted China, some jewellery, enamel work, nothing like Fabergé though, drawings, paintings, there were a couple of Malevichs as I recall. There were lots of scenes of happy workers, tractors, assembly lines; some of it was uncomfortably like the German stuff being turned out before the War."

"That's not surprising. One kind of totalitarianism is much like another. We'd need a Russian expert."

Davenport was shocked that Gerald was prepared to entertain a thought thrown out in desperation. "Who would buy it though?" he queried.

"You'd be surprised," Gerald said, echoing the woman whom Davenport had met that morning. "It's about time for a revival of radical chic. That kind of stuff might go well on the wall with a Che Guevara poster and a Rothko. Give it some more thought. We'll talk again." Gerald spoke as if he were leaving on a sea voyage by sail. "Yes, we'll talk again," he repeated.

5

The Lure of Russia

When Olga had come into Rupert's gallery for the first time she had looked disapprovingly at the cracked ceiling, the perilous staircase, the dusty basement, and the pictures on easels – as well as those stacked against the walls. Only after she had looked at most of these had she spoken.

"Like Moscow except pictures not as good."

"I'm sorry?" Rupert had inquired.

"This old building like Moscow construction of 1930. Everything crumbling."

"I'll have you know this building was built in 1870."

"Time for bulldozer then."

"It's got good bones this building."

"Needs new skin. Pictures not much better."

There were in the stacks, some ten or so pictures Rupert thought were good, including an early Brangwyn, a Clausen of a young field hand, three circus drawings by Dame Lura Knight, and a possible Sickert.

"You'd need to know something about British art before you could make that judgement."

"British and art, contradict each other. There is English word for that?"

"Oxymoron."

"Sounds right. Good art is good whoever make it. Bad art bad whether French, Eskimo, or Russian."

"I'm not aware of any Russian modern masters."

"You not heard of Malevich?"

"Of course I have, but he's been dead a long time now."

"Who buys this stuff?" Olga's eyes had disparagingly swept across the whole room.

"Collectors, occasionally another dealer, decorators, especially the still lifes."

"If you want pictures for decorators I know where there are thousands, very cheap too."

"I don't handle lithos or prints of any kind."

"Not prints, paintings, oil paintings on canvas panels made by artists taught to draw and paint."

"I'm well aware that in Hong Kong and places like that there are assembly lines of workers daubing paint on canvas, but they're not making pictures."

"Not Hong Kong, Russia, everywhere, St Petersburg, Moscow and all capitals of the old Soviet republics – even in central Russia."

"How do you know this? What's your interest in art?"

"I studied at art school. I could draw a little but not paint. I become art historian instead. Many good artists in my family, one especially."

"Obviously you're Russian. What part of Russia do you come from?"

"Near St Petersburg."

"May I inquire what you're doing in London?"

"Teaching art history part time at high schools. Waste of time. No one interested, still get paid though."

"Why London? The iron curtain's collapsed. There must be opportunities in Russia now."

"All opportunities taken by the Mafia. One day perhaps it improve, then I go back."

"What brings you to this particular part of London?"

The Lure of Russia

"I give lesson twice a week at school two blocks away. I walk past your place. Always interested in art. Today I decide to have closer look."

"Well, in view of your opinion about the pictures, I suppose you won't do that again."

She must have caught a glimpse of a corner of one of the drawings by Knight because she had walked over to it and extracted it from the stack. "Good drawing. Who did this?"

Rupert had told her, and then explained how the artist specialised in drawing and painting Gypsy, theatre, and circus scenes.

"Even England, then, has some good artists."

"Well, I have to admit that you seem to have a good eye to pick out the Knight." Rupert had looked at his watch. On impulse he'd said, "I'm about to get a coffee. Like to join me?"

"Here?"

"No, at the café three doors down."

Olga had asked for a Turkish coffee but had to accept a short black espresso. She had ladled three spoonfuls of sugar into it and stirred until the mixture had become as viscous and dark as sump oil.

"Do you always teach two days week?" Rupert had asked.

"I'm a supply teacher, on call. On average I get about ten hours a week. To teach art history to English students is endurance test. So far I survive. It help me learn English, anyway."

"Do ten hours give you enough to live on?"

"This is very expensive city. But anyone who brought up in Russia, learn to be a survivor."

"Are you really qualified as an art historian?"

"I have certificate from University of Fine Art, St Petersburg. The Education Department have accepted my qualifications."

"I have to tell you that's hardly a recommendation these days." Rupert had paused to think. As he did, he'd seen again how beautiful the woman was. But it was not just her beauty that had been attractive. She had about her an air of recklessness, danger even; an indifference to authority that, back then, had struck a

55

chord with him.

"Would you be interested in working for me part time?" he'd asked.

Olga had looked at him suspiciously. She'd been the recipient of many propositions, some less ambiguous than others.

"In the gallery I mean. You see, I'm away quite a lot. I have to go to auctions in the country, house sales, and minor auction houses all over England I do have two other employees, a temp, Julia, and Lawrence." Rupert had wondered how he might explain the latter. "He does deliveries mainly; goes to the conservator and the framer for me, odd jobs. Sometimes he's, he's..." Rupert searched for a word. "Disconnected."

"What is disconnected?"

"High. Out. Substances."

"Your gallery opium den or something?"

"Of course not. I haven't even smoked a joint for twenty years. I'm a family man, respectable, law abiding. I've had my differences with the Inland Revenue of course, but who hasn't. I've a son. I wouldn't let Lawrence in the place if he had any substances on him."

"What would be my duties?"

"Dealing with people, clients when I'm not here mainly. You might do some tidying up of the place, help me do a proper catalogue of what I've got, look out for saleable works...generally make yourself useful."

"Tidy up overdue I think."

"I don't have any trouble finding things...usually that is."

"How many hours and how much you pay?"

"Well, you'd want to keep your other job. Perhaps we could say a minimum of fifteen hours a week, and Saturday sometimes if I want to get away for the weekend. Pay? I don't know? What do you think?"

"Education authority pay thirty pounds an hour."

"I could pay thirty five."

"You know nothing about me except what I tell you."

"Well I haven't told you much about myself. Let's regard each other as being on probation for the first two weeks or so."

"Disconnect. Probation. Why you use difficult words?"

"Probation means on trial. Each can call it off if we're unhappy."

Olga began to relax, then, and had asked whether she might have another coffee. "You will need my details. I will write them down." She had taken a pen and a piece of paper from her handbag and proceeded to write her name, telephone number, and address on it. "What else you need? I am twenty five years old. I came here with my mother. She was naturalised and received British pension. Now dead. I have grandfather and distant family in Russia, and cousin in London." Her face had screwed up in distaste when she'd mentioned the cousin. She had said nothing about her grandfather. She had handed Rupert the piece of paper. He had handed her his business card.

"Were you serious when you spoke of thousands of paintings for sale in Russia?"

"I tell no lies about art."

"They're not dear?"

"By standards here, cheaper than bad prints."

"A competently painted landscape, an interesting one by an acknowledged Russian artist, two feet by three say, what would you pay for that?"

"Forty, fifty American dollars."

"Seriously?"

"I tell you, I not lie about art."

"Selling them here, that would be rather like retailing mass produced goods."

"You do not understand. Russia, all the Soviet Republics very big country. Many art school academies. Communists start off with big idea that culture belong to masses. Opportunity must be given to all with talent. It is true that painting styles not evolve, or not much. But artists receive full classical training. Good artists given time and money to paint. Subjects limited. Many, many portraits of Lenin and Stalin, narrative pictures of the revolution, Russian ships, battles – old battles even, oriental scenes, still lifes, nudes, not erotic communists say, but how you paint good nude without being erotic. Paintings of miners and machinists and people working in the fields, dock yards. Work of proletariat for proletariat."

"Even that sort of stuff, at fifty dollars, might be an investment. Would it be hard to get out?"

"When my mother left Russia we brought a dozen unstretched pictures in our suitcase."

"No one asked any questions?"

"No."

"What did you do with them?"

"We sold them in Paris."

"Were they hard to sell?"

"We took them up to Montmartre and asked a Russian looking artist to sell them as his own. They were much better than what he was doing. He agreed, for half the proceeds. He did stretch them. He sold them within few days."

"I don't know whether English people would buy them."

"They were bought by tourists, some of them English tourists."

"American decorators come to London all the time. I wonder if they'd be interested." By this stage Rupert had finished his coffee. "We can speak about this when you start work. When would you like to come in?"

Rupert had spent the next few days thinking about Russian paintings. He had noticed a falling off in interest in the sorts of paintings he ordinarily sold. He had never been to Russia but, at the same time, he often dreamed of becoming a great entrepreneur. All of these thoughts had milled around in his mind. But above all there had been a wish for adventure.

The evening before Olga was to start he had told Cecelia about her as she prepared his usual whisky and soda.

"A Russian girl, why would you do that?"

"She's an art historian, very knowledgeable. She's got good contacts in Russia."

"What's the use of that?"

"I'm thinking of doing some business in Russia."

"Business in Russia. That should be interesting." Cecelia was used to Rupert's grand plans that rarely went beyond the conceptual stage. "What sort of business did you have in mind?" She had handed him his whisky and soda.

Rupert had tasted the drink and held it out to Cecelia. "Needs a little more ice." Cecelia had carefully extracted one cube and lowered it into his drink.

"What were you saying?"

"I asked what sort of business you thought you might do in Russia."

"Art business at first. I've heard there's some very commercial stuff to be picked up for a song. It also occurs to me that it might be worthwhile buying some property there."

"I'd worry about how secure titles would be there." Cecelia always responded as if Rupert had every intention, and the capacity to carry out his grand schemes.

"You'd need to have cash. Probably have to be prepared to pay some bribes but there's nothing unusual about that. Corruption begins at Calais," Rupert had mused.

"And gets worse the further east you go."

"St Petersburg's a Western city. They're just like us."

"St Petersburg's where you'd be going then?"

"At first. No doubt I'd be branching out once I've got the feel of the place. Olga says..."

"Olga? Who's Olga?"

"I told you. The Russian girl who's coming to work for me."

"I didn't know you were looking for anyone. I could have worked for you full time, I still could."

"But you couldn't get access to a cache of cheap Russian paintings."

Cecelia had seen no point in discussing the matter any further. Like Rupert's other schemes this one would be stillborn in a week or so.

But Cecelia had been wrong this time. Over the next eighteen months Rupert made two trips to Russia and the new central Asian republics, each time returning with a couple of hundred or so unstretched canvases of just the kind that Olga had described. Most of them sold well at the prices that Rupert was able to ask. With Olga's assistance, he began to learn something about several of the artists which he confidently retailed to potential buyers with only a little embroidery. He never disclosed to Cecelia the risks that he and Olga had run in towns and in the countryside in which local chieftains and the Mafia jostled for power, and the discomfort of louse infested hotels and appalling service in even the safe areas.

6

Gloria by the Ganges

Just as Gloria was about to leave her room, the telephone rang. It was Walter.

"I thought you promised not to swan off without me again." He must have followed her to the hotel.

"I changed my mind." What a bore Walter had become.

"A promise is a promise."

"What do you want Walter?"

"Don't book out until I arrive. I'll come up straight away."

"I've no intention of booking out, and don't come here. I'm going out."

"All I want is to use the bath."

Gloria could understand that. Only yesterday they had seen three corpses floating down the river in the midst of the dead cattle and other flotsam that it would be wise not to investigate. "Last time we shared a room in a hotel in India you used both towels and you know they only replace them weekly."

"I promise to use the hand towel only."

"Walter, I came here because I need to spend time on my own. That means I don't want to see you until I'm ready."

"Please Glor."

In their early days together Gloria had put up with Walter calling her Glor. It was the same pet-name that Davenport had used. She had not liked it then, and had come to dislike it equally now when Walter used it. Nor did she like the wheedling tone in his voice. He was coming to depend upon her, not just for money, but also for guidance and support in everything. His financial dependence was particularly irritating. They may not have spoken directly of his contribution, but in various ways he had led her to believe that he had enough money to fly to India and live comfortably at the Ashram. Right from the beginning he had been her debtor. He would repay her for his air ticket as soon as a term deposit matured, he said. Would she pay his fees to the Master in the meantime? The meantime became all of the time. The wretched bank had misunderstood his instructions and put the money on deposit for three months again. He always needed something: new sandals, clothes, money for meals. There was no end to it. She had not budgeted for these, or for the extras that the Master said they must pay if they wished to remain. After paying for everything here, and the final instalment on the new townhouse she had bought in Australia, the money that she had received in the settlement with Davenport was almost exhausted.

"Just this once then, Walter. And do use only the hand towel, and don't take the soap. They only provide one cake every three days. I don't want you to be here when I get back. I told you," she said, using the cliché that Davenport had found obnoxious: "I need some space". She put the telephone down and headed for Mr Keynon to begin, what she knew would be the prolonged, torturous, and as satisfying for him as they would be exasperating for her, negotiations for a half-reliable car and a two-handed driver.

Mr Pickford stood a few paces back as she closed, what he would later describe, as the deal.

"Gasoline Mrs Jones, is an extra. It is necessary to charge fifteen percent on top of the bowser price."

"Why?"

"The selection of an honest supplier who does not adulterate the refined product requires much skill and experience."

"Taxi drivers don't seem to worry. They pull in wherever they are when their tanks are low."

"Taxi drivers do not go on long journeys as you and Mr Pickford will today."

"We're only going down the road."

"The road you go down is a singularly bumpy, winding road with much dust on it. To be stationary on that road would be a most unhappy event."

"Five percent on the bowser price."

"Seven and a half."

"All right," Gloria accepted.

Mr Keynon looked disappointed. "Everything is agreed then. Ah, you have not said which you prefer, premium or standard gasoline. The journey will be smoother and surer with premium."

"Standard." There was steel in Gloria's voice.

"Very well then if you must."

Mr Pickford was relieved when the negotiations were concluded. Gloria told him the agreed costs and added. "It will be more than that of course. It always is. I dare say it's a lot less than it would be in America but it still adds up." She said nothing of her own miscalculations.

They walked to the door. The hotel had been built – and its grounds laid out – in 1913. The Hun would not then dare to seek to enlarge its empire, India would continue to be the jewel in the British crown and to provide a livelihood for tens of thousands of English and Scots forever and ever.

A gravelled drive swept through the tall gates and the overgrown gardens to an imposing portico on which the paint was peeling like the soft outer covering of a paperbark tree. In the middle of what had once been a manicured lawn, a fifty foot tall banyan tree had anchored itself with a hundred sinuous roots. The smell of the ubiquitous marigold blended with smoke from dung fires beside the road, strong curries, and other unthinkable scents.

"A first-class country for second-class people. Who was it who said that?" Mr Pickford asked.

"I don't know," Gloria replied.

But Mr Keynon, who was standing behind them, did. "Noel Coward," he said. "It was no account that he was talking of Malaya and not India. It doesn't matter, India or Malaya, the man hit the nail on the head every time. A very clever author. Even the British soldiers who came east only did because they couldn't afford the fashionable regiments."

"They brought you democracy," Gloria countered. It was as if she and Mr Keynon had to express polar views on everything.

"Not true madam. We never had any democracy until they left."

"That's what I mean, they left you the framework of good institutions, a free press, fair courts, parliament, free elections."

As Gloria spoke a very large, old black car began to make its way slowly up the drive.

"It arrives. It is on time," Mr Keynon announced triumphantly. "I look forward to continuing our discussion Mrs Jones about the British heritage, such as it is, in India."

Gloria was unable to resist one final shot. "You, Mr Keynon, as a fluent and a grammatically correct speaker of English, must acknowledge the gift of language bequeathed to you by the British."

Mr Keynon chose not to hear what Gloria had said as he opened the back door of the old limousine when it came to an uncertain stop. In an aside, Gloria said to Mr Pickford, "I've been here too long. I'm beginning to speak English like them."

Mr Pickford read aloud the name on the car, "Humber Super Snipe. What a name for an automobile."

"The best of British internal combustion engineering," Mr Keynon stated.

"That's reassuring," Mr Pickford said as he stood aside to allow Gloria to enter the car.

"The driver is a second cousin of mine. He is young but reliable. I vouch for him. You can talk freely," Mr Keynon reassured them as if they were about to discuss state secrets. "He has not the gift for English language. He understands go, stop, and slow down. The last is very important. He does have a regrettable tendency to put the proverbial foot down." He slammed the door with a flourish and called out, "Setram, go."

The leather in the car was old, and the springs in the seats devoid of all springiness. Setram turned round and stared at them as the car moved off towards what had once been a rose garden.

"I don't travel by car very often," Gloria said. "But I find when I do, the best thing is never to look ahead and never to look to the side. Just keep your head down. If I had my way, the passenger seats in this country would face backwards so you could see all the dangers and near misses after you've escaped them."

It was sweltering inside the car, even with the windows down. Each time they stopped, people would stick their heads in and offer them pieces of fruit, or bunches of flowers, or swatches of crimson and golden sari silk.

"I meant to congratulate you on your negotiations for the car. That man seems to love an argument."

"It's all very amicable but quite exhausting. I think my time here is up. If I have to go through that to hire a car I don't envy you trying to buy, what, ten thousand or so dollars worth of materials."

"Not ten thousand, ten million more like, but over three years."

"As much as that?"

"If the quality and price are right, yes."

Gloria looked at Mr Pickford with heightened interest. "Yours must be a very big business."

"The biggest of its kind in the States."

"You've never bought here before?"

"No, but I've seen samples. They were very good."

"No talk about prices?"

"Vaguely. Figures have been touched upon, but nothing firm."

"Your wife, she doesn't travel with you?"

"I've never married. What about you, are you married?"

"It's been all over for a long time. He was a very selfish man."

"I'm sorry to hear that."

"He was only interested in himself. He was an arts bureaucrat – very ambitious." Gloria lowered her eyelids. "He neglected me."

"A woman, like you, capable," Mr Pickford lamented, "and so

attractive. You're here alone then; what I mean..." He blushed, recalling that there may have been mention of a platonic travelling companion.

"Yes, well, that is, a former colleague travelled with me, and is taking some of the same courses as I am."

Mr Pickford looked disappointed.

"I've no idea what his plans are. As I said, I'll be leaving soon," Gloria added.

Mr Pickford cheered up. "Another course, more travel, what are your plans?"

"Self-betterment."

"Is that what you've mainly been doing here?"

"Self-betterment and ascetics."

"You mean aesthetics?"

"No, ascetics. The right way is the austere way, renunciation of all but the basic bodily functions of living, and thinking."

"I don't get it. The hotel, where you're staying, I know it's not the Waldorf, but by local standards I wouldn't call it ascetic."

"The Master, the course master that is, said I had denied myself too much for too long. He prescribed two nights away from the Ashram."

"Did he prescribe the whisky you recommended too?"

"No. That was for a stomach upset."

The car was approaching a great pile of a building constructed mainly of rusting corrugated iron. A large sign in English on its façade stated, 'Pandit Silks and Fabrics Company.'

They were met at the entrance by a brisk young woman in western clothes, and taken into an air conditioned board room. Its carpet and furniture were modern, and unlike the exterior of the building, in good condition. After a minute or so, Mr Pandit himself entered. He was a small, alert man in middle age, with a wide smile. He greeted Mr Pickford effusively and looked inquisitively at Gloria.

"This is Miss, Miss..."

Gloria finished the sentence, "Jones."

"A venerable English name," Mr Pickford said. "But you are not

English."

"Australian."

"Another esteemed member of the great Commonwealth. Miss Jones is...?"

"My personal assistant and translator for this trip."

Mr Pandit could not conceal his look of disbelief. Recovering, he observed, "It will not be necessary for Miss Jones to translate. As you see, my English, although sadly deficient by the standards of a Brahmin of the East Coast of the United States such as yourself, should suffice. I am not myself a Brahmin of India, simply a modest businessman." He tapped loudly on the table and two workmen appeared carrying many dozens of samples of different materials.

Even to Gloria, who had been in the country long enough to know how tortuous the simplest of transactions could be, marvelled at the loquaciousness of Mr Pandit, and his unwillingness to state prices and delivery dates. She also marvelled at how well Mr Pickford handled the negotiations, which were punctuated by frequent invitations to take tea. On the third of these, Mr Pandit launched into a digression on the tea trade.

"You are aware, Mr Pickford, of the dishonourable association of the Indian tea trade with the cultivation and sale of that dangerously addictive derivative of the poppy flower?"

Mr Pickford showed no interest in the matter. Mr Pandit persisted. "The English, who were the largest consumers of tea, were forced to go to China to buy it because in those times the Middle Kingdom had a monopoly over it. The English paid for much of it with opium cultivated in India. The trade converted many Chinese into addicts. In time, the plant was stolen from the Chinese and transplanted in the verdant fertile hills of northern India. Drink up. I have heard it said that it is the beverage that cheers but never inebriates."

"Quite so. Now, there are some twenty samples or so that I'm interested in. Do you think we can return to those?"

"You are a true American businessman, anxious to do the deal. I understand that. In America time is money. In this country, as our former masters used to say, take time for tiffin. That expression

The Russian Master

reminds me of a book by another of our former masters about our neighbour, Malaya as it used to be called. You have read the works of Mr Anthony Burgess?" When Mr Pickford shook his head, Mr Pandit looked to Gloria. "Not even *The Clockwork Orange?*"

"I saw the film, nasty, violent thing it was."

"The book of which I speak was not a particularly violent one. There was some violence in it of course. The violence was the violence of the Chinese communist insurgents in Malaya. That insurgency was quelled by the skill of the British general, Templar. You have heard the name?" For a moment, Mr Pandit lost his train of thought, but then he continued. "Where was I? Yes. Anthony Burgess, the book, *Time for a Tiger*. Hence, in this country, time for tiffin. 'Tiger', as you may also be aware, is the brand of a beer made in the Malay States, as then they were called."

"Mr Pandit I really do need to get firm prices, quantities, and shipping dates if we are to do business."

"I am sorry. Again I have been seduced by my love of literature. Does it strike you as odd, disloyal perhaps, for an Indian to have a love for the language and literature of the people who enslaved this country?"

"No. Can I get those prices and dates?"

Like Mr Keynon at the hotel, Mr Pandit could recognise an ultimatum when it was delivered. With a sigh he reached for his notebook and pen, and began laboriously to write the code number and colour of each cloth, and the price of each roll. When he had finished he handed the notebook to Mr Pickford.

Mr Pickford very deliberately took his Mont Blanc pen out of his pocket, unscrewed the cap, and briskly wrote a lower number beside each of Mr Pandit's prices.

Mr Pandit slowly and painfully read Mr Pickford's numbers. Again, he sighed before writing a new price, in each instance about fifteen percent below his first price. He returned the notebook to Mr Pickford.

The American stood up. "I am sorry to have taken up your time. I am unable to do business with you at those prices." He signalled to

Gloria to come with him and made for the door.

"In order to clear some surplus stocks, and because I hope for a long and mutually profitable future, I am prepared to accept your prices," Mr Pandit paused and looked to the ceiling for inspiration, "Plus five point seven five per cent."

Mr Pickford stopped. "It is high, but because I similarly hope for a profitable association, I agree."

Gloria was mistaken, however, in thinking that the negotiations were concluded. As Mr Pickford explained later, "Quality control, date of production, and assurance of delivery, are critical. Never pay before you've tied them down. The terms of the letter of credit and a trustworthy person to inspect, insure, supervise, and certify delivery and shipment are vital."

"I'd stopped listening. It gave me a migraine."

"That's just business."

"Is it always like that?"

"Pretty much. Every country has a different style."

"Well I'd find the Indian style intolerable if I had to do it."

"It could be much worse. You heard him talking about English literature and history. You wouldn't find many American businessmen who could do that."

"It seemed like a diversion to me, to put you off. Not that you were. You were very clever."

It was a long time since anyone had told Mr Pickford that he was clever, let alone very clever. "I'm sorry it was so boring for you."

"You didn't need me. I didn't do a thing."

"Just having you there was a help. He knew you had been living in India. Your presence was enough to stop him from putting anything over me."

The traffic was heavy. At one point they were stationary for twenty-five minutes. At last the car drew up in front of the hotel. It came to a stop like an amateur dancer teetering on her toes. It was half past three already.

"I feel like a drink," Mr Pickford said. "You'll join me?"

"I've a better idea. Why don't you bring a bottle of whisky and

The Russian Master

soda water up to my room. That way Mr Keynon won't bother us. Just give me half an hour to have a bath. Room 414."

"You're sure? I can pay you then too." Mr Pickford blushed at the implication of going to a woman's hotel room to pay her for services provided. "You're...there's no problem about my coming up there?"

"Of course not. And you don't owe me anything."

"We'll see. Half an hour then."

Mr Pickford went ahead. He outflanked Mr Keynon who had been trying to encircle them before they separated. He was left with Gloria.

"Everything was satisfactory, the car, its performance?" When Gloria nodded, he continued, "It was the gasoline, pure and unadulterated that ensured the smooth ride. And the business, all transacted to Mr Pickford's satisfaction I trust?"

"You'd have to ask him. I'm not a businessman."

"You will be dining together tonight?" A salacious smile appeared on his lips. "By the way, a Mr Walter was here. He wanted your key. 'By what authority?' I asked. He said he wished to use your room. 'For what purpose?' I said. I would not repeat to a lady like yourself the violent language that he used. I stood firm, like the proverbial Rock of Gibraltar, that great imperial fortification at the western mouth of the Mediterranean. I thought he was about to strike. Then I recalled that it was true that twice, I am right in saying twice am I not, twice before I had seen you walking in the town with him in an apparently friendly way. I felt obliged therefore to allow him the access he sought. But I warned him," Mr Keynon shook his finger at Gloria as if to admonish her, "that he should be careful because I had an inventory of all hotel property in the room."

"You did the right thing Mr Keynon. I take it he's gone."

"I was not at my desk but I saw him leave by the back door two hours ago. Your key madam." Mr Keynon handed Gloria a key from a pigeon-hole.

Upstairs, Gloria washed away the dust of the day with the half cake of soap that was left. She was too tired to be angry with Walter for the theft of the other half. She was furious, though, when she saw that he had taken her shampoo. "That does it," she said to herself. "It's finished." She forced herself to be calm. Walter's sponging and this latest petty theft were ample excuse for severing the tie, and for doing with Mr Pickford whatever she could persuade him to do. She wondered, in thinking he might need persuasion, whether she was being a little unfair to herself. She was still young, her body, as she surveyed it in the bath, was firm and shapely, and she was not a woman without interests or other attractions. Mr Pickford might be twenty or so years older, but he seemed a strong man, virile intellectually and physically.

Gloria dried herself and dabbed a drop of scent on her neck. She chose a loose fitting, low necked, long, vaguely sari-like dress, that she had bought in the bazaar.

She looked around the room in irritation. It was so plain. Still, she must make the best of it. She closed the curtains and turned off the lights except for the lamp on the bedside table. She pulled the coverlet off the bed, and turned a corner of the sheet and blanket back away from the pillows. She would have liked to turn on some soft European music but all that the radio offered was a succession of loud Bollywood songs more apt for energetic, non-proximate, outdoor dancing than the natural and inevitable proximity that she had in mind.

Five minutes later there was a light knock on the door. Mr Pickford was outside with whisky, two bottles of soda and two glasses. "I didn't bring any ice, thought it might be a bit risky, is that all right?"

"You have good judgment in all things," Gloria offered. "Come in."

"You must think me terrible," she said as Mr Pickford sat down, "A whisky drinker. I don't imagine decent women drink whisky in Indianapolis."

"By the gallon, at the Country Club. Don't stand between them and a pitcher of Bourbon Sours."

"Unless you've got the royal suite in this hotel, you'll understand that I can't offer you a better chair than the one there. You take it and I'll sit here on the bed."

The Russian Master

Gloria sat down at about halfway along the bed. If she were to fall, or be gently pressed, her head would be upon the pillow with her hair artistically spread beside and under it.

"That was a very impressive performance today," she said, as she allowed Mr Pickford to remove the seal from the bottle and pour two whiskies before adding soda water. "There's a theory," she continued, "I don't hold with it myself, that the whisky would kill any germs in the water anyway. It's not worth the risk in my opinion."

"Cheers," Mr Pickford said.

"Why don't you take your coat off?" Gloria suggested. It did not seem to her that Mr Pickford was accustomed to strange women's bedrooms. "How much longer will you be staying here?" she asked.

"Only another day or two. I'll need to talk to some local shippers and a lawyer. Doing business in foreign countries has taught me you have to have a local lawyer as well as your own. But by God, on the assumption that any lawyer can out-talk any businessman, I shudder to think how long a consultation will take. I expect they do time charging here too."

"There's such a lot you must have to know to be a successful businessman. Here, let me freshen that up, freshen-up a drink, isn't that what they say in the USA?"

"Er, thank you. Yes in some places."

As Gloria added half an inch of whisky to his glass her inner thigh made a slight but unmistakable contact with his knee.

"Are there many other westerners at the, what do you call it, the Ashram?" Mr Pickford inquired.

"Not as many, apparently, as thirty or so years ago. A lot of the pop singers came here, not the biggest names though. They mainly went to Katmandu. This place would be too intellectual for them. Transcendental meditation, getting to know the inner self, is a hard, tiring activity." The whisky was already going to Gloria's head. She made meditation sound like a day in the salt mines. She leant back and kicked her sandals off. "This must seem very different to you."

"A little on the exotic side perhaps," Mr Pickford gallantly said.

Mr Pickford was getting the lie of the land now. He took off his shoes and socks.

"Stretch out your toes and then your feet, then your calves, and last your thighs. You'll feel the strength and the power flow through them. Then relax, starting with your thighs and going through, slowly, to your toes. Have you ever seen a panther when it wakes up? It stretches, slowly, luxuriantly, beautifully," Gloria advised.

Gloria lay back upon the pillow, and slowly, languorously began to lift one leg, her skirt riding high on it. She was not wearing any underclothing.

Mr Pickford stood up. He came across to Gloria, lay down beside her, and cradled her in his arms. He was about to kiss her when there was a noise outside the door. It opened. Walter stood on the threshold.

"Gloria," he shouted. "Stop that."

Mr Pickford fell off the bed.

"What are you doing here? I told you not to come back. And, and...you stole half the soap."

"It's just as well I did come back."

"Where did you get the key?"

"I asked the boy for the key. I told him I'd left the other one in the room."

"Just when you need him that Keynon's never there. Leave the key on the dressing table and get out."

Mr Pickford managed to pick himself off the floor. He searched around for his shoes and socks. He found only one of each but headed for the door."

"Don't go Mr Pickford," Gloria pleaded.

"I'll fix you up for today later. I'll leave an envelope at the desk."

"So that's what it's come to has it, Gloria?"

"What do you mean?"

"You know what I mean, doing tricks for foreign tourists. What do you charge? I suppose it depends on what you need at the time."

"What's your problem if I am? Not getting your share? You've got all the instincts of a pimp."

"You're disgusting," Walter shouted.

The Russian Master

"And you're a parasite. It's a wonder I'm not on the game. You haven't paid for a thing for months."

The deception and then betrayal of Davenport, the anticipation of the divorce settlement, the giving of notice, and the journey to India – all that excitement – were well and truly behind them now. Any physical attraction, in the heat and dust of the harsh Indian climate, and beset with the strange and urgent desires which manifested themselves in the bowels, had been the first to go. Respect, interest, and liking were not long in following. The fag end of the affair sputtered and went out there and then that early evening in room 414 of the Blenheim Hotel in Rishikesh on the Ganges.

The next day, as Gloria booked out of the hotel, Mr Keynon handed her a thick envelope. She opened it in a secluded corner of the dining room. Inside were Mr Pickford's business card with the words "for services rendered" written on it in neat handwriting, and two hundred and fifty US dollars. A tear of chagrin fell from Gloria's eyes as she put the money in her purse.

Back at the desk she asked the number of Mr Pickford's room. "Three hundred and twelve," Mr Keynon leered. He waited until Gloria had reached the lift before he announced, "Mr Pickford checked out half an hour ago."

Gloria went first to the Air India booking office where she booked a cheap flight to Paris. She was in no mood for long negotiations. At the Ashram she packed the few belongings worth taking with her. She spoke to neither the Master, any of his staff, nor Walter before she left for the airport.

7

At the Swinging Gate

Davenport, although a generous man had never been an extravagant one. He blanched at the furniture catalogues Elena insisted he read. For a start it had never occurred to him that there could be so many different varieties of beds and mattresses, and springs and slats, and bed linen and pillows.

"Buy the practical things first," Elena said.

"I don't see how a bed that oscillates like a gentle tide can be very practical." He pointed to the illustration in the catalogue. "Nor spending three thousand three hundred and ten pounds plus VAT."

"There's no need to go for the top of the range. Look at this one, French Cherrywood and brushed steel, extra length and width. I like the look of it. It would fit with old or new."

"At two thousand four hundred, I should hope so. All right, I've seen the top of the range. Now where's the bottom?"

"That's hardly the Londys spirit."

"Nor was the case of whisky I saw going into Gerald's room yesterday afternoon. It was not a label known to many men."

"He'll put it in a decanter, and few will know the difference. But there's no hiding a bed, Davenport."

Davenport couldn't decide whether Elena was being suggestive.

On balance he thought it was better to give her the benefit of the doubt. "I don't know why people get fussed about beds. Back in Australia there were times when I slept on a blow-up plastic mattress." He congratulated himself on being free of those days when Gloria would banish him to his den, as she called it, whenever she was troubled by her headaches, or whenever Davenport had committed one of his unintended but deeply offensive transgressions. "I'm quite comfortable on the mattress that was left in the flat."

"A blow-up mattress!" Elena's mind was still focused on his earlier comment. "How very nineteen seventies Earls Court," she scoffed. "Australians are much more upmarket these days; what, with Booker Prizes and chief executives running British companies.

"It's not as if I expect visitors or will need to entertain clients at home," he protested.

"You don't know who you might be entertaining, Davenport. No, cheap and nasty won't do. It isn't you anyway."

"I'm very grateful for your interest, Elena, but I don't think you should waste your time trying to make me fashionable."

Elena was not to be deterred. The next Saturday they set out for the trendy shops of South Kensington. By two o'clock he found himself the owner of a new, budget model, king-size, adjustable, flexible, laminated, slatted bed with a swept back, powder coated aluminium head board, an 'Eternal Bliss' mattress, three sets of Egyptian cotton sheets and pillow cases, a sheepskin undersheet, three cashmere and wool mixture blankets – relatively cheap because they were made in China, a set of never-tarnish stainless steel flatware, a dinner set for eight of Worcester (another bargain because it was a seconds from the Reject China Shop), a Romanian Khelim, and a Pakistan Ghul pattern rug, all for, as Elena stressed, the remarkably low sum of seven thousand three hundred and ninety five pounds and forty nine pence. He had stood firm against a new stove, refrigerator, and other kitchen appliances.

"And for all that money I've got nothing decorative, or anything I particularly like."

Repeatedly, Elena had to draw him away from the windows of the

At the Swinging Gate

picture and antique dealers in the area.

"You can think of that later. Right now there are more practical things that you need."

"Such as?" Davenport grumbled.

"Pots and pans, pyrex dishes, I told you, appliances. There's nothing in that flat except the leaking refrigerator, a stove that looks as ancient as a First World War field kitchen, and a few beaten-down electrical items. And those central heating pipes don't look the best to me. Two or three oil heaters won't go amiss. However, that's for after lunch. I'm famished."

When they had ordered, Elena said, "You'll thank me for this Davenport, especially in January when you're huddled under your cashmere blankets on your Eternal Bliss mattress with the oil heaters glowing away and the winds howling outside."

"You make the mattress sound like a sarcophagus. It was kind of you. I don't mean to be ungrateful," his habitual courtesy compelled him to add. The prices on the menu seemed a trifle expensive but after his earlier profligacy, not worth complaining about. He glanced across to her. "I'm taking up your whole Saturday."

"Not yet. There's a place in Old Brompton Road where they sell superceded model appliances. If you are determined to be a cheapskate we can try there I suppose. We'll have to get a cab, though. Nowhere to park there."

"Sounds just right," Davenport gratefully agreed.

They were finished their shopping by half-past three. The goods that he had paid for were described by the salesman as made on the 'just-in-time' basis, which, it became apparent to Davenport, meant that it would be some time before he got them. Elena stood on the footpath expectantly. Unfortunately Davenport didn't know what she was expecting. What he did know was that he was almost exhausted, financially, he reminded himself, as well as physically.

"I'll get you a taxi," he said, although by now he was beginning to realise that Elena had something else in mind. "Here's one," he announced, throwing himself in front of it.

"For Christ's sake gov'nor," the driver shouted, "You after compo

The Russian Master

or somethin'?"

Davenport pretended not to hear as he flung open the door and ushered Elena inside. He handed the driver a twenty pound note, waved, and hurried away.

He hailed another taxi and gratefully slumped into it, asking the driver to take him to his new flat. The journey took him along the road where earlier in the week he'd spoken to the Russian woman outside the small, art dealer shop.

As he passed the shopfront, he saw that the portrait of Lenin had been replaced by an even larger painting. It was a narrative scene in which several gaudily uniformed senior officers, some guards, and civilians in frock coats appeared to be watching a test flight of an old biplane. The aeroplane was flying out over the sea, and in the foreground was a competently painted landscape. He told the driver to stop, paid him and got out.

Davenport drew closer to the window. The faces and postures of each of the men were quite different. There was character and expression in the eyes of those in the foreground. One man had his back to the viewer. He was leaning upon his cane in an entirely natural posture.

Totally absorbed, Davenport wasn't aware that someone was standing beside him, until he saw the reflection in the window.

"Not bad is it?" Rupert asked.

"Not bad at all," Davenport replied.

"Two thousand one hundred, including delivery, and it's yours."

"I wouldn't have a place for a picture as big as that. What is it?" Davenport asked.

"I'm calling it 'Test flight by Bleriot'."

"But what is it really?"

"God only knows."

"But you must know something about it. Who's the artist?"

"A top Russian."

"Yes, but what's his name?"

"You'll need Olga for that."

At the Swinging Gate

"Olga?"

"My assistant, Russian, art historian, expert. You see there's a signature in the lower left corner. It's in Cyrillic. You don't read Cyrillic by any chance do you?"

"No."

"I thought you might be able to. You're not English are you?"

"Australian."

"I should have guessed. You never know in this city anymore. Most of the foreigners I meet who speak English have been educated in the States. It's the worst of all worlds, a Czech or a Japanese trying to speak English, but doing it with a hybrid Czech-Yank accent. I could let you have it for nineteen hundred."

"I'm afraid I couldn't afford it at nine hundred."

"You Aussies are shrewd bargainers, I will say that."

"I'm not trying to bargain with you."

"That's the art of it, bargaining while you deny you're bargaining. I couldn't go below fifteen hundred. Are you interested?"

"In the picture, and the artist, but not in buying it."

"Well, as I said, you'll have to wait for Olga for that. You're interested in art?"

Davenport was in two minds whether to admit that he was. "In a manner of speaking."

"What's that mean?"

"I work for Londys."

Rupert stood back to appraise him. "You don't sound like Londys. You don't look like Londys either." Rupert noticed Davenport's expression of concern. "That's not an insult. It's a compliment, actually."

"It's a very old firm."

"Old, experienced, and devious. Do you answer directly to Gerald de Pyne?"

"As a matter of fact I do."

"I was at Brenton with Gerald. It was obvious even back then that he'd make a good confidence man...or an art auctioneer."

"But you're in the art business yourself."

"No honour among thieves. You should know that. How is Gerald? It's a while since I've seen him. He's too high and mighty these days to call on a little art dealer at Worlds End."

"He's well as far as I know. I've only been at Londys for a few weeks."

"How do you come to be working for Londys?"

"Gerald asked me."

"Headhunted?"

"That sounds too grand for me. Only chief executives or chief financial officers are headhunted."

"You must have some special talents. Are you a tax lawyer? That's what Londys would be after. I'm looking for a tax shelter myself. Any good tax shelters in Australia?"

"I'm not a tax lawyer but I don't think there are any good tax shelters in Australia."

"You're an accountant then? Gerald would also need an expert to help him cook the books."

"No." Davenport thought Rupert was more inquisitive than a Sydney taxi driver but decided to continue. "I'm in the painting department, late nineteenth early twentieth century European art, Spanish more than the others, but mainly topographical."

"How would you know about Spanish art, living, and I assume studying, in Australia?"

"I've travelled, and I'm also the London expert on Antipodean art, although I don't expect to see much of that here."

A look of enlightenment appeared on Rupert's face. "I think I read about you, in *Jove*, is that right? You've got some strange name, 'Stoke on Trent Smith', something like that?"

"Davenport Jones."

"That's right, the Divera expert. What about a drink?"

Rupert led the way to the Swinging Gate, a pub five doors from his shop. The air inside was heavy with old tobacco and the smell of two hundred years of spilt beer. Through the dark, smoky air, Davenport thought he could discern three dogs on leads, all wearing muzzles. "Good pub this, one of the few in London where you can bring your dog. The coursing people like it. "Are you a betting man, Jones?" Without waiting for an answer, he added, "I'd have a hundred each way on 'Goldilocks' if I were you." He pointed to a yellow bitch oblivious to the noise and smells around her.

"She doesn't look very fast to me."

"Course not. She's trained to look sleepy. That's what the punters are supposed to think. Not that it matters whether she's vigorous or not. The other dogs in her race will have been fed salted pork all day. They'll be so thirsty that they'll drink half a gallon of water before they're taken on to the track. But she'd beat them on merit anyway. Two weeks ago she caught the mechanical hare. All the lights short circuited. Good dog that. Bitter?"

"Just a half thank you."

When Rupert returned with the drinks they found a table and two chairs near the wall. "How did you come to be interested in Divera?"

"He spent some time in Australia. You know all art is related. He got something out of my country and left something in return. You can see the influences if you look hard enough."

"It was a good story. There were two women weren't there, an old one and her niece? Has anyone ever heard anything of them since?"

"There are rumours they went to Buenos Aires. Even if they could be extradited from there, the Director of Public Prosecutions doesn't think there's a case against them. They never specifically said the picture they sold the museum was a Divera."

"Caveat emptor."

"Exactly. As it always has been."

"Like Londys's promise they'll refund your money if you can prove the painting's not what they have sold it as. Ever tried it?"

"I don't think I'd put myself in the position of competing with the firm's clients."

Goldilocks had awakened and was slowly but purposely moving towards Rupert and Davenport. She put her muzzled snout on Davenport's groin. He stroked her gently as she subsided back into sleep.

"You've got a way with dogs, too. I thought all you had out there were dingoes."

"You've got some strange ideas about Australia. You ought to go there, see it for yourself."

"Going to Russia is bad enough. I take it you've never visited that great social experiment?"

"No, but I'd like to."

"I'm thinking of going again myself."

"I thought you must have been there."

"Because of all the Russian pictures in the gallery? I did, but Olga found them for me. We did get to Uzbekistan, though; a bit hairy but I managed to pick up some reasonable stuff. You have to ask yourself whether Russia's ever going to be ready for democracy. Still, chaotic times are times of opportunity. Why don't you come next time? We could share the cost of hiring a van."

"I've just started in a new job. I can't go anywhere. Do you think there's anything else there? I mean anything other than proletarian art and pale shadows of nineteenth century impressionism?"

"You're a bit hard on my stock."

"No, in its way it's not bad, just not very original although I concede some of it has something."

"You've got to admit it's not expensive."

"True. But surely the party couldn't stop everyone from experimenting."

A wily look crossed Rupert's face. "Do you know more than you're letting on?"

"I don't know what you're talking about?"

"Do you like Rothko?"

"Not much."

"Nor do I. I wouldn't mind having a few though."

"Why did you ask me about Rothko?"

"No particular reason. I might as well have asked your opinion about Pollock or de Kooning. Your round."

Davenport went to the bar and returned with two drinks. When he sat down, Rupert asked, "Have you heard of the Spoliation

At the Swinging Gate

Panel?"

"No."

"It's a panel, a committee of art experts presided over by a High Court judge. It functions as a kind of a court or arbitrator. It's not perfect but it's a lot better than going to law. Isn't anything?"

Davenport, recalling Gloria's legal assault upon his property when they divorced, enthusiastically agreed.

"The panel has other uses."

Davenport was curious but thought it better to wait to see whether Rupert would explain. But he didn't. He quickly finished his drink, rose to leave, and said, "Look in next time you're passing." As he stepped away, Goldilocks lunged at his heel but was unable to bite him through her muzzle.

"Bloody dog," Rupert exclaimed.

Goldilocks's owner came over and secured her with a lead.

"She's a bit restive before a race. She's a cert. you know, probably start at twelves. I've been slowing her down the last few runs. She likes you. You should bet on her. How much money have you got on you?"

Davenport instinctively went for his wallet. He opened it to check, and took out six five pound notes to count them. The owner reached across and extracted four of the notes as smartly as a skilled surgeon would extract an appendix. "I'll put it all on the nose. No point in an each-way bet." As quickly as he had taken the notes, he, the other two dogs and Goldilocks disappeared through the side door.

Davenport tiredly made his way towards his new flat. There were no lights in Rupert's window now. Nearby, the cafés and bars were bustling with young women with bare midriffs, and men in black suits without ties, and with their shirts loose about their trousers. Davenport felt as out of it as he had at school when he had been mocked for tucking his T-shirt into his trousers. The kerb was lined with BMWs and Italian cars he could not name. One of them was a convertible. Its hood was down. Davenport wished for rain.

In his flat he undressed and prepared to bed down on an old couch

The Russian Master

left by the previous occupant. All that he had for entertainment was an ancient-looking transistor radio. He turned it on. A country and western singer was crooning a sad song about his dog that had died from a bait a neighbouring rancher had put out for the coyotes. It was a particularly long song. Davenport tried to change the station but the selector switch was jammed. He turned it off and composed himself for sleep. When it came it was restless and dream filled. There were three women in the dreams – Elena, Olga, and Gloria. They appeared and re-appeared but sometimes it was Olga's head on Gloria's body, with Gloria in her neat, scrubbed jeans going off to school, or Elena in her business suit with Olga's face. When Davenport woke at six o'clock in the morning he was just as tired as when he had turned off the light nine hours before.

He heard an urgent knocking on his door. He threw on his dressing gown and went to investigate. Elena, carrying two large shopping bags was on the threshold. She lurched past him.

"You look awful. What were you up to last night?" She put her head around the door to the bedroom, nodded in approval of its monastic solitariness, and strode towards the kitchen.

"Men never really learn how to look after themselves. I bet you've got no food of any kind here." She placed the bags on a bench and began to unpack them. "Coffee, tea, milk, butter, bread, some lamb chops. I assume you like lamb. All you Australians do I imagine, all those sheep roaming around, what else could you eat? Paper plates and cups, knives and forks. Sugar, bacon, some potatoes, tomatoes, cheese, and eggs. Can you boil an egg, Davenport?"

"Of course I can. How much do I owe you?"

"Forget it. I began to feel guilty last night about how much I made you spend. You can take me out to dinner when you're flush again."

"As a matter of fact I might have made a few pounds on the side. You didn't happen to bring a paper with you did you?"

"Is the Sunday Telegraph all right?" It was the last object in the bags. She handed it to him.

Davenport turned to the sports pages. "You wouldn't know

whether they publish the dog results would you?"

"Dog results, what on earth do you mean?"

"Coursing dogs, racing dogs."

Elena took the paper from him. In a few moments she'd found the results. She handed back the paper. Davenport searched for the name. "Goldilocks," he found it. She had won by three lengths at twenty-two to one.

"I think I've won more than four hundred pounds," Davenport said.

"I never thought of you as a betting man, Davenport."

"I'm not, but a man in a pub promised to put twenty pounds on Goldilocks last night for me."

"A man in a pub, you'll never see the money."

"He owned the dog."

"So?"

"I think he's a friend of Rupert."

"Who's Rupert?"

"A man I had a drink with in the pub last night."

"Just what did you get up to last night? I had a feeling when I left that you wanted to get rid of me."

"No, not at all. You see I was looking in that art dealer's window when he came out. We got to talking and he invited me for a drink."

"And you went, just like that? Look Davenport, this isn't some little Australian town, this is London. It's full of deviants. You know what I mean by deviants?"

"Well Sydney isn't actually Vatican City either."

"You can tell me all about it over breakfast. Coffee? Eggs and bacon, toast?"

Davenport was in favour of all those. He had greatly missed them during the health regimes Gloria regularly used to impose on him. "I'll just go and change."

"No. Stay as you are. It's your house. You're entitled to be comfortable. I'll just slip this off myself." She removed a light cardigan she had been wearing. Underneath it was a low cut shirt that finished about two inches above the top of her jeans. "Go on, read the paper. There's nothing you can do here."

Elena was as efficient as a cook as she was an accountant, even on the stove which the previous tenant had not thought worth taking. In no time she had the gas alight and the bacon and eggs crackling away in the pan. When breakfast was prepared, she put it on the paper plates and carried it out on to the balcony on the side of the flat. The former tenant must have thought the two chairs and metal table there also not worth taking.

"Quite a picnic," she observed. "I sometimes think it would be good to use throw-away utensils and plates all the time. Could you imagine Gerald doing that? He's fastidious to the point of boring. Now tell me about your art dealer and the dog owner."

When Davenport had given an account of his meeting, Elena said, "This man Rupert sounds a bit of a chancer to me. London's full of people like that. He didn't try to sell you a painting did he?"

"Yes, but not very hard."

"Well you're the expert on art. I'm just the bookkeeper."

Davenport smiled. For the first time since leaving Australia he felt the sun on his bare feet. Elena was leaning back to expose her full face to the warmth.

There was silence for a time. Elena broke it. "I love lazy Sunday mornings. We should have the papers, not for edification but to read the travel section and plan foreign holidays." Davenport was inclined to think she meant holidays together. "What do you do for holidays in Australia, Davenport?" she asked.

"Nothing special, not after Gloria and I were divorced."

"Before you were?"

"Once she sent me to a health camp."

"You don't look as if you needed that. Was it a spa?"

"No, it was literally a camp. I had to pitch my own tent. It was in the mountains, in the middle of a rain forest. It rained the whole time. If ever there was a misnomer, it was health camp. I was freezing the whole time. I caught a dreadful cold and got food poisoning."

"Why was it supposed to be healthy?"

At the Swinging Gate

"The inmates, guests that is, were taught self-dependence. Physical and spiritual well-being they claimed. We had to confront our demons, extend ourselves: meeting the challenges of nature would teach us to meet the challenges presented by our own inadequate personalities. I can hear Gloria reading the brochure now. She drew the tariff out of our joint account, fifteen hundred and seventy dollars for the week."

"Why didn't she go?"

"She said we couldn't afford for both of us to go and my need was much greater than hers."

"It sounds as if whatever it cost to get in, it would be worth more to get out. Surely you didn't stay."

"I had no choice. We drove to a pick-up place at the foot of the mountain and had to surrender our car keys. Then they drove us up the mountain in four-wheel drives. They didn't have to blindfold us. It was dark by then. There was no way any of us could find our way back. After a few days, I tried to start a revolt. They phoned Gloria on their mobile – they'd impounded ours – and told me to speak to her. She cried and told me how ungrateful I was. There were only two days to go. I stayed, and had to spend three days in bed when I got home."

"I thought Australia was a place for wonderful holidays?"

"The myth of the bronzed surfing Aussie. Don't believe it. I had to be rescued from the surf by a lifesaver once. They say they're volunteers. He extracted quite a lot of money out of me afterwards. Where do you take your holidays?"

"A lot of Britons go to Spain. Not me. I like to go to less conventional places. Bulgaria, Croatia, Turkey. I went to Marrakesh via Casablanca once. Now that was romantic, the palm oasis and the orange groves with snow on the Atlas Mountains behind. You'd like that, Davenport." She stretched, luxuriating in her recollection of the heat, the snake charmers, the Souk, and the exoticism of it all. "Let's go inside and tidy this up."

She stood, picked up the plates and cups, linked her arm in his and drew him inside. There she threw the paper implements and the remains of their breakfast into one of the shopping bags she had earlier emptied.

Nervously, Davenport said he had better change. Whether she had heard him or not he did not know, but she followed him into the bedroom. She came up behind him and put her arms around his waist. She undid the cord of his dressing gown and flicked it off. Davenport concluded that anything other than submission was not an option.

Afterwards, Elena assured him that this was not something that she did as a matter of course. "You're attractive you know, Davenport, in a rather hopeless fashion. Now don't take that the wrong way. I mean that you're the sort of man women feel they need to look after, lead almost."

"Boss you mean."

"No I don't, although I must say your Gloria sounds rather like a sergeant major."

"That would be about the right rank. But, thankfully, I'm out of that regiment now."

"Do you ever hear from her?"

"I should hope not. We're not like your aristocracy, forgive and stay friendly. Gerald told me he was going to a fiftieth birthday party for a friend of his. The other guests included the man's first two wives, his present wife and his current two mistresses, all of whom knew about the others. Gerald denied that the man was a Muslim or a Morman."

"We're just more tolerant."

"If you say so."

"It is true we do some things differently here. But they're different in France and Germany again, different everywhere in Europe. There's something to be said for the new world, however. You're a refreshing addition to Londys."

They rose at about twelve o'clock. Davenport said he'd like to go to the Swinging Gate to collect his winnings.

Rupert was in the bar with Cecelia but there was no sign of Goldilocks or her owner. Rupert waved them over. He introduced

At the Swinging Gate

his wife and Davenport introduced Elena. As he did Rupert winked at him admiringly.

"You haven't seen that man who owns Goldilocks have you?" Davenport asked.

"Shouldn't think so. He'll be in a casino somewhere punting the winnings. You do know the bitch won don't you?"

"Yes. What do you mean he'll be punting the winnings?"

"The man's an incurable gambler. Can't be trusted with cash, anyone's cash."

"He said he'd put the twenty pounds I gave him on Goldilocks."

"Bad luck. You won't see that twenty pounds again."

"Four hundred odd. She started at more than twenty to one."

"You're in the art trade. That's a casino if ever there was one."

Cecelia spoke for the first time. "I'd prefer Rupert to be in a respectable business." She laughed but there was more than a hint of seriousness in her voice.

"What, back to pestle and mortar and potions, no thanks."

"Don't be ridiculous Rupert, it all comes off the shelf now."

"Well who wants to be a shop assistant in a white coat?"

"He's a hopeless romantic you know, full of schemes and projects," said Cecelia. There was affection in her voice.

"Speaking of projects, I could have one for you, for Londys that is."

"I assume you're suggesting you might be able to put us on to some good stock?" Davenport said.

"It's a possibility. Of course any stock worth having won't be cheap or easy to acquire."

Money was Elena's department. "Londys are always ready to pay a finder's commission. But if you're on to something good why would you be prepared to let someone else in on it?"

"This project will require capital."

"Londys isn't an investment bank."

"No? Well what about those finance deals it did for some of its clients five years ago? The purchasers were given five years to pay two thirds of the price at three percent interest when the bank rate was seven point five. The clients were accordingly able to pay right over the odds. Londys benefitted from the higher buyer's and seller's premiums and inflated the market for the artists concerned. The seller was satisfied because he got a much higher price. It was the ultimate, mutually satisfactory deal."

"I'd only just started there," Elena explained. It appeared she knew what had happened. She looked at Rupert with new respect.

"This is a perfectly reputable project, nothing like that."

They waited for Rupert to tell them about it, but he was not ready to do that yet. "The dogs are probably sleeping in after their big night. I can't believe you gave that man twenty quid. Bloody thing tried to bite me," he told his wife.

After their drink, Elena said she must go. Davenport agreed to walk with her to the bus which she insisted on taking. "That's something you'll have to get used to in London Davenport. People use public transport even if they have cars or can afford taxis. It's just as quick. Sometimes quicker."

"What do you think Rupert's project might be?" he asked.

"Obviously you haven't known him for long. But with your experience in the business you must have met others like him. He probably wants to pass off a lost Stubbs or something. It'd be like your Divera all over again."

"He doesn't seem dishonest; disarmingly frank in fact."

"They're the most convincing."

"And you're just an over cautious accountant."

"I wasn't too cautious this morning," Elena reminded him.

A bus pulled up and she climbed aboard it. "See you tomorrow," she said, and waved.

Davenport turned to walk back to his flat. Events had moved rather too quickly for him since he had arrived in London. He did not think he was quite ready for an in-house mistress, or for the tenancy of a flat, which, when restored under her directions as she threatened, would be larger and grander than any place he had previously occupied. The best way of avoiding worry about such matters – as he had found in the past – was to put them out of his

At the Swinging Gate

mind.

    He did that and thought of Rupert's project. It, and the Spoliation Panel to which he had referred, intrigued him. He suspected that the two were connected. When he reached his flat he got out his laptop and searched the internet for the Spoliation Panel. Its role was exactly as Rupert had described it. The relevant web pages boasted of the numerous settlements the panel had effected. The names of several famous artists were mentioned.

8

Solutions Required

Just as impulsively as she had decided to leave India, Gloria concluded that it was time to leave Paris. The article about Davenport was very unsettling. Gloria was not one to acknowledge mistakes, but perhaps she had been too hasty in jettisoning him and heading for India with Walter. And what had that all come to? She could not yet bring herself to admit that the Master was a charlatan. She had paid him too much money for that. If asked, she would say that the experience was interesting but expensive.

Paris too had failed to live up to expectations: all those chauvinistic Frenchmen smoking strong cigarettes, Japanese tourists endlessly snapping photographs in the Rue de Rivoli, the inescapable smell of exhausts and essence, and the French obsession with cream sauces. She was sure she had added, despite her tight budget, at least two kilos since she had arrived.

She bought the cheapest ticket available for the train to London. Then she took her clothes out of the wardrobe to pack. What had seemed so appropriate and bright in Rishikesh looked cheap and garish in the thin light that filtered through the frosted window of her room. The sandals she had bought only a few weeks ago from a stall in the market were frayed and misshapen. She could see now that what had looked like leather was in fact plastic. She began to

Solutions Required

put aside objects that were either too worn, too bright or too coarse for wear in London. What remained barely filled half her suitcase.

When she had finished, Gloria sat on the narrow bed and looked around. The natural light had faded but she saw no point in switching on the room lights. For a moment she wondered what might have happened to Walter. But the thought soon passed. What a mistake he had been. She was prepared now to concede that. Suddenly, she burst into tears.

The crying didn't last long. Gloria was rarely given to self-pity. She began to calculate. At London prices, even her very carefully husbanded remaining money might last only three weeks. She had heard that it was easy for Australian school-teachers to find work. Fortunately her mother had been born in England so she would be permitted to work in the United Kingdom. If she couldn't find a position immediately as a school teacher, she should be able to land a job as a governess, or as a tutor of children of the rich. That might be better...in the beginning, anyway. She might even be able to obtain board and lodging in such a job.

At about eleven o'clock on Thursday morning the porter called Davenport. "There's a couple at the front door who say they want to see you. The man's pretty scruffy looking. The girl's all right though. A lot younger, and a real looker. She speaks with a foreign accent."

"What are their names?"

"They won't give them. I'd say he was a solicitor if he wasn't so untidy. All he'll say is he wants to tell you something to your advantage. You weren't expecting to inherit a little something were you Mr Jones?"

Davenport suspected that the last was not sincerely asked. The porter had made common cause with the self-important guardians on the front desk – all of whom thought an Australian not quite right for Davenport's position.

"I'll come out," Davenport got up from his desk and went through the main sale room to Londys's Mount Street entrance. The porter, as tall as a guardsman and as officious as a sergeant in the Military

Police, was standing menacingly in front of Rupert and Olga, as if daring them to make a run for it.

"I thought you'd never come," Rupert said. He glanced up at the porter. "Bloody man, must have done his apprenticeship in the Hitler Youth." He darted past before the porter could respond. Olga stood firm. "NKVD more like." She pronounced the letters slowly and distinctly. Only when she was sure that the porter had heard and understood did she start to move. She was not prepared to move around him, however. She motioned for him to stand aside and then walked past him as if he had ceased to exist.

The three of them walked towards the disapproving stares of the two women on the front desk. Rupert stopped as he reached them. "I have a small drawing signed by Gontcharova, a crayon sketch of a group of dancers, precisely ten inches by fourteen. Please tell me the nationality of the artist, period, and approximate value of the work."

Neither woman could conceal her ignorance of the artist.

"I also wish to have some information about a small oil, predominantly blue in colour, signed Van Dongen. What can you tell me about him?"

Again the women's ignorance was apparent.

Davenport took Rupert firmly by the arm before he could continue his quiz. Once seated in Davenport's room, he said, "They couldn't tell a Renoir from a Turner, and it's not as if they're even attractive."

Rupert began to explain his visit. "You remember I mentioned I had a project. Well, I've decided to cut you in on it, that is, you and Londys." He made it sound as if he had just presented Davenport with a bowl of frankincense.

Olga beamed at Davenport and added, "It is opportunity once in lifetime."

"Art auctioneers are told that every week. People turn up with a picture they've had for many years. 'It's very valuable,' they say. 'It's by Flint. The family's owned it for two generations. We read that one sold last week for twenty thousand pounds. This one's bigger,

Solutions Required

not a mark on it. We'd expect at least thirty'. You're almost certain it's a print. You, or at least some of the people here, want to let the owner down gently. 'I'll need to verify it's a Flint'. They begin to get angry then. 'It's signed R. Flint, can't you see? Are you saying we're trying to pass off a forgery?' 'Not at all. But we have a responsibility to the buyers. If we say it's a Flint to them, then we have to stand by our word.' 'Grandfather always said it was Flint and it's signed Flint.' 'Look, I don't want to offend you. If you'd like to take it around the corner to have Shaws look at it, we won't be upset'. 'But you're looking at it now'. 'Not as I'll need to if I'm going to verify it'. 'I wouldn't want you to interfere with it'. 'All that I'd do is lift these tacks at the back, gently take out the back board and examine the texture without the glass on it'. Usually they agree at that point although they'll still be suspicious. You take it out, see straight away it's a print and invite them to touch it lightly near a corner. 'See how smooth that is. See how the texture of the image is exactly the same as the texture of the paper outside the image. Look at the back of the paper. There has never been a trace of watercolour in this picture. I'm afraid it's a print'". Davenport paused for a moment and then continued. "It's like a surgeon telling a patient the baby's just died on the operating table. People have threatened to assault me. If that's the project it's not for me, and I'm sure, not for Londys."

"God, you're a Jeremiah," Rupert sighed.

"What is name of person who buries people?" Olga added.

"An undertaker," Rupert answered.

"Yes, undertaker. You are burier of hopes, Mr Davenport," Olga said.

"It's a long story," Rupert added.

"Whether it's long or short, I'm not interested."

"I don't believe that, Davenport. You're a famous art detective. You won't be able to resist." Rupert eased himself back into his chair. He had taken a little trouble with his appearance today. He was wearing a yellow tie over a checked shirt with a buttoned-down collar, a dark suit with unfashionably narrow lapels and a pair of black brogues.

Davenport resigned himself to listening.

"Have you heard of Kruffinski, Vadim Kruffinski?"

"Of course I have, the last of the New Utopians."

"He is my grandfather," Olga announced.

"He's still alive?" Davenport was surprised by Olga's use of the present tense.

"Barely," Rupert said. "He's been in hospital in St Petersburg. What a constitution he must have to survive so long. What else do you know about him?"

"You mentioned Rothko the other day, the painter of floating panels and bars with blurred edges."

"That man decorator only," Olga stated.

Davenport continued. "Kruffinski did the same sort of thing, but better. Under the layers of paint there were exquisitely drawn figures and scenes and flowers, barely perceptible. Wasn't there a political problem, wasn't he sent to a gulag?"

"Well, you know more than most of Londys's staff, not that that's saying much. He was born in nineteen seventeen. His father was killed fighting the Germans in the first war. He was minor nobility. Hence none of his children could be trusted. Nonetheless, Vadim managed to get into art school. The curriculum was limited except for a brief period of influence by the Utopians in the thirties. Artists were given some freedom then so long as they could argue that in some way their works would have an educative purpose. Even Russia was not unaffected by modernity."

"Modernity? And all the time Georgian monster butchered autocracy and middle classes, and starved peasants."

"Yes Olga," Rupert was used to Olga's interruptions. "So the artists said that what they were doing, was painting designs for fabrics and decoration of public spaces. The alternative was to paint Paris style eighteen eighty. Vadim said he was doing designs. That was all right until one of the local party members visited the art school. Perhaps it was the time of day, or the angle of the sun, but he could see the scene that Vadim had inscribed before he had applied the layers of the panels. The effect is quite remarkable I can tell you.

Solutions Required

Unless you're at the right angle in the right light you wouldn't know what was there. Anyway the party official thought the underlying scene highly seditious?"

"It showed brave white Russian officers on fine horses chasing communist rabble," Olga explained.

"Well yes, it was a battle scene. That was the end of Kruffinski's art classes. Next thing he knew he's an infantryman. Before invading Poland they gave him some experience on the Finnish border. He was wounded in the leg there but that didn't mean he was unfit for duty. He must have had a hell of a war. After Poland, he was at the siege of Stalingrad. He loses two toes from frost bite there."

"He say they can cut off legs if he keep eyes and fingers."

"Quite so, Olga. Despite distinguished war service he's marked not to be trusted, ever. He asks to go back to art school after the war, to teach. Nothing doing. He gets a pittance of a pension and marries in 1946. His wife Natasha is a biologist. There is still no job for him. But Natasha worships him. She manages to buy him paint and canvases, until again they see what he is doing. This time they send him to a gulag."

"My grandfather slow painter. What is word, Rupert?"

"Meticulous. He waited for each layer of paint and glaze to dry before he applied the next one. He did the most detailed preliminary sketches before painting the underlying scenes on the canvas. I suppose because he had nothing else to do, he could take his time. Nobody knows for sure how many large paintings he actually completed in his lifetime. There's no catalogue. Benezit's dictionary suggests no more than two hundred. The preliminary sketches, though, there were plenty of those. They'd be worth a great deal of money themselves."

"Where's this heading?" Davenport asked.

"Patience, Davenport, patience. I said you'd hear something to your advantage."

"Kruffinski still has in his possession forty major canvasses." This statement silenced Davenport.

The thought of forty fresh signature works out of two hundred or so of a total *oeuvre* was, to a genuine art lover and dealer, heart stopping.

"Plus hundreds of sketches, some very finished," Rupert added.

"I may have seen one once in reproduction in an obscure book about Russian revolutionary arts. It looked interesting I must say." Davenport was not entirely immune to the commercial lessons that he had been taught. "There's a curious story about the American post-war abstractionists and expressionists. It goes that it was the CIA that made their reputations – especially Pollock's. They chose non-representational artists because they were the opposite of Russian contemporary artists. Everything Russian was wrong during the Cold War. Anyway, they had Rothko, and they wouldn't be interested in a foreign lookalike, even if the similarity was only superficial. That's why your grandfather isn't as famous as he should be."

"You can't blot great art out, Davenport. Cover it up for a while, but blot it out forever, no. Let me assure you, he's about to become very famous."

"His name will be restored, but there are complications," Olga said. "Always there are complications."

"Let's talk about the restoration of his name first. I mentioned the Spoliation Panel the other day. Well that's where his reputation is going to be redeemed. For some reason best known to himself, Goering conceived a great liking for Kruffinski's work. You know how he extorted works out of their owners all over Europe?"

Before Rupert could continue, there was a perfunctory knock on the door and Gerald entered. He could not conceal his surprise at seeing Rupert there.

Rupert was equal to the occasion. "De Pyne, I haven't seen you for years. The last time must have been at Bermondsey Markets at five o'clock in the morning, about fifteen years ago? You were working as a runner I think, for an antique dealer in South Kensington. We were at school together," Rupert added.

"Not so, I've been here for fifteen years," Gerald sniffed.

"Time flies, must have been sixteen years ago then."

"Nothing seems to have changed for you though," Gerald fired

Solutions Required

back.

"No, no sellouts for me. I like my independence."

"I'm sorry to break this up, Davenport, but there is something I need to talk to you about," Gerald offered a further apology but not to Rupert. "Forgive me Miss, Miss..." He broke off when no one attempted to introduce Olga, and left the room quickly.

"You could see why they never made him a prefect," Rupert said.

"Were you a prefect?" Davenport was unable to keep disbelief out of his voice.

"No, but then I didn't want to be. I suppose that means we'll have to postpone our talk."

"If it's heading where I think it is, I doubt whether there's any point in resuming it anyway."

"Don't be hasty. Just keep on thinking of forty stunning Kruffinskis and hundreds of sketches in pencil, watercolour, and oils. And there are some etchings too." Reluctantly, Rupert stood up. "Why don't we have lunch at the Swinging Gate next Saturday?"

Davenport was about to refuse outright but then he remembered Goldilocks and his four hundred pounds. It had been the first time he had ever won a bet and its proceeds had assumed a special importance in his mind. Rupert suggested a time. Davenport said he couldn't promise but that he might be there.

When Rupert and Olga left, Davenport hurried to Gerald's room. Elena was seated opposite Gerald and was holding a sheaf of papers with figures on them. Davenport blushed when he saw her but Rupert was too preoccupied to notice.

"Things are getting serious around here," he opened. "Elena's been helping me with the figures for tomorrow's board meeting. We've got good turnover of items, but nothing in big numbers. We need a great spectacular, something to put Londys back on the map. It doesn't have to be paintings. I wouldn't mind getting my hands on some Fabergé piece. The Russians are the new Mellons and Morgans, buckets of money and determined to pay whatever they have to for the best of their own. It's a pity, but not surprising, that the Russians didn't produce a decent painter from nineteen twenty on. Now, Davenport, what are we going to do? You're the stuntman in this place. That's why I put you on. This time though we need a real Divera, and not a forgery."

"I am working on it, Gerald," was the best that Davenport could offer.

"It's a bit rough to put the onus on Davenport. He's only been here five minutes," Elena said.

"What was that fellow doing here anyway?" Gerald asked.

"I don't know. He was about to tell me when you came in."

"Let me give you a warning, Davenport, he's a very unreliable person – some would say, dodgy."

"From something he said, I gathered there might have been some tension between you two at school."

"What did he say?"

"I've forgotten now, but that was the impression I got."

Gerald thought about this for a moment. But another, deeper, concern prevailed. He seemed to be staring at Davenport's chest. "Where did you get that shirt?"

"In Singapore, on the way over. A tailor in the basement of my hotel ran three of them up in a couple of hours. What's wrong with it?"

"It's a commercial traveller's shirt. It's got a pocket. Next thing you'll have a propelling pencil sticking out of it."

"Leave him alone, Gerald. It's a perfectly respectable shirt," Elena said.

"And useful," Davenport was encouraged by Elena. "You should get one. You can carry reminder notes and dry cleaner's slips in it. That way you won't forget to pick up your dry cleaning."

"Londys people don't wear them."

"I'm thinking of buying a pair of bottle green suede shoes." Davenport's recollection of a gossip writer in a novel by Evelyn Waugh had floated into his mind. It was immediately obvious that Gerald had never read the novel (and might never even have heard of Waugh), and he glared uncomprehendingly at Davenport.

Solutions Required

"It's a joke, Gerald," Elena said. "Something a journalist in a work of fiction made up."

"Well, fewer jokes and application are what are required around here."

"I do have one suggestion," Davenport offered. "We could include more Australian pictures in our next topographical sale."

"Assuming you're right, where would we get them?"

"I've got a theory about that. Twenty years or so ago not many Australian dealers were aware that the London auction houses occasionally sold Australian works – or any non-European, or non-English material for that matter. Those who did often picked up works cheaply which they could resell for plenty in Australia. All countries are parochial about their own artists. Even today, with the exception of perhaps a pretty Venetian scene, or a Cassis landscape by Bunny, paintings by Australian artists of overseas landscapes, no matter how well done, sell for less than inferior Australian landscapes by the same artists. Today, all of the astute Australian dealers watch the London catalogues for works by Australians. They still think, however, that they're buying better here than in Australia, even though they're often bidding against one another. They believe they're getting works fresh to the Australian market because they've been hidden away in English collections. Remember how all those Arthur Steeles surfaced a short while ago. They'd come into the possession of his niece who lived in this country and had never been seen in Australia. They went back there but if we'd got them they would have brought more than they did in Australia when they were sold there."

"That's the point, Davenport, we didn't get them and nor did our competitors. There's competition now from dealers in the UK as well as the other auction houses. Everyone's in the market. If it's not in a dealer's room or an auction house, it's on bloody eBay."

"I know where to get Australian pictures," Davenport asserted.

"After a few weeks in this country you say you've unearthed a cache of Australian art?" Gerald snorted. "I can't believe that."

"I'll get them in Australia."

The Russian Master

"What? And bring them here to sell? What's the sense in that?"

"We'd have to be discreet, deal with a reputable dealer who could be utterly trusted."

"Reputable dealer, trust. That's a joke. Are you seriously saying that Australian dealers would pay more at auction in London, including our very reasonable buyers' premium, than they would in a dealer's gallery in Sydney or Melbourne."

"We wouldn't publish any provenance at all in the catalogue: just 'Morning Harvest by Hans Heyson, circa 1927.' We'd have to be careful we sold nothing that had been illustrated in an Australian catalogue for say, fifteen years. There's still a cachet in buying in London, and the dealers, most of whom hadn't been in the game for more than fifteen years, will think they're getting a bargain."

"You're more crafty than I thought," Gerald said admiringly. "But it can't work, or not for long enough to make it worthwhile, even assuming that we could get the stock." Gerald's brow furrowed as he continued to consider the proposal. "If you could get your hands on a few really choice pieces, it could wash, I suppose."

"I've another idea," Davenport said. "Why don't we advertise for Australian works in the provincial newspapers in England."

This time Gerald was genuinely horrified. "Londys, advertise for stock, like a barrow boy! Unthinkable. Next you'll say we should hold car boot sales."

"That's not quite accurate," Elena interposed. "What about when we place a notice in local newspapers saying we're going to be in a town on certain dates and we'll do appraisals there?"

Like most inconvenient truths, Gerald distorted it. "Merely conventional practice. All the major houses have been doing that forever. We help people by advising them that their works need conservation, let them know whether they've got something very good, or let them down gently if they haven't."

"Come on Gerald," Elena replied. "It's not altruism. If they've got anything worthwhile we tell them we'll get them a villa at St Tropez on the proceeds if they'll let us auction it."

"I didn't have in mind to use the Londys name," Davenport was at last able to get a word in. "I thought perhaps we could use my name, or Elena's, or someone else's, and ask people to bring their works to a hotel. Or I could go out and look at them."

"I'll give it some thought," Gerald said. "But it couldn't be a complete solution. We need something bigger, sooner, and surer than that. Still, it'll give me a talking point for the Board meeting." Gerald ended the conversation.

Elena nodded to Davenport to follow her to her room. He said he would be along shortly.

In his own room he recalled that he had already broken the vow that he had made to himself in Australia when his marriage had fractured and the fake Divera was unmasked, to shy clear of strong and demanding women. He resolved to stand up to Elena, to let her know that he was not a man to come at the beck and call of any woman.

Behind her desk, with spread sheets neatly arranged in front of her, and her laptop glowing and winking with authority, Elena, immaculately groomed and dressed, was immediately in the ascendant.

"Gerald can't handle pressure." She said calmly. "He's starting at the wrong end. The way to make profits is to cut out the deadwood. I would do it like that." She made a sweeping motion with her shapely left arm. "Take those desiccated debs at the front desk. I'd get rid of them first. That isn't what I wanted to talk about however." Her efficient manner evaporated. "You were very sweet last weekend," she said. "I really enjoyed myself."

There was only one response possible. "Me too."

"We must do it again."

"Yes."

"Soon."

"Of course."

"Next weekend?"

"If you think so."

"I do, and I've been doing other thinking too. You know my lease expires in two months?"

"I thought leases were easy to renew here, that you had some kind of protected tenancies."

"Not my lease."

"Would you stay in the same area?"

"It's a different area I had in mind."

Only then did Davenport realise exactly what she did have in mind. "I'm a terrible person to live with, untidy, disorderly, inconsiderate, hopeless, you name it."

"But very sweet. That's a big flat, plenty of room for two people to do everything either might want to do without worrying the other. Anyway I'm a very orderly person."

"I'd drive you mad."

"You're far too self-deprecating." She was about to come round to Davenport's side of the desk when the telephone rang.

Davenport jumped up as she answered it. "Have to go," he said as he waved and darted away.

9

A Violent Encounter

When Gloria came out of Waterloo Station on to the Strand, that deceptively light London rain that can soak you and curl your hair in five minutes was falling. Lines of cars interspersed with gleaming, wet, red double-decker buses stretched for hundreds of metres in both directions, barely moving. The natural light was fading, and in the distance, the streetlights which had turned on, glowed through the mist. People hurried past her, uninterested in anything except their private affairs and escaping the rain. The bustling scene reminded her of the hundreds of Parisian scenes painted in a wet twilight by the pot-boiler French artist of whom Davenport had been an admirer, and whose name she struggled to remember. 'Galien Lalou,' that was it. She was pleased with herself, but the pleasure was momentary. She contrasted her loneliness with the brisk cheerfulness of the artist's scenes. As she recalled, the people in them always looked happy, couples out shopping, families with well-fed and smiling children, unaccompanied people obviously heading for happy assignations in the French way, and even the vehicles looked new and shiny, their wheels never splashing water on the happy pedestrians. Gloria had ventured too close to the kerb. A lorry with a smiling face painted on its side sped past, throwing a cascade of water over her suitcase and her shoes.

Anger began to well up: anger at the Ashram, at Walter, at Australia, at London, and at her lot. But most of all at Davenport. She could picture the scene. There he would be, expensively dressed, generously paid, respected for his professionalism, living no doubt in a good hotel, greeted each morning at work by adoring secretaries, and probably indulging in some affair with a like minded, equally overpaid, over-groomed female executive he'd met at a fashionable nightspot. How dare he!

She steadied herself. That was no way to think. This was not the time for temper or haste. Still, she did need to be aware that Davenport would have changed, and to try to adapt to the changes. She looked in despair at her wet and battered suitcase, and fingered her by-now unruly hair. She had no idea where to stay, even for a night or two. This was hopeless, she thought. She signalled a taxi. The driver, even though his vacant sign was on, ignored her as did the succession of other drivers whose cabs were full of people as intent as she of getting out of the rain.

Gloria began to walk. She came to the Savoy, its top-hatted porter opening and closing taxi doors, and furling and unfurling umbrellas like a circus juggler. She dared not even ask the price of a room for the night. A hundred metres along the road she saw a grand building with a neon sign with the letters 'Covent Palace' incompletely lit up on it.

Gloria went into the foyer which was full of Japanese and American tourists sheltering from the rain. She threaded her way through them to the reception desk. A receptionist looked disapprovingly at her wet clothes, hair, and luggage.

"How much does it cost per night?" Gloria asked.

"I think we're full up," the girl said.

"If you weren't what would it cost?"

"There could be a suite left."

"I couldn't possibly afford a suite."

"That's what I thought," the girl turned dismissively to a Japanese who wanted to know the hours of the Imperial War Museum and in which rooms he would find the war in the East. "You could ask the concierge," she said, and then after a glance at the empty concierge's desk, she added. "Tomorrow, he should be in then."

"Would you please check whether there's a small single room vacant, anywhere, in the basement or the attic, it doesn't matter where?"

The girl took pity on her. "Eighty pounds, on the front, first floor."

"You couldn't make it sixty could you?"

"Where are you from?"

"Australia."

"We get a lot of Australians. The others could subsidise you I suppose. You can have it for seventy." She handed over the key.

Some water had entered Gloria's suitcase. The colours of her few remaining dresses that were wearable in London had run. But there would be no more self pity. She unpacked quickly and hung some of her clothes on the chair and headboard of the bed. Then she undressed, bathed, and washed her hair. She dressed quickly, and searched, unsuccessfully, for a hair dryer. She telephoned the housekeeper's number. There was no answer. She called the reception desk. She recognised the voice of the girl who had given her the room.

"We don't provide hair dryers. Aren't you the woman I just booked in?"

Gloria ignored the inquiry. "I thought this was a superior hotel. There must be a hair dryer somewhere?"

"Well, I'm sorry, there's not," Gloria heard the word 'gratitude!' before the handpiece at the other end was loudly replaced.

With a towel around her head she sat down with the business directory in front of her and a pamphlet she found on the dressing table which contained a map of the city, bus and tube routes, and a timetable. She took her pen out of her purse and placed it beside the sole piece of hotel stationery in the drawer.

She looked first for Londys and entered its address and telephone number in her neat schoolmistress' hand on the top of the page. She turned then to employment agencies, selecting those that claimed to specialise in nannies, school teachers, and governesses, noting the telephone numbers of half a dozen of those with the most modest assertions of successful placements.

Gloria had visited London once before, after she had qualified as a teacher but before she had been given a position by the Education Department. It had been a quick cheap trip of which she could recall little except the Tower of London, the Tate and the National Gallery – both of which Davenport, who had just then begun to court her, said she must see, and Harrods. The thought of the last reminded her that, back then, after she had confirmed that there was nothing in the shop that she could afford, she had walked west where there seemed to be row after row of Georgian facades behind which there were small hotels that advertised cheap rates in their ground floor windows.

She looked at the map. Harrods was prominently marked, as was the Knightsbridge tube station immediately beside it. Tomorrow she would take the underground there and walk west until she found a hotel that she could afford.

When her hair was dry, Gloria got into bed. She had a great deal of calculating to do: first, the extent of her rapidly diminishing funds and the order in which they could most usefully be applied, and second, how to best approach Davenport. She knew little of grand English firms like Londys but enough to understand that they and the people who worked in them would have manners as superior and condescending as Edwardian butlers. To get past them she would need to buy some better clothes, have her hair styled and cut, and buy some make-up. The Master had thrown out the cosmetics she thought she had concealed from him and had told her that she had no need of them there. After laying her plans, Gloria fell into a deep, exhausted sleep.

Try as he might, Davenport could not put out of his mind the interrupted conversation with Rupert and Olga. He decided that he would meet them for lunch on Saturday.

Violent Encounter

On Friday afternoon Elena came into his room carrying an overnight bag. "I brought this in so we could go straight to your flat," she said.

Davenport looked at her in dismay. "What's wrong?" she asked.

"Nothing." He racked his brain for an excuse. "I can't do it, not tonight," he said. He was certain that Rupert, Olga, and Elena would not make an amicable trio.

"Are you programmed or something?" Elena inquired.

"I don't mean that. Of course I could if I had to."

"Had to! Well, if that's the way you feel about sex with me, Davenport, forget all about it," she made no attempt to leave the room.

"I don't mean... Look, Elena, you've got the wrong end of the stick. What I'm trying to say is that I have to go somewhere else tonight."

"I thought you didn't know anyone in London."

"It's a second cousin of my mother." He was about to say that he had received a note from her but he wouldn't put it past Elena to demand to see it. "She rang me this morning. She asked me to stay with her, in ... Buckinghamshire. Until tomorrow afternoon."

"I suppose I could drive you there," she offered.

"She's going to meet me, in town, drive me down herself."

"I could collect you," Elena sounded decidedly suspicious.

"Her son's going to bring me back."

"Well, you'd better give me your key so I can let myself in."

"I wouldn't recommend it, not tonight. That's why I was pleased to get the invitation. The fumigators have been in all day. No one's to sleep in the place for twenty-four hours. Heaven knows the poisons they use these days. The agent says she always arranges it for new tenants."

"If I didn't think you were such a nice, simple person Davenport, I'd be very sceptical about this invitation, and the fumigators. You are telling me the truth aren't you?"

Davenport, who had never been a scout, held up the palm of his hand the way they did in American court room television dramas, and said, "Scout's honour."

"When will we be seeing each other then?"

"After five o'clock tomorrow. I'll make sure I'm back by then. I'm looking forward to it very much."

Elena picked up her bag and moved slowly and sceptically towards the door. "I hope so Davenport, I hope so."

Davenport cautiously looked up and down the street before he left the porch of his block of flats. Only when he was sure that neither Elena nor her dark blue BMW was anywhere to be seen, did he step onto the footpath and head towards the Swinging Gate. As he did, he occasionally, insouciantly he hoped, stopped to look in shop windows to see whether Elena was reflected in them.

When he reached the Swinging Gate, he scanned the bars in search of Goldilocks and her owner. They were nowhere to be seen, and nor were Rupert and Olga.

Davenport took the opportunity to ask the barman whether he knew a dog named Goldilocks.

"A bear, did you say?" the barman asked, "Do you mean that white polar bear that Australian rum company uses in its advertisements?"

"A dog, a coursing dog."

"Why didn't you say so? Everybody knows that yellow bitch. Bite your balls off it she takes against you."

"I'm looking for her owner. He owes me more than four hundred pounds."

"Join the queue. You could hold a creditors' meeting of all the people in this pub as are owed money by Jack Smythe."

"The dog won. He would have got the prize money and whatever he bet on her himself. I don't see why he'd want to keep my four hundred."

The barman guffawed. "You won't see him here for a while. It'll be a new story if you do. Last time he said when he got to the track all the smart money was on Jezebel, or Rover or something, and that's where he put the money: thought it was only fair to do so.

Violent Encounter

Tricky fellow that Jack Smythe. Bloody good dog, though, when she's trying." The barman finished wiping a glass, blew on it and into it, and gave it a final rub of the dirty tea cloth. "I'll tell him you asked if I see him." He didn't bother to take Davenport's name and address.

Rupert came in wearing his casual clothes, a scuffed leather jacket, faded blue corduroys, a pink shirt, and moccasins that once had sported heels a quarter of an inch thick but now hugged the floor. Olga was dressed as if for church, in a demure dark green dress, stockings, and high heels – which elevated her three inches above the top of Rupert's head.

"Knew you'd be here," Rupert said.

"I was passing. I thought I'd look in to collect my winnings on Goldilocks, from Jack Smythe."

"That's the name he's using these days is it?"

"That's what the barman said."

"Ever heard of an actor called Lon Chaney? They said he was a man of a thousand faces. Jack Smythe's a man of a thousand names. Bitter?"

"A half gin and tonic if you don't mind. Plenty of ice."

Rupert turned to Olga. "Your usual?" When she nodded, he said, "You're as much a stage Russian as a Dubliner is a stage Irishman. You don't know where that vodka comes from. They make it out of anything these days."

"Large vodka, from refrigerator," Olga insisted.

"Get a table, outside if you can, away from the noise," Rupert ordered as he went to the bar for their drinks.

It was now a perfect day in the sunshine but Davenport would have preferred the interior. Olga was surprised when he jostled past her to the seat against the wall which commanded a long view of the street and footpaths in both directions. He wished he had brought a hat to tilt over the top of his head and eyes.

"Where were we?" Rupert asked when he brought the drinks. "Always was a rude bastard, de Pyne. Don't let him push you around Davenport."

"He is the chief executive."

"It was better when they called them general managers."

"Everyone in Russia in party a commissar in bad old days. No more, except some, what they say ... resurrect themselves as businessmen. Gangsters!"

"Calm down Olga, you won the counter-revolution. We've got something a lot more important to talk about. Did I mention Olga's cousin? Doesn't matter. He's the most avaricious Russian in Europe and that's saying something. His name is Oleg, Oleg Kruffinski."

"Black sheep of Kruffinski family. Party member until 1988, now capitalist."

"Quite," Rupert continued. "He's the only son of Olga's mother's sister. He took the name Kruffinski to ingratiate himself with the old man. He's not interested in art but he's got a fair idea of what a well publicised major Kruffinski would bring."

"Friend of Mafia, that what he think. Client more like. Big gambler. He owe them money."

"We can't be sure of that, Olga."

"You think what you like, Rupert. I know."

"True, up to a point. Now, we are certain about one thing. He did locate the Kruffinski that Goering took during the war. There's quite a lot of documentation about it. There's a photograph of it hanging at Karinhall before the house was destroyed. It went where a lot of that stuff ended up, to Geneva, in a banker's house."

"Swiss," Olga said contemptuously. "Where Swiss when Great Patriotic War raging?"

"I didn't expect to hear you, an anti-communist, call it that," Davenport mildly offered.

"When Russia was invaded, communist, capitalist, man woman child, all must resist."

"Quite so," Rupert agreed. "The trail is a bit murky after that. It probably went through the French auction house, Druots in 1963. There was no illustration of it in any catalogue of that year but two pictures were sold as school of Kruffinski."

"School of Kruffinski, bah! Never a school of Kruffinski or circle of Kruffinski. My grandfather have to paint in secret. Tell no one, or Commissar of Art appear on doorstep and send him back to gulag."

"I thought he *was* sent there," Davenport said.

"For three years, soon after war. Sent back to St Petersburg then. He didn't know why. In Russia in those days no logic in anything. When something good happen, don't ask."

"Returning to Paris, Olga is right. There was no circle, no school, and therefore an absence of imitators. Those pictures were almost certainly the real thing. The Goering one was called 'Finnish Tundra'. It was painted in purple and yellow, shading into red and gold, the midnight sun. There's a landscape and a city beyond. The etched figures underneath were soldiers in white on skis. It was obviously inspired by his participation in the war against Finland. Perhaps he painted it then. Perhaps some German soldiers looted it and passed it on to Goering. So far as we know he never painted any other major work in those tones."

"And after Paris?" Davenport was interested now.

"Monte Carlo, where else? It was hanging in the house of John Greenland."

"The playwright?"

"None other. There's no doubt he believed it to be a genuine Kruffinski, and that he came by it honestly. He has all the papers, including a certificate and a receipt from the dealer in Nice from whom he bought it. He was quite a collector."

"So was Somerset Maugham. Someone said he knew the price of everything but the value of nothing."

"That very true of many people," Olga said. "True of Oleg who only interested in money."

"I'm afraid I don't understand." Davenport was bewildered. "Someone in Nice owned a probable Kruffinski he came by honestly. Kruffinski's still alive and still has most of his other paintings, and Olga's cousin is venal. What's the point?"

"The Deptford people bought the picture by private treaty from Greenland's executors. Oleg has produced all the evidence he can

The Russian Master

find to the Spoliation Panel. I admit that he's done a good job tracking it down. He wants the panel to declare that the painting was looted, and that it should be returned or its owner reimbursed. He's produced an authority to act in his grandfather's name."

"How does that help Oleg and what's it got to do with me...and you for that matter, Rupert?"

"He say he has written authority from grandfather. It is a forgery." Olga was dismissive.

"Probably," Rupert added, "but it doesn't matter. What Oleg wants to achieve is this: first and mainly to get a lot of publicity, to put the name Kruffinski in lights in the art world. Secondly, he wants the Spoliation Panel to put a value on the picture. They always do, even though not at the top end of the range because that would make it harder to negotiate a settlement. But that doesn't matter. Even the bottom of the range will be a half to a million pounds. Everyone knows the panel is conservative. Whatever value they nominate would put a floor under Kruffinski's prices. Oleg will probably get a payout, but his main game is to get his hands on the rest and sell them in a blaze of glory."

"But you say his authority is a forgery."

"Oleg like Rasputin to my grandfather."

"Olga, tell Davenport about your grandfather."

"He is old, vulnerable man. You would be too. Hard life when his father died, then the Finnish front, the rest of the war, the gulag, always he have to stay quiet. When grandmother die, like many Russians, for a time vodka his best friend."

"What Olga means is that her grandfather does not always act rationally. He might well have signed an authority. Perhaps at the time he knew what he was doing, perhaps not. What is clear is that, so far, the Spoliation Panel has been prepared to deal with Oleg as duly authorised."

"I would have thought every country would have had a law of undue influence."

"Russia have many laws, too many laws. No one except poor obey them, if they know what they are. In communist times no lawyers except criminal lawyers working for state. No private property, no need for lawyers. After Wall go down, suddenly many lawyers, lawyers everywhere. Not many know much law. Those who know law not be trusted."

"Well, it's an interesting story. I'll buy a round and then I'll have to go." Davenport went into the bar and brought back their drinks. As he put them down on the table he thought he saw a yellow tail disappearing around the corner of the building. "Goldilocks, Goldie, Goldie, Goldie," he called out.

"Do sit down Davenport. You're making a spectacle of us."

Davenport ignored Rupert and hurried to the corner. No one and no dog were there. He returned to Olga and Rupert and sat down. Thinking the Kruffinski story finished, he asked, "Expecting any new stock from Russia yourself?"

"Yes, dozens of Kruffinskis and a few hundred drawings."

Davenport laughed at Rupert's joke. Rupert didn't laugh. "I want those pictures."

"You and every other dealer in Europe."

"But they don't have Olga."

"Well, good luck with them."

"We want them to be your good luck and Londys's."

"If you can't get them out of Mr Kruffinski, what makes you think Londys could?"

"We don't just want practical help. We need money. We want this to be a joint venture."

"I don't think this is Londys's style. Try the other houses."

"I'm going to be frank with you, Davenport. We have and they turned us down. Londys is our last resort."

"There seems to be some antipathy on Gerald's part towards you. I'm sure he wouldn't be interested."

"That's why we're talking to you. You're a kind of a middle man, neutral."

"You art historian but not want write historic account of great Kruffinski! And not like money? Rupert, we came to wrong man."

"Calm down Olga. He needs to think it over."

"I have. The answer is no."

"You haven't heard the proposal. Realistically we need about a hundred, perhaps two hundred thousand pounds. We'll need fares to get there, the money to buy a reliable van in Helsinki, travelling expenses, bribes, and we may need to buy some protection in St Petersburg. If we get the pictures out, Londys can sell them, most of them that is. There'd need to be two auctions. We would want to tantalise the market with some sketches first. In return for financing the venture, we'd pay a commission of twenty-two percent. We'd also repay Londys's investment, with interest at seven percent. Think of the prestige, Davenport. You could write a monograph, a book even. If I were you I'd be looking for a personal cut from Londys. Of course, Londys would also get the buyer's premiums. This could be a twenty to fifty million deal for Londys."

"There are a few problems you haven't mentioned. I couldn't imagine the Russians letting the pictures out of the country."

"Grandfather owe Russia nothing. Russia owe grandfather everything."

"We didn't have in mind to go through any recognised border crossings."

"Corrupt border guards let Fabergé egg through for carton of American cigarettes and six months supply of Viagra pills."

"Only a slight exaggeration," Rupert said. "The borders are rather porous. I think we could get them out legitimately, or for some relatively light bribes. Because his pictures haven't been in circulation in the auction rooms or with the dealers, his name hasn't gone on the heritage list or whatever they call it in Russia. The border guards probably wouldn't know anything anyway."

"They say," Davenport suggested, "that most failures stem from incompetence rather than corruption."

"Bullshit baffle brains," Olga was delighted with her command of the idiom.

"That sort of thing," Rupert agreed. He seemed to be unfailingly tolerant of Olga's interruptions. "He will go on the register, eventually, there's no doubt about that. But the new Russian bureaucracy while it is as inefficient as the old, lacks power and ideological commitment."

"You don't think the blaze of publicity that Olga's cousin is looking for would precipitate a listing?"

"Not in Russia, not before we could get the pictures out, anyway."

"But Oleg has the authority. He's the one in contact with the old man. Why would he let you get your hands on the works?"

"That's where Olga comes in. She used to be his favourite grandchild. She last saw him in Russia in 1995. There's every reason to think that he would trust her more than her cousin."

"Particularly when I show up Oleg's forgery. Please understand though, Mr Davenport, we not wish to cheat grandfather. We wish to let the world see his works. We charge him only fair commission, ten percent to arrange everything. Full proceeds otherwise go to grandfather. I know he will give or leave me some pictures."

"The arrangement I have made with Olga is that I may select ten of the paintings to sell from my gallery at full dealer's commission, thirty three and a third percent. Olga has also agreed to pay me three of the ten percent for setting up the deal. Who are Londys's solicitors, Davenport?"

"I don't know, why?"

"All of this will have to be documented."

"But I told you, Londys..."

"Davenport, I thought you were in Buckinghamshire?" Engrossed, despite his strong reservations about Rupert's proposal, he had not noticed Elena as she had walked towards their table. "Were you ever really going there?" Elena glared at Olga.

"Been there, and just come back," Davenport lied.

Elena's eyes, like a Spanish Inquisitor's, probed his for deceit and heresy. "A neighbour had to come up to London early this morning. To save trouble, I got a lift with her, him that is."

"What are you doing talking to these people?"

"To Rupert and Olga you mean?"

"Whatever they call themselves."

Olga stood up. She was three inches taller than Elena. "You are very rude woman. You interrupt important business discussion."

"Since when has fifty pounds for a fuck in a car on a vacant lot been an important business dealing?" Elena turned to Rupert. "What's a pimp get these days?"

Olga wound up her right arm like one of those baseball pitchers Davenport had seen on late night cable television. The blow she delivered to Elena's left cheek was not a slap in the Hollywood style, with the flat of her hand. It was possible to see immediately the four red knuckle marks on Elena's cheek as she slumped, as shocked as she was dazed, to the footpath.

"Bitch," Olga said, as she looked round for Rupert. By now he had crossed the road and was trying to hide behind a lamp post. Without hurrying, Olga moved to join him. When she was ten metres away, she called out to Davenport. "We continue our discussion later. Think about it until then. It is good scheme. It make everyone happy." She paused, "Except that swine, Oleg."

Davenport bent down and helped Elena to her feet. Four or five of the people nearby looked concerned but the incident had been over in a few seconds. No one, except Elena, Rupert, Olga, and Davenport knew what had actually happened.

Davenport assisted Elena into a chair. "A brandy, that's what you need. I'll get it. Don't move."

"Has that foreign slut gone?" Elena asked warily.

"Don't move," Davenport unnecessarily repeated as he went to find the barman. Having regard to recent events, and what he feared lay ahead, Davenport thought it prudent to make the brandy a double. He was not disappointed to see Elena finish it in a few gulps. He insisted she have another. She agreed and finished it as quickly as the first.

"Truman's got a lot to answer for," she angrily said.

"Truman?"

"For stopping Patton. He should have been let loose to exterminate those barbarians."

Davenport was surprised that she knew anything of World War II history. "To accuse her of being a prostitute might have been a little on the provocative side."

"I know her type. Watch out, Davenport."

He was relieved that she seemed to have lost interest in interrogating him about Buckinghamshire. "As a matter of fact, it *was* a business discussion we were having. Rupert was at school with Gerald you know."

"When public school boys go bad, they go really bad. Look at Lord Lucan."

"I think you ought to lie down. Do you feel up to walking now?"

Elena rose shakily to her feet. Davenport took her arm and guided her along the footpath. It seemed to take ages to reach his flat to which all of his purchases had now been delivered. He helped her upstairs and into the spare bedroom. She made no protest when he told her to sit down on the first of the wide couches to arrive and which she had insisted he buy in case one of his friends from Australia visited him. He undid the buckles on her shoes and gently pushed her down on to it.

"I'll get a pillow." He brought one from his own bedroom and put it under her head. He lifted her feet and legs on to the couch and placed a light blanket over her. He could see her eyes beginning to close as the brandy took hold. He started to tiptoe out of the room.

"Don't go, Davenport," she said.

"You need to sleep, Elena."

"Not yet," she tried to keep her eyes open. "Just sit with me for a while." Davenport sat on the end of the couch.

"I didn't understand about Buckinghamshire, how you managed to get back this morning."

"A neighbour was coming up to town. I told you."

"Odd you running into that pair."

"Well, I was looking for Goldilocks, actually."

"Davenport, I have to ask you this. Did you tell your wife stories like that before she left you?" Elena's eyes closed and stayed closed before Davenport could think of an answer.

10

The Return of Gloria

It was only when Gloria pressed the security button near the lift that she recognised the name, Jeremy Baker, the popular author who had made millions from his sequential novels about a London entrepreneur who joined Scotland Yard after making his fortune. Gloria recalled that some critics had suggested his plots were thinly disguised thefts from Conan Doyle but his public didn't seem to care.

She pressed the button again and spoke her name into the device. A very formal voice told her to enter the lift and to come up to the third floor. When the doors opened she was met by a man of about her own age dressed in a black coat, silver tie, and striped trousers.

"Mr Baker," she said, and held out her hand.

"Barnes, butler," he replied in a condescending voice. "Mr Baker will interview you shortly." He pointed to a couch of austere Georgian lines that had been brightly gilded and covered in a fabric of peacock green. Gloria sat down. On the wall facing her there was a fine, large painting. Making sure that she was alone, she approached it to try to find a signature. It was a Bonnard. Now that was a name she had heard Davenport mention. She examined the rest of the hall, taking in the thick, heavy, Turkish rug and the centre table topped with a green striated stone – malachite, she remembered. There had been a ceremony at the museum where Davenport once worked, to acknowledge the gift of a malachite table, much smaller than this, from a rich widow. The value, for taxation purposes, had been many thousands of dollars.

A door at the end of the hall opened. A man of slightly less than average height swept through it. His clothes, even though they were casual, looked as if they had been sewn on to him. He wore an old fashioned green eyeshade over his eyes.

He was not content to let the affectation speak for itself.

"I wear this whenever I am writing. I'm in no way visually impaired. I find it helps to focus my mind." He shot out his right hand. "Ms Jones."

"Mrs Jones, actually."

Baker's eyes flashed to the vacant fingers of Gloria's left hand. "We'll go into the living room. You've brought your references?"

"Yes." Gloria followed him down the hall into a grand room with large windows. They overlooked a small green square and other expensive residences, but none so tall as this building.

"You like it?" Baker asked. "Most of my friends have been kind enough to say they do."

The decoration was in the same expensive but florid style as the hall: an enormous rug that could have been by Aubusson or, on the other hand, by eastern child labour, gilded side tables, deep sofas, a petra dura centre table from either Florence or Delhi and, beyond question, a beautiful Monet of a haystack in a ploughed field in a fading sunlight. Gloria couldn't take her eyes off it.

"Yes, it is a Monet. I bought it in New York on my last lecture tour of the States. Museum quality I'd say. Like the view? I bought the top three floors of the building in 1989. Some of my friends said I was insane to have paid so much. Why not, I told them. Where else in London can you look down on Mayfair. It's freehold of course. They've changed their minds now, my friends I mean. Well, I suppose we'd better get on with it. I understand that you were a primary school teacher in Australia?"

"Yes."

"What have you been doing in the meantime?"
"Travelling, Paris, living for a time in India."
"I won't tolerate hashish."
"I have never taken drugs. I don't believe in them."
"Alcohol?"
"Practically never."
"I make an exception for Cristal and the Widow."

Gloria had no idea what he was talking about. She decided to look interested, aware, and a little on the prim side, keeping her knees as close together as a bull dog clip.

"It goes without saying then that you like children."

Involuntarily, Gloria almost said, 'Well-behaved ones', but quickly thought better of it.

"I had a very disciplined upbringing myself. If I hadn't I couldn't write my three thousands words of prose a day."

Gloria had not heard his works described as prose before. But so long as he was content to talk, she was content to say nothing.

"There are two children, but no doubt you already know that."

Gloria, who didn't know whether there were two or five...or ten, nodded knowledgeably.

"Everyone knows of the children even though I've done everything I could to shield them against the consequences of my fame."

Gloria, who now had a vague recollection of a spread of photographs of Baker and his family in *Salute Magazine*, again nodded.

"Polly and Cassandra, ten and eight, the dearest little girls. They attend day school. You'd have to take them and collect them each day. I'm pleased you're a teacher. You'll be able to make sure they do their homework. They have activities at weekends: art lessons, ballet, museum outings, tennis coaching. Do you like sport Mrs Jones? I did, still do. I played rugger at varsity, scrum half, half back as you Australians insist on calling it."

"Not me. I don't like the game."
"You've no objection to tennis I hope."
"It seems harmless enough."

The Return of Gloria

"I should like to read your references. Look around while I do. There's a more than passable gouache by Picasso in the dining room, nineteen twenty-one the experts say; a very strong period." He put his glasses on and began to read Gloria's references. They were mainly from friends but he wouldn't know that, and it was unlikely that he would call Australia to speak to any of them. Gloria walked silently around the room and into the adjoining dining room. The dining table had a thick lucite top, and the chairs, in a faux Graeco-Roman style, were of the same material. She found so much transparency unnerving.

Hearing a step behind her, she turned to see Baker holding her papers. He didn't look as if he had found much of interest in them. But then Gloria suspected that there was little of anything that he found interesting anywhere except in himself.

"One of my guests asked me if I was a moralist or a prude. You can see why." Baker waved his hand at the table. It was unnecessary for Gloria to say anything. He continued, "Clear table top, no groping under it." He laughed as if he had made a very clever joke. "These seem all right. I am not prying, but I won't compromise where my daughters' well-being is concerned. This job is, as you know, live-in. So I need to know about Mr Jones. I will not allow any man except Barnes to have regular contact with the girls. Your husband, you say he is your husband, would not be permitted to sleep over. Indeed, his presence here would not be welcome even for short periods. You will have, if I offer you the position, which I am inclined to do, a kitchenette and a small sitting room, bedroom, and bathroom. None is adapted – intended, may be more apt – for entertaining."

"My husband is a senior executive at Londys. He is quite famous, a world expert on the Central American painter Divera. As a connoisseur I would have thought you would have heard of him. Do you read *Jove*?"

Baker was tempted to lie. Gloria could see it in his eyes.

"I find I am too busy to read it."

"Davenport was featured in it recently. He travels a great deal for the firm. He worries about me being alone all the time. 'Take a live-in position', he's been saying for ages now. 'We can spend weekends together when I'm in London'. You wouldn't expect me to work every weekend I take it?"

That had been Baker's expectation but even he had come to realise that no one would be prepared to do it. "Every second weekend, I suppose. You could finish at midday on alternative Saturdays after the girls' activities. You'll have a lot of time of your own when they're at school."

"That's very demanding. The agency said you were offering four hundred pounds a week and free accommodation. I had no idea there would be so much weekend work. I'm afraid I wouldn't be interested for that amount."

A look of desperation crossed Baker's face. But before he could respond, Gloria moved on to the front foot. "And what about Mrs Baker, anyway? Wouldn't she want to interview me? And surely she'd want to do things with the children at weekends."

"Like your husband, Mrs Baker is a very busy woman. And like him, she travels a great deal. We agreed some time ago that I should have the responsibility of the practical arrangements for the children. I could go to five hundred plus a loading of one-twenty for each full weekend worked."

"Are you offering me the position at that amount?"

"I suppose I am. Yes."

"Thank you," Gloria said, as she took her references from him and stepped around him to walk to the hall. "I'll think it over. Can I let you know in twenty four hours?"

"I can't hold the position for that long."

"So long," Gloria corrected him. "If I miss out, I miss out. I will call you by this time tomorrow. Good afternoon."

Gloria went immediately to a telephone box. She must, she told herself, buy a mobile phone as soon as possible. She took the agency's card out of her handbag and dialled its number.

"Mrs Outright?"

"Dulcie Outright speaking."

"It's Gloria Jones. I've just been interviewed by Mr Baker."

"That's good dear. Did you get the job?"

"Why didn't you tell me he was the popular novelist?"

"I thought you would have known – those pyramids of his latest novel in all the bookstore windows. Did he engage you? You know you have to pay us your first week's salary, after tax of course, and seven and a half percent thereafter."

"How many other women have you sent to him?"

"I don't think I could disclose that information, dear."

"Well, if you don't I wouldn't even consider working for him."

"That means he did offer you the position."

"But not that I have taken it. How many did he interview before me?"

"Why do you ask?"

"He seemed like a desperate man to me. Apart from his appalling conceit, what's wrong with the job? Are the children monsters? Is he some kind of sex fiend? And why isn't Mrs Baker in evidence?"

"He's seen seven of our girls."

"How many refused an offer of the position?"

"Five, I think. He seemed a perfectly decent man when I spoke to him on the phone. Young people do have unrealistic expectations these days. I thought as a more mature person you would be suitable to him, and the position suitable for you."

"Thank you. That's all that I wanted to know."

"You will be taking the position then?"

"I'll let you know. If I do, I won't be paying the commission you charge. I imagine you're like the art auctioneers my husband works for, charging both parties."

"You signed an agreement."

"And you chose not to disclose some highly relevant facts to me."

"Five percent after the first week?"

"One half of the first week's salary and three percent thereafter."

"You Australians are hard people. We'd be bankrupt if we had to submit to those terms."

The Russian Master

"Well I won't take the job except on those terms, and it doesn't look as if anyone else will on any terms."

"How much did he offer you?"

When Gloria told her, Mrs Outright said, "That is a very good offer." Gloria could almost hear the woman calculating her commission.

"Very well. I'll confirm our new arrangement in writing."

"Provided I take the job of course."

Gloria waited until the next day to telephone Baker. "I would be prepared to take the position, for a salary of seven hundred pounds a week and two hundred pounds for each weekend worked."

"That's...that's out of the question."

"I doubt it. You'll probably describe me as a secretary or something else that's tax deductible. Besides, I've told the agency about yesterday's offer only. There's no need to tell them about our new arrangement. That will reduce the commission you'll have to pay them."

There was a long pause before Baker spoke. Gloria sensed that chagrin at being outsmarted as much as meanness, was the reason for the delay.

"When could you start?"

"Tomorrow."

"What time?"

"Assuming the tube is working, nine o'clock."

"I would need a trial period, a month say."

"So would I. That is satisfactory."

Gloria went back to her room to pack. She would not now have to move to a small hotel beyond Knightsbridge. She counted her money. She need have no qualms now about spending – or 'investing' might be more appropriate – a substantial part of it. She telephoned a manicurist, a hairdresser, and a facial cosmetician. When she had packed she took the tube to Oxford Circus and walked to the dress department of Pickers and Holmes. There she bought two new outfits in the sale she had seen advertised in the *Daily Telegraph*. In turn, she visited the other women's departments to buy the balance of a new wardrobe, inner as well as outer.

On Monday morning, Davenport knocked on Gerald's door. When he entered, Gerald continued to study the proofs of a catalogue. "Modern photography, digitalisation, whatever they call it, and they still can't get the colours right. Do you know how much a year we pay for printing? Tens and tens of thousands of pounds."

"Digitisation," Davenport corrected him as he sat down and examined the proofs that Gerald passed to him. "They do seem to have a rather heavy hand with the puce."

"You'd think from this," Gerald held up a reproduction of a Braque, "the artist used mud instead of paint. This is our biggest sale of the year, 'Major Impressionists'. If it bombs then it's goodnight Irene. These will have to go back." He threw the proofs into an untidy pile. "What bad Monday morning tidings do you bring?"

"Good tidings, actually. At least I think so. You remember those people I was talking to last week when you came in, the woman and your old school friend, Rupert?"

"Not my old school friend, Davenport. The man became a pharmacist."

"What's wrong with that?"

"I really do despair of you sometimes, Davenport. Anyway, what about them?"

"They had a rather interesting proposal I thought."

"I'd doubt that. The man's little more than a barrow boy. He should have stuck to pestles and pills."

"Just be patient till I finish."

Davenport told the full story of his visits to Rupert's gallery and his discussions at the Swinging Gate, omitting only Olga's demolition of Elena, and his fruitless search for Goldilocks's owner.

Gerald heard him out without emotion.

"You must have heard of Kruffinski?" Davenport pleaded.

"Oh yes, I know quite a lot about Kruffinski."

"About his present circumstances?"

"Yes."

"Well, shouldn't we try to get them, get in ahead of that Oleg fellow?"

"Do you think so?"

"The pictures won't come here if he gets his hands on them."

"Au contraire."

"What do you mean?"

"I've an understanding with Oleg Kruffinski."

"But he's a crook."

"You've only got his cousin's word for that. Oleg has a different story I can tell you."

"Why didn't you say something to me that when I was speaking to them? You must have guessed what we were talking about."

"I thought it would be good training for you. I know you had a great triumph with the fake Divera, but that was in the colonies. For every fake Divera in Australia there are ten thousand fake impressionist pictures in Europe. They've got a technique now for printing reproductions on canvas with the texture of oil paints. You and I wouldn't be fooled Davenport, but there are many who will be. And they'll be bringing them in here expecting us to sell them for hundreds of thousands. This city is a great clearing house for the fraudulent and the over ambitious. So far, the only case against your friends is over-ambition, but that could lead to much worse. No Davenport, for this transaction, Oleg is our man."

"Olga struck me as a very sincere young woman."

"I do believe you've got the hots for her Davenport. I had no idea you were so energetic."

"Energy doesn't come into it."

"Again, au contraire. Ask Elena."

"I don't think that's any of your business, Gerald."

"It's not just my business, it's my duty to know about staff entanglements. Not world's best practice for office workers to sleep together you know."

"I don't think that line would work in an anti-discrimination tribunal."

Gerald frowned momentarily. "Don't ever threaten me

The Return of Gloria

Davenport... But enough of your torrid love life. I have an important task for you. Tomorrow, the Spoliation Panel is going to hold a public hearing to trace the ownership of Oleg's Kruffinski."

"Is that usual?"

"No. This is the first public hearing they've held. There are some judges who crave publicity. The judge who's the current chairman of the panel had the secretary place a public notice in the *Telegraph*. It invited any interested persons, or anyone who might know anything about the picture to attend. The panel secretary handed out a press release. We got our copy by email, talking the usual nonsense, public interest, transparency, public record, and community participation. Nothing about grandstanding. It might be amusing to attend, better than dealing with bloody printers and avaricious vendors at any rate."

"I looked the panel up on the internet. But that didn't tell me much."

"It consists of five people, the chairman, who is a High Court judge – Sir Richard Stedley in this case, a senior curator of a museum with no interest in the object under consideration, an Oxford or Cambridge history don, a 'people's representative' – whatever that means but it's fashionable to have one on everything these days, and a senior public servant from the Department of Media, Arts and Sports – the 'bread and circuses' department."

"You're making the last up."

"Certainly not. The Department of Media, Arts and Sports finances the panel. It's effectively part of the department. What a delightfully Orwellian name for a department. What a wonderful constellation of activities – something for everyone. If you don't like the art, have some sport, the government will provide. I don't know where the media fit in though. The panel's probably got a mission statement."

"So do we, don't we?"

"Yes, but no one takes ours seriously. Everything about the panel is pretty high minded: the restitution of pillaged heritages, the protection of private property, the assessment of fair compensation, the imposition of high standards of integrity on public museums, and so on. It's legerdemain of course."

"I don't understand."

"Well, they don't, can't actually order anyone to send an object back. They encourage them to do so. It's a kind of mediation. I suppose it's better than the courts, and trying to get around statutes of limitations, and having to prove title. What they do is assess a value, not a current one unfortunately, and recommend the museum pay it or return the work."

"That doesn't sound too bad."

"Not too many original owners are going to get an object back. The museums all say they're forbidden by law to part with museum property. It's a classic Catch 22. I'm no lawyer but I've always understood that you can't get property in stolen goods. The Nazis probably compelled their victims to sign a sale contract or something. Anyway, Stedley's going public this time. Good show for us. The media will be there – the department will make sure of that – and Stedley will be playing up to them. It means the Goering-Kruffinski story will get a lot of publicity."

"Who has the picture at present?"

"The Deptford Institute. It's a teaching and exhibiting institution in Bloomsbury. They have a good, mainly central-European collection. No one else in London has much of that kind of stuff. They won't be anxious to part with their Kruffinski. Until recently no one paid any attention to it. That's enough for now Davenport. The hearing begins at ten-thirty tomorrow at Somerset House. By the way, I'd stay away from Rupert and his Russian mistress that you're lusting after. Just because the Cold War is over, doesn't mean the Russians have stopped setting honey traps. That reminds me. What have you done to Elena? I've never seen her so angry: something to do with the Russian woman and you, I gather."

"Me? Nothing." Davenport escaped as quickly as he could. He crept into his room, weighing up whether he should look in on Elena. When she had woken late on Saturday afternoon, she had left in a fury, refusing to speak to him. He decided it was better to leave well alone.

Just as he left Londys the next morning, it began to rain. He had intended to walk but now he was coming to understand why the English always carried umbrellas. He huddled under the dripping awning as the porter tried to find him a cab. The truth was that Davenport rather liked riding in London cabs. Unlike in Australia, the drivers always knew the way, could speak English, and kept their vehicles clean. But, as in Australia, when it rained, they disappeared as if they were water-soluble.

He borrowed a Londys umbrella from the porter and started to walk. Skirting round the corner, he hurried past the Bentleys in the show rooms at Berkeley Square. He doubted that any self-respecting nightingale would have perched in any of the skeletal trees there long enough to sing a song these days. By the time he reached the Burlington Arcade, the cuffs of his trousers were soaking. It was five to ten already. As he broke into a jog in the arcade, he heard a thunderous voice behind him. "Stop that man. Thief!" The few early morning window shoppers ignored the command, but its speaker, a top-hatted porter, called out again, this time loudly enough to alert his companion at the Piccadilly end of the arcade.

Davenport lengthened his stride. He turned his head to see whether the porter behind him was following. As he did he collided with another, the Piccadilly porter who had interposed himself between the entrance and the footpath. This porter was of a size consonant with the dignity and importance of the famous shopping arcade. Davenport was a slight person. He rebounded half a metre before coming to a halt. The porter pinioned his arms. He was soon joined by his companion who glowered at Davenport, daring him to make another run for it.

"Got the bleeder Sid. Just as well you called when you did. What's he got?"

"That's what I'm about to find out. What's yer name?" he demanded of Davenport.

"Davenport Jones."

"And I'm Winston Churchill. I think he's an Aussie, Fred. You an Aussie?"

"Yes."

"All the same these Aussies, they're either spin bowlers or thieves. No wonder we got rid of them. Got any ID?"

"My Australian driving license."

"Useless. It'd be stolen."

"It's got my photograph on it," Davenport said indignantly. "Look, I've got an urgent appointment at ten-thirty."

"You're right about that: with a Bow Street magistrate."

"Let me get my licence and phone out."

"They won't impress us. It's easy to forge a licence and put a photograph on it. Sid, get them to ring the police." Fred pointed to the nearest shop and tightened his grip on Davenport's arm. "Don't try anything funny just because I'm on my own."

"I work for Londys, the art auctioneers. You've heard of them. Ring them. And look, I haven't got anything stolen on me. Check my pockets."

"Honest people don't sprint down the Burlington Arcade." Sid paused, though, as he spoke.

"I was only jogging. I was running late. Go on, search me."

"I'm not falling into that trap."

"What trap?"

"Taking an arm off you. You'd be away in a flash."

"I have nothing of value on me."

"Course not. You would have got rid of it as soon as Sid called out. A diamond ring or a brooch, you probably dropped it down a drainage grate."

"Would you please call Mr Gerald de Pyne at Londys. He'll vouch for me."

"Londys, the auctioneers!" Fred said derisively. "Your associates are more likely to be fences in the Bermondsey Markets."

Davenport vaguely recalled a court case that had been reported in the newspapers in Australia in which a customer sued the owner of a department store whose security guards had mistakenly retained

The Return of Gloria

her on suspicion of shoplifting.

"If you don't let me go I'll sue you for unlawful arrest, and, and assault." Davenport sensed a loosening of the grip on his arm. "You could be up for a lot in damages." He wondered whether these porters had the same capacious overcoat pockets as the porters at the grand hotels. He had noticed tourists who photographed the porters at the arcade tipping them for the privilege.

"Couldn't be unlawful," Fred rejoined, "You were running, hard as yer could, down the arcade. That's suspicious. That makes what we did reasonable."

"Unless you ring Mr de Pyne immediately, that will be for a jury to decide."

Fred motioned for Sid to use the telephone. Davenport could hear only Sid's end of the conversation.

"What's 'e look like? ...average I suppose...'ard to see anything distinctive about 'im... Yer say that, what, that yer can't otherwise describe 'im. Is 'is name really Davenport Jones, though?"

Fred loosened his grip on Davenport a little more. "Blue pin striped suit, tie with foulards, short hair, about five feet ten." Sid was looking anxious now, and Fred was smiling obsequiously at Davenport. Sid put down the handpiece and came over to Fred. "Seems e's who 'e says 'e is."

"Misunderstanding it appears sir. With all these terrorist bombers, we can't be too careful. Let me find you a cab."

Sid strode out into the middle of Piccadilly and majestically barred the path of an approaching taxi. As he flung open the door and stood aside for Davenport to enter, he said, "No 'ard feelin's sir."

Davenport arrived at Somerset House at twenty-five minutes past ten. He was directed to a large room overlooking the Thames and Waterloo Bridge. It had been set up as a kind of courtroom with a sort of bench on an elevated platform at one end, and a number of tables aligned in a row in front of it. There were five chairs behind the bench and one in front of it for the secretary. Nearby was another table with a tape recorder on it. Behind the tables and chairs facing

The Russian Master

the bench were about thirty chairs for the public. At right angles to the bench was a long table with the words, 'Media Only' written on an improvised sign. There were five reporters and two camera operators at this table. About half the chairs for the public were occupied. At the end of the front row of these were Rupert and Olga. At the other end was a man of between thirty and forty, with a closely shaven head.

Davenport went over to Rupert and Olga. They invited him to sit next to them. "Better not, might have to run," he said. "Leave early I mean, not actually run," he added, recalling the trouble running had just caused him. He toyed with the idea of telling them of Gerald's rejection of their proposal but decided that now wasn't the right time.

"Oleg, the communist swine, at other end of row," Olga made sure that the man heard what she called him. "His proper place Lubianka."

At that, Oleg turned his head towards Olga. Words were not necessary to convey his triumphant superiority.

There was a knock on a side door which then opened and through which the panel entered, preceded by the secretary. Nothing was said for a minute to enable the camera operators to take their photographs, an event which the chairman seemed in no hurry to abbreviate. When he was sure that they had taken their fill, he looked down at a file in front of him and cleared his throat before beginning to read.

"This is the first public sittings of the Spoliation Panel. We are constituted today by Professor Trilby of Cambridge University, an historian; Mr Lumptage, a senior official of the Department of Media, Arts and Sports; Ms Currey, curator of modern Slavic Art at the Solehanger Museum; Mrs Laddle, community representative; and myself, Justice Stedley of the High Court.

"This is an occasion of some significance because it is a public one. Long gone, happily, are the days when tribunals did their work behind closed doors. Our proceedings, I would emphasise, however, are not adversarial. Their purpose is to investigate the facts. Only

The Return of Gloria

when we can be confident that we know them will we be able to recommend what should be done in respect of the object in question, and mediate the differences between the stakeholders." He smiled with satisfaction as he used the fashionable term. "The last two stages cannot, of course, be public ones. Mediation is a process to be undertaken sensitively, and away from the harsh light of publicity." As he spoke the last sentence the chairman beamed at the reporters and the camera operators to show that he bore them no ill-will personally. Naturally, when we have made our decision and have decided on our recommendation, we will publish it. Mr Soames, QC with Mr Lile are here to assist us. Are there any applications for leave to appear?"

Two men stepped up to the line of bar tables.

"My name is Rawlins, I am a solicitor and member of the firm of Rawlins and Sons. I seek leave to appear for Mr Oleg Kruffinski."

The other man then spoke. "My name is Stevens. I am a barrister briefed on behalf of the Deptford Institute, the custodian, or, as the institute would prefer to say, the lawful owner of the relevant object, the painting by Mr Kruffinski."

"You both have that leave."

The two men sat down at the table.

"Is the painting available?" Sir Richard asked.

The secretary of the panel left the room and soon re-appeared carrying a hinged wooden crate. He undid it and removed bubble-wrap and tissue paper to expose one of perhaps the only two Kruffinskis known to be in the United Kingdom.

There were sighs and faint expressions of awe and approval from the public as the journalists and camera operators tried to assume knowledgeably admiring expressions. Sir Richard made a show of leaving his chair and coming round to examine the painting closely, as if he were the only person there capable of verifying its authenticity. As he returned to his place, those close-by heard him say, "A remarkable piece of work."

Davenport quietly moved to the side of the room furthest from the high windows overlooking the river. From his new position he was able to see the intricate incised drawing underneath the rectangular plane of heavy purple paint which shimmered and merged into a perimeter of bright yellow. He estimated that there could have been as much as a quarter of an inch of paint on the canvas, made up of layer after layer into which a detailed, but elegantly simple landscape with a city behind at twilight had been incised and overpainted. This was a picture which both required and deserved for its understanding and appreciation, a trained eye and careful examination. Each time Davenport's eyes passed across it he saw something innovative or different from what he had noticed just moments before. The painting was intrinsically contradictory. At the same time as the mind was drawn to the incised buildings and figures in the landscape, the eye was captivated by the luminosity of the overpainting. And when there was the slightest change in the light, the city-scape could be seen to be more than a mere drawing. There were faint tones of pink and brown, and the murky orange of foggy street lights to be seen – the midnight sun behind, and then not seen, as the light changed again. Davenport was irrevocably captivated. Kruffinski immediately and completely supplanted the great Divera in his pantheon of geniuses. Shaken, he returned to his original seat. Nothing, he thought, could induce him to leave it now.

The judge nodded to Soames who rose to his feet and began to speak.

"This panel has to trace the movement of the painting now produced and made by Vadim Kruffinski between 1938 and 1939. There are two claimants to the work, Mr Oleg Kruffinski, the grandson of the artist on behalf of the artist who is too ill to travel to London, or even to make a coherent statement about the picture and how it came to leave his possession, and the Depford Institute in whose possession it has been for thirty-five years.

"Some matters are not in dispute. The institute bought the picture in good faith from the executors of the estate of the playwright Greenland thirty-three years ago.

"All of the executors are dead.

The Return of Gloria

"The picture was offered to the Leningrad Fine Arts Museum in 1941. There is a letter from the director of that museum dated nineteenth of June 1941, an official translation of which I will read.

"The Peoples' Advisory Committee for the administration of the Leningrad Fine Arts Museum have discussed your offer of the painting by you entitled, 'Midnight Sun'. The offer is rejected. The painting was considered to be a decadent bourgeois work unsuitable for a people's museum. The committee wishes to express its concern that work of this kind is being done in the Socialist Republic. The scene, imperfectly concealed under overpainting, can be understood only as an exhortation for a return to the failed capitalist system before 1917. The overpainting can be seen to be not just an attempt to conceal the drawing beneath it, but as a derivation of meaningless Western abstraction. You are commanded to collect the picture within seven days. You should give two day's notice of your intention to do so. You will be required at the time of collection to report to the party advisor to the museum.
Signed..."

Soames explained that there was a signature in Cyrillic which could not be deciphered. He put down the letter.

"As the whole world knows, shortly after the date of the letter, Hitler launched a massive assault on the Soviet Union.

"The Leningrad Fine Arts Museum was located on the outskirts of the city in an area which remained in German hands throughout the siege which followed soon after the war began. Some of the works held by the museum were able to be withdrawn before the Germans surrounded the city with a ring of steel. Just what these works were is unknown. It is possible that they were dispersed throughout the city. Who knows? The siege lasted hundreds of days. Tens of thousands starved. A loaf of bread would have been more valuable than a Rembrandt in that beleaguered place. Access to it in winter was across the frozen lake. In summer the assault intensified. Conditions were chaotic. The last thing on anyone's mind was art.

"What does seem likely is that Mr Kruffinski would not have had time to collect his painting, and therefore confront the party advisor, before the attention of the authorities would have been directed to the siege and little else. It is more likely that Mr Kruffinski very studiously kept away from the museum and the party advisor who was so anxious to speak to him.

"This too may fairly safely be assumed, that a piece of decadent art by an outcast artist would not have been high on any list of priorities for dispersal or preservation.

"Let me return to matters which can be unequivocally stated. The Leningrad Fine Arts Museum was pulverised in the siege. It was never rebuilt. No catalogue of its contents exists. There are no manifests of items safely removed from it. So far as we know, there is no person alive who can give any reliable account of the dispersal and what, if anything, was done about works which could not be removed.

"At this point let me suggest that the possibilities are these:

"Mr Kruffinski recovered the painting – unlikely. His infirm condition now has deprived him of any memory of the events of those days.

"The painting was removed before the siege – unlikely.

"The painting was destroyed by the Russians – possible.

"The painting was looted by the Russians – unlikely, because in Russia at that time no one would have thought it of any significant value.

"The Germans destroyed the painting – possible. In fact, until recently – that is until it was established that a somewhat similar picture in the Berlin Modern Museum was painted in 1939 or thereabouts – this seemed the most likely fate. The risks of destruction during bombardment were very high. It has also to be remembered that many in Germany, a fascist country, and Hitler himself, regarded any form of non-representational art as decadent, and held such art with as much contempt as the communists. Ignorant Germans were perfectly capable of deliberately destroying it as a depraved piece of work.

"Mr Oleg Kruffinski, however, advances this plausible theory. It starts with the proposition that Goering was a true connoisseur who paid lip service only to totalitarian architecture and representational reactionary art. Bear in mind that beneath the surface of the Kruffinski is a beautifully sketched piece of impressionist art, a style to which the marshall was attracted. The painting somehow reached him.

"There is support for the theory. Many knowledgeable people who visited Goering's hunting lodge, Karinhall, were surprised to see impressionist, modern, and even cubist works on its walls - as well as Cranachs, Rembrandts, and high renaissance art.

"It is also well documented that many generals were well aware of Goering's avarice and interests, and in order to curry favour with him before he fell out with Hitler, plied him with paintings and other treasures looted from the fallen countries.

"The theory goes that a German general or other senior officer - even a Gestapo officer - may have become aware of the picture, and taken it from a soldier who had appropriated it, and sent it back to Goering.

"There was found in Berlin, in Goering's office, a partial catalogue which listed as stored in Karinhall, ten, unnamed contemporary Russian masters. We know that he held for a time a Malevich and a Tatin. The Kruffinski could probably be described as a contemporary Russian master - at least in the making.- even then.

"On the other hand, the Deptford Institute advances this theory: either Kruffinski did retrieve the painting, in the confusion of the early days of the siege when the party advisor, in the way of political officers generally, had fled. Alternatively, the artist may have painted a replica. The institute points out that Kruffinski, like many other artists, did this from time to time.

"How then, if the institute's theory is so far feasible, did the painting find its way into the possession of a resident of Nice years later? The institute frankly concedes that it cannot say. But, it adds, it does not have to. Once the picture or its replica was in the possession of its owner, he was fully entitled to dispose of it as he saw fit. The institute bought the painting in good faith. It bought it from reputable people. Mr Kruffinski is unable to give any account of the war years. If the possibilities are evenly balanced, the institute says that there should be a presumption in its favour, not only because of its purchase in good faith, but also because no one has questioned its entitlement during all the years that it has owned the painting and publicly displayed it. If its title were to be challenged, it should have been done much earlier. Property rights should be asserted promptly. This is not a case in which theft, or other unlawful dispossession can be proved, let alone with the rigour which the law traditionally requires when serious misconduct is alleged.

"What I have said is enough to indicate the unusual nature of this matter. It is one, in substance, in which the panel will be asked to choose between competing theories rather than to make a decision based upon hard evidence."

The chairman thanked Soames for his admirable summary. Davenport's reaction was the same as the reactions he had always had to legal advice whenever he had been obliged to seek it, complete uncertainty.

Oleg looked pleased. So did the journalists who were scribbling away. Of course, Oleg would be pleased. Publicity was his aim. Who ended up with the Deptford Kruffinski, as the journalists would come to call it, was of little importance to him. He had more, bigger, and better where that one came from.

The chairman adjourned the proceedings until two o'clock. The journalists hurried out of the room. Oleg smiled derisively at Olga and Rupert, and took his time leaving. Olga followed him with Rupert trailing.

On the footpath of the Strand, Olga strode up to Oleg. Davenport was not close enough to hear what she was saying. He turned to make himself scarce but before he could, Olga saw him out of the corner of her eye.

"Davenport, come here, call policeman, arrest this thief and forger."

Davenport looked around for Rupert. He saw him walking quickly with his head bowed, across Waterloo Bridge.

Olga repeated her call. In the way of the English, passersby were, for the time being, acting as if nothing unusual was happening. When Olga raised her handbag to strike Oleg, however, three Japanese tourists stopped to enjoy the spectacle, and a well-dressed Englishman paused. Reluctantly, Davenport covered the width of the footpath and took hold of Olga's arm before she could strike Oleg who shrugged and walked unconcernedly away.

"Pig," Olga snorted. "What was meaning of all those words?"

"I think, that no one knows how the painting got to France and nobody ever will."

"What happen then? That man in the middle, how he will decide who owns painting?"

"He's a judge. Judges do that sort of thing. It is not for a mere mortal like you or me to understand the mysteries of judging. What you need is a strong cup of tea, or whatever it takes to calm a very angry Russian down." He took her arm firmly and led her across the road to a small restaurant.

A waitress came to their table. For a moment Davenport thought that Olga was about to order a vodka.

"Water," she demanded, and turning to Davenport said, "Need clear head to deal with deviant."

Davenport looked around to discover the deviant.

"Swine Oleg. Thief, also deviant."

"That might be drawing rather a long bow don't you think?"

"Long bow? I talk about criminal, not symphony orchestra."

Davenport started to explain but quickly realised the futility of it. "Just relax. Now, what would you like to eat?"

Even after she had ordered, Olga remained angry. With her high Slavic cheekbones, round blue eyes, flushed cheeks and ash blonde hair, she was very beautiful. When Davenport as an adolescent was going through his pulp fiction phase, all of the femmes fatale were blondes, and the heroines ash blondes. Olga was the first definitely ash blonde he had met. He was tempted to say as much, but wary of misunderstandings, drew back.

"I think it's going to be very difficult for the panel to make a confident finding."

"I tell you, Oleg not care. The more uncertainty the more publicity. What your manager say about our proposition?"

"Chief executive," Davenport temporised.

"Whatever he call himself not matter. What he say?"

"I know he thinks your grandfather is a very great painter."

"The proposition, what he say about that?"

"I'm afraid he's not interested."

Olga shook her head in disbelief. "Davenport, you tell truth now."

"That is the truth. Gerald has a board of directors he has to answer to. Probably, they thought the whole thing too speculative. But I have been giving the matter some thought. Why don't you try the two smaller auction houses again, Bonds or Regency? It could be very attractive to them. Because they're wanting to expand, they'll see this as a great opportunity."

Olga played with her knife and looked sheepish. The truth dawned on Davenport. "You've already done that haven't you, tried again and been turned down?"

Olga gave no answer, pretending total absorption in the serrations of her knife. Only after Davenport repeated the accusation did she reply. "But we always wanted Londys."

Davenport considered telling Olga that Gerald had already made an arrangement with Oleg: better to do it now when Olga was on the back foot than later. He sensed, however, that a crowded restaurant at lunchtime was neither the place nor the time for provocative confessions.

"Do you intend to watch the whole proceedings?" Davenport asked.

Olga treated the question with contempt. "Of course."

"What do you hope to achieve by doing that?"

Olga was beginning to be exasperated by Davenport. She made no attempt to conceal it. "What you there for? Londys not interested in good proposition. What happens now not your business."

"I like the painting." It was true. Davenport had already seen enough of the proceedings to understand their nature, and even to predict an ambiguous outcome of them. "Apart from some Rothkos..." he could see Olga's mouth opening in protest, so he hurried on, "which are, of course, much inferior to a Kruffinski, I have never seen a painting like that one."

"It is good work but not grandfather's best work. He simplify later works. Incised scenes became semi-abstract. Sometimes he painted under borders and bars. Some scenes surreal. As Russia deteriorated, so did morale. Beneath stunning colours and glazes he sometimes paint a search light, or low aeroplane in night skies. Sometimes he paint cubes and blocks of boxes underneath. One painting has portrait of my grandmother beneath last layer. There are still lifes, landscapes, seascapes, cityscapes, portraits, everything. Grandfather not like other painters. He paint better as he grow old. You not want to help us, buy your own book on Kruffinski."

"I would if I could. But you said it yourself. He is not nearly as well known as he should be. Perhaps after this, Oleg will arrange for a book to be published."

"Never. I slit canvas end to end before that happen."

At that point, to Davenport's relief, the waitress brought their food. Despite being aware that Olga would be, as Silas Morning used to say back in Australia, high maintenance, he knew he was beginning to fall in love with her – despite having earlier eschewed for all time, any association with argumentative, strong women. He suddenly felt protective towards her even though he knew that Olga was well able to care for herself.

"Do you know why Rupert scurried off?" Davenport asked.

"Rupert like make trouble, not deal with trouble. He come back. Like you, artist interest him. He was angry when he hear you not interested in proposition."

"Not me. Gerald. I'd be happy to be involved if it were left to me." At that moment there was little that Davenport would not be prepared to be involved in, if Olga were part of it.

She looked at him quizzically. "How much money you have?"

"Not a great deal I'm afraid. I've just taken a lease of an apartment and have to spend a lot on it."

"You have assets. You could borrow?"

"Not enough security for that. I'd say."

"Something turn up." She then focused on the rump steak she had ordered.

Davenport toyed with his omelette. He thought he had detected a look of contempt on Olga's face when he had ordered it. Perhaps virile Russian men didn't eat omelettes.

When Olga finished her steak she looked around for a menu. A waiter brought one. She read it quickly and pointed to the profiteroles. "Coffee also."

Davenport ordered tea. Olga made no effort to restart their conversation. As they waited, Davenport speculated again about her relationship with Rupert. Olga and Rupert spent their days together. Sometimes they travelled together, although Rupert had said that he needed Olga so that the gallery could be kept open when he was away at auctions in the country. Davenport recalled the building, with its cramped spaces, stacks of paintings and dangerous stairs leading to a dank basement full of old frames and paintings bought in haste and regretted in leisure. Not even the most determined adulterers would find the space there comfortable. Cecelia seemed to keep a close eye on him. Davenport was already thinking like a jealous lover. He stopped himself.

Olga ate each of the profiteroles and then circumnavigated the plate with her spoon and fork ensuring that not a speck of chocolate sauce or a dollop of cream was overlooked. She misinterpreted the expression of admiration on Davenport's face.

"In Russia, food terrible: often stale, hard to get. English food not marvellous but much better. Olga not intend to be hungry ever again." She glared at Davenport daring him to contradict her.

"Quite. Perfectly understandable. Would you like something else?"

"Not now." She stood up and waited at the door as Davenport paid the bill.

Out on the Strand, Davenport asked her again if Rupert would be returning to the hearing. She shrugged her shoulders. They started to walk back to Somerset House.

He inquired whether the gallery was closed for the day. Olga said that it was being minded by Cecelia. Davenport had to suppress another surge of jealousy. As he was about to take Olga's arm to guide her across the road, his mobile phone rang. It was Gerald.

"Where are you now?"

"In the Strand, heading back to the panel sittings."

"There's no time for that."

"But you told me I had to be there."

"That was this morning. This is the afternoon. Something's come up. I want you here." Gerald raised his voice as he gave the order. Olga could hear every word of the conversation. "Kruffinski's there I take it?"

"Yes, at least he was this morning."

"Well he can tell us if there are any surprises. I'll see you very shortly." He terminated the conversation.

Before Davenport could say that he would have to go, Olga struck. "What this talk of Kruffinski?"

"That? Gerald was just inquiring whether he was there."

"More than that. He say Oleg tell you if there are surprises. What surprises? Why Oleg talk to you or de Pyne? What you have to do with Oleg?"

"I, I, really can't say."

"Davenport, I thought you Australian gentlemen, what you say, cricketer. All Australians good cricketers, not like English. But you make deal with criminal Oleg Kruffinski."

"Look, I'm sorry. I really do have to run. You'll be able to find your way back. It's just over there."

Davenport turned quickly like a guardsman making an about turn. From a standing start he moved off in a brisk walk. The English seemed to have some strange ideas about running in public places. Now was not the time to be apprehended by a policeman or a conscientious porter. He headed up the hill and skirted around Covent Garden. Only when he was in the middle of a throng of tourists in Leicester Square did he look around to make sure that

Olga had not followed him.

"You took your time getting here," Gerald said.

"I couldn't get a cab."

"Never take cabs in the West End or the City. I told you, you have to master the underground."

"What's the urgency?" Davenport asked.

"We have been presented with an opportunity. You've heard of Maltbys? No? They were a firm of merchant bankers. Why are there no ordinary bankers these days? You know, Davenport, that's what I should have got into. That's where the real money is, in money. Not for Maltbys though, in the end. They set up in the City seven years ago. Took the place by storm. Into everything: infrastructure – when it was the fashion, margin loans, hedging, investments no one had ever heard of before. Very ingenious. They were Americans, or so they said. That's why they took such an English name. Very British all round, except when they opened their mouths to speak. Never seen in anything except a Bentley or an Aston Martin. They couldn't quite get their suits right. A bit like you, Davenport. Colonials and foreigners never learn. They never wake up to the fact that a red stripe on a black cloth looks brown: a suit for a night at the dogs. Now I think of it, that explains something. You're a coursing dog fancier yourself, Davenport, aren't you?"

"A man owes me my winnings on a dog called Goldilocks."

"I thought so. I'd give the dogs away if I were you, Davenport. The art market's risky enough without other betting. Where was I? Yes. The inevitable happened. Maltbys collapsed. Something to do with a subordinated debt scheme. The principals have folded their tents: the talk is they may, in fact, have originated east of here rather than America. The city's ringing its hands. They're saying the losses make the Lloyds debacle look like petty cash. Of course, whatever wasn't nailed down they got away with themselves. Peter Lanson thinks it could be a much as fifty million."

"Who's Peter Lanson?"

"A chartered accountant, a company liquidator, an old school friend, and presently a person of very great importance to Londys and yours truly."

"I suppose at some stage you'll tell me why?"

"Patience, Davenport. When they set up, the brothers Maltby, there were three of them. God knows what their real name was. Anyway, they built and furnished the most sumptuous Palace of Money - that's what they called it, London had ever seen. Fortunately, they had a better decorator than tailor. Everything was the best. Obviously, they didn't choose any of it themselves, furniture, glassware, porcelain, and - best of all - paintings. The decorator may have let them have a say about some of those, probably the Olympians. You're aware of the Olympians?" Gerald could not conceal a note of condescension.

"Naturally. I'm very familiar with them. There are several in the Art Museum of New South Wales. They're very good in a Cecil B. de Mille sort of way. The public love them."

"Well, let's hope the British public, particularly the cashed up members of it, do too. There are two of those, including a practically unknown Alma Tadana, six feet by nine, 'The Triumph'. It's full of elephants and tigers and prisoners and chariots and slaves, and enough nubile Roman maidens for every harem east of Istanbul. The boys must have also liked the Impressionists. There are ten of those too: a Renoir, a Manet, two Monets, a Fantin-Latour, and, to establish their Britishness again, a Brangwyn - a huge history picture. Come to think of it, it's pretty apt that an Australian like you will be handling this deal. It's of convict hulks on the Thames. There're also a couple of Sickerts and two Laverys. I think that there are some Rodins as well. Most of it is big. It seems there was also some small stuff, but like anything else that was portable, they're gone."

"You said I'd be handling the Brangwyn."

"Not just the Brangwyn. That reminds me, there's a Conder too. Another coincidence. Didn't your run-in with the fake Divera start because of something you thought you saw in a dodgy Conder?"

Davenport was well aware that most of Gerald's questions didn't require direct answers. "You said Londys were being presented with an opportunity."

"Good old Peter. All the art work has to be sold. But not immediately. You can imagine the pressure the competition's been applying to get the sale. It'll hardly need any advertising. Something like this is just what the market needs now."

"Your old friend, he's fixed it for you then?" Davenport was also coming to realise that friendships made at school, like the enmities there, were the ones that endured in this community.

"I wish you wouldn't say 'fixed', Davenport. This isn't one of your dog races we're talking about. Peter has to proceed very, very carefully. The other houses' offers will continue to be very competitive. I wouldn't put it past them to offer to forego seller's commission entirely. Exclusivity for us has to be justified. It has to stand up to the most careful scrutiny. Even if I do say it myself, the scheme, no, business plan, no, not just a business plan either, my enlightened proposal for orderly disposition of the Maltby collection, is, to use that deplorable expression, a win-win proposition. I have made these offers to Peter that he cannot refuse. We will postpone all of our scheduled sales in the main room for six weeks. All of the collection will be exhibited there for that period. We will refurbish the Gallery before the works are hung. We will advertise the exhibition at our own expense. Public admittance will be fifteen pounds, and whatever concessions the GLC gives to pensioners, seniors, students, the halt and the lame. All the proceeds will go into a special fund to buy the big screen Alma Tadema and one of the Sickerts for donation to the National Gallery. And, most munificent of all, Londys will donate one fifth of its usual selling commissions to the fund."

"How can you be sure our rivals won't do better than that?"

"It'll be a fait accompli by the time we announce it. Also, there's something else. And this is where you come in. You're a qualified curator, a famous figure in the art world. You're part of the package. We've offered you too. The exhibition will be curated, catalogued and mounted by you, a trained and experienced curator. I'll get *Jove* to write you up again. The other houses don't have a trained and experienced curator."

"I don't think you realise how much work is involved in curating a major collection: checking condition, transport, insurance arrangements, conservation, verifying provenance, and writing a catalogue."

"There's no need for a doctoral thesis. Elena's up to date with her work. She can help you with anything financial. You don't look very enthusiastic, what's wrong."

"What I said. I'd need at least six months to do the job even half properly."

"This is commerce, Davenport, not the indolent world of the faculty of fine arts. The creditors are anxious for whatever they can get. Besides, Peter can't get paid until the assets are liquidated. You've got a month from today."

"But what about the Kruffinskis?"

"This is much more important. I can keep my eye on those myself. This is a great coup, Davenport. We can't afford for anything to go wrong. This sale could nett seventy or eighty million. Even with reduced sellers' commissions, total commissions with buyers' premiums could be as much as twenty to twenty five percent of seventy to eighty million. Think also of the prestige. And better, think of the fury of our competitors."

"You can't expect me to prepare a proper catalogue in that time."

"Davenport, we're talking about famous artists here. Millions of words have been written about each of them. You don't have to write anything original. You're wasting time talking about it. Get on with it. Speak to the head porter about transport and hanging. Elena can help you with the insurance. Here's our favourite liquidator's card. Deal direct with him about pick-ups, etcetera. Come on Davenport. This is another opportunity for you. 'The Divera Expert presents the Maltby collection'. And get your mind off that little Russian vixen. That mountebank she's working for has already taken her anyway."

There was no point in further resistance. Davenport took the accountant's card and turned to leave.

"Davenport, have you been holding out on me? You told me you weren't married."

"I'm not. Haven't been for some time now."

"A woman's been here looking for you. I didn't see her myself. She didn't get past the front desk. She said her name was Gloria Jones. Quite attractive apparently, but also, it seems, quite aggressive."

"I was married to a Gloria once. Aggressive, you say?"

"You seem to attract them, Davenport. Or perhaps it's just that you bring it out in them. Elena was a lot more placid before you arrived on the scene."

Davenport ignored Gerald's last remark and hurried to his room. He had put out of his mind ever having to speak to Gloria again. Surely she was still in India with her lover. He had thought the property settlement in which she almost bankrupted him would be the last transaction in which his affairs would, in any way, be mingled with hers. Perhaps it was all a mistake. Perhaps one of the girls on the desk had misheard the name. But Davenport knew in his inner heart that this was Gloria, attractive but aggressive. How had she found out that he was in London? The damned internet. There was no privacy anywhere anymore. What was she after? More money? Surely it couldn't be him she was after – not again. It was very unsettling.

Elena knocked on his door and entered. He could see no vestigial evidence of Olga's haymaker. Nor did there appear to be any scars.

"You're going to have your work cut out doing the Maltby collection. I just want to tell you immediately I'm ready to do anything to help."

Davenport was still preoccupied with Gloria's apparent arrival in town. In a strange kind of way he was grateful to her for leaving him. The relief at the time had been enormous. The property settlement she had insisted on had, as it turned out, almost been worth it. Now he could feel all the old tensions returning.

Elena noticed his preoccupation. "Don't you want my help Davenport?"

"Of course I do."

"Well, let's draw up a plan."

Elena was as good as her word. She left and returned with

her lap-top. She numbered the steps that would have to be taken, then systematically dissected each of them into sub-categories. She allocated each task to a member of the staff. Then she prepared a critical path and graphs. By the time that she left to collect the sheets from the printer, Davenport's head was swimming. For a moment he thought that he might slip away, but already Elena was back, beaming and holding a sheaf of papers.

"I've made a copy for each of us. We can both study it and refine it tomorrow. Davenport, have you thought any more about...you know, our seeing more of each other out of hours...? I mean, my moving in with you?"

"I don't think we're going to have much time until this is finished, in or out of hours."

"That's my point. The only spare time will be late at night, or early in the morning, travelling, travelling to work together that is. You haven't forgotten I'm about to be evicted?"

"No, not at all. I'm fully aware of that."

"Well...?"

Davenport was both in and out of luck these days with telephone calls. He picked up the handpiece as the phone rang. "Jones," he said in the way of busy, well-known people in films. As soon as he recognised the voice he half-turned in his chair. He put his hand over the mouthpiece. "This could take some time," he said to Elena.

She continued to sit opposite him. Then, suspiciously and reluctantly, she got up and left. Davenport put the handpiece down and rushed to close and lock the door behind her.

Olga never missed a beat. "I never thought you traitor Mr Davenport Jones. You like typical English spy. You the Philby of art trade or something. You worse than Philby. At least he spy for Russians. You spy against your Russian friends. Some English writer say, better to betray your country than your friends. You betray friends." Davenport could hear her crying.

"Look Olga, it isn't what you say. Do you think we could meet so that I could explain."

"I never want to see you again. Who say first, 'perfidious

Albion'?"

"I'm Australian not English."

"English, Australian, Canadian, Americans, Indian, all English speakers same. Never trustworthy. You tell me one final thing Mr Jones, how much Oleg promise Londys."

"I don't know. I'm trying to tell you that I only just found out myself that Gerald had an understanding with your cousin."

"Likely story!"

Davenport heard the crash of the phone's handpiece at the other end. He tested the door and went back to his desk. It took him only a few moments to find Rupert's number.

"A bit late in the day for you to be ringing me," Rupert said.

"It's all a misunderstanding. I tried to explain to Olga but she wouldn't let me. Is she there now, with you?"

"Her movements are no concern of yours."

"I had nothing to do with any arrangements with Oleg Kruffinski. It's all Gerald's doing. If Olga's even half right about Oleg, it's bound to come to grief."

"Well, I must say I'm very disappointed in you. There's nothing more to be said."

"Could I just ask you a question?"

"That depends. What is it?"

"Did Olga say anything to you about spying, or about the English being born spies?"

"That's a bloody silly question, Jones." Rupert became the second person to hang up on Davenport that day.

He unlocked his door and made sure that Elena was nor lurking in the corridor. He tried, but was unable to concentrate on the documents. Feeling beyond redemption he put on his coat and turned off his light. Then, like a ghost, he silently glided down the corridor to the back entrance through which he passed as quickly as he could. He noticed that the billboard for the *Daily Revealer* was proclaiming in large letters, 'Russian masterpiece looted by Gestapo.'

The Return of Gloria

He wondered whether the evidence in the afternoon had somehow established that, or whether, Oleg had offered the newspaper some other, far more interesting, inside story.

11

Londys on the Move

Rupert had not returned to the hearing in the afternoon, but Olga explained to him what had happened. "The criminal give evidence. Told everyone he not communist, never. He member of underground resistance. But I know the only time he go underground was to cellar to steal vodka. He say he protect his grandfather. NKVD looked for grandfather. That part true. They destroy his paintings if they find them. Oleg great hero: save grandfather, save paintings. Ask nothing for himself." Olga's rage made her pause.

"Why you not come back after lunch, see for yourself?"

"I thought you could handle it yourself."

"Then Oleg tell greatest lie of all. He say many years ago cleaner of museum tell him day before Germans overrun suburb, he conscripted to help museum staff load paintings and sculpture on trucks. He say he go down to basement to check. He see room full of paintings, lying on floor, stacked against walls, some damaged. He go upstairs tell museum director. Director say, leave there. All rubbish. Pictures sent by bad artists to get money from state. 'Hurry. Last truck leave now,' he say – firing getting closer as truck drive away."

"All hearsay," Rupert said, and then regretted it because Olga insisted he explain what hearsay was, and why courts generally paid no attention to it."

"You think so. That judge very interested. No one say he should ignore it."

"But it doesn't prove anything."

"That what woman on the panel say. But then man in middle, judge, he ask Oleg whether the cleaner could describe paintings in basement. Guess what criminal say. Only that one of them on floor was like plain sheets of colour unless you look closely at it. He not have much time. He think someone paint over it to cover up drawing underneath. He say something about yellow and purple."

"A likely story," Rupert observed.

"It get worse. Criminal say cleaner tell him he see patch across back top left corner of canvas. Of course he say that. Panel look at back of painting. It have patch in top left corner."

"Everyone in room get excited. Reporters run out, get on mobiles."

"Did the barrister for the institute get a crack at him?"

"Not today. Judge say something about inquiry, not adversarial. What he mean by that?"

"I would say that he doesn't want any of the barristers to get rough with the witnesses."

"I like ask questions of criminal."

"Perhaps we should have asked for a right of audience, you particularly as a grand daughter of the artist. If Oleg really hasn't got a proper authority from him, you have an interest which might entitle you to be heard. It's all rather contingent though. I didn't think we could afford the expense of getting legal representation. Spending the money on bribes in St Petersburg and on the border would be a better investment. I think you'd better go again tomorrow to see what happens."

Olga had every intention of doing just that. Indeed, she intended to do somewhat more than that.

After Gloria had been told at the front counter that Davenport was out, she had gone to the racks in the foyer where the catalogues of recent and future sales were kept. She was surprised to notice that each of them was secured by a small but strong chain, like coathangers fixed to a rod in an inferior hotel. And Londys was supposed to be a superior place. She was minded to say something cutting to that effect, still smarting as she was at the condescending way in which the receptionist for the day, a new woman, the Hon. Deborah Fairwether, had spoken to her. You would have thought Mr Jones, as she pointedly drawled – Gloria having asked for Davenport Jones, was the most important and unapproachable person in the whole of the art business of the country.

After she and Davenport were married she had seen catalogues he had brought home from Londys. She remembered that on the inside cover there were usually listed the names of the firm's employees who were the experts in the field of the art in the catalogue, and who were in charge of the sale. Whether Davenport's name was in one of the important ones would be the measure of his importance there. She pushed aside the catalogues concerning sales of fine furniture, of Chinese porcelain, of the contents of a gentleman's residence in Hereford, of ballet materials of artists of the Austrian Secession, and of Australian Aboriginal art, pausing only to recall that she had once said to a sceptical Davenport that there might be some money in Aboriginal art some day. Well, that certainly wasn't the only thing that Davenport had been wrong about.

One of the brochures on the racks caught Gloria's eye. On the front, was a mission statement containing all of the usual clichés, 'serving our clients', 'good corporate governance', 'workplace safety', 'excellent industrial relations' and 'world's best practice.' Gloria wondered how the last was measured. Was there some international board sitting at Geneva to pass judgment on all the people who claimed to follow world's best, not merely better, practices? The Master has expressed his aspirations in mystic language, but in the end it came down to the same thing, ripping off your clients to the greatest extent possible without risking gaol.

She turned to the inside of the brochure. It contained photographs of the executive staff and the expert employees, together with a short biographical note on each. She passed quickly over Davenport's. It told her nothing that she didn't already know.

Elena's photograph was at the bottom of the left corner of the inside of the first page. She had either forgotten to remove her glasses or had determined to look serious and efficient. It was almost impossible to see her eyes behind the bottle glass spectacles which she used for close work on small numbers.

Gerald's photograph was the biggest. He was presented as a cerebral chief executive who nonetheless was maintaining his youthful good looks, if not to say, 'baby face'. The biographical note enthusiastically described his rapid ascent to his present position and implied an aesthetic knowledge of which Berenson would be proud. It said nothing about his marital status. Gloria was minded for a minute to demand that the woman at the desk summon Gerald to see her. She decided, however, that today was not the time to do that. As she walked out the front door the image of Gerald stayed in her mind. That she was attracted to young looking, baby-faced men was hardly her fault.

Davenport locked himself in his flat. He pulled the blinds down at the front and turned on only the light in the kitchen. He opened a tin of spaghetti and poured himself a small whisky. He ate and drank in front of the television set that Elena had rented for him.

The program was one of those carefully scripted series in which the man is the mythical, understated Englishman, and the women, his wife, grasping and from whom he is separated, and his secretary, impossibly efficient, well meaning but lacking completely in emotional judgement. It was mildly amusing but Davenport's mind kept slipping away from it.

He had thought that, with distance, his life would be improved. He was aware that he was not the first person to make that mistake. How many hopes, he wondered, had been dashed, how many ambitions thwarted or left to wither away, in London in the last one thousand, one hundred...ten years even.

He felt tense, threatened. The beautiful, mercurial Olga might be capable of anything when her temper – fury more like – was raised. Nor was Elena a woman to be taken lightly. But more worrying was the presence in town of Gloria. Why would she be asking for him? If ever there had been a book closed shut it was surely their marriage. She could not be looking for money, he reassured himself. Apart from taking almost everything he had as part of the divorce settlement, she had retained her own not inconsiderable savings. And as for wanting to see him for old times sake, or any other benign purpose, that was inconceivable. He was as restive as a tiger, no, not a tiger, a deer being stalked by a tiger...in the jungle.

He looked at his watch. It was only seven-thirty. He found the newspaper and turned to the entertainment section. There might be a film that he wanted to see. On the opposite page there was an article about a new night club that had opened in Chelsea. Already it was the place for fashionable models and American film stars in town to be seen. There was no reason why he shouldn't do the same, be there, be seen. He was a single man, reasonable, affluent, well, almost affluent, and on the fringe of the entertainment business himself. That was probably an understatement. He remembered a performance artist in Australia who used to run across hot coals in his bare feet, and construct installations with suspended claypots in which various flammable liquids burned. One day he had caught fire and incinerated himself. The leading art critic on the *Sydney First Voice* had written that the artist, in one brilliant stroke of self-immolation, had erased the faint and shifting border between art and entertainment.

Davenport looked again at the pictures of the habitués of the new night club. The girls not wearing jeans appeared to be wearing the sort of flimsy lingerie that wedding shops display on dummies in their windows. The men wore black t-shirts or light cotton or linen jackets fashionably crumpled, and with their sleeves rolled to a few inches below the elbow. He decided that night clubs were out unless he were to exchange his current wardrobe for a new one, cut in fitted styles and probably made, like the first fortune of the Maltby brothers, at least several hundred miles or more to the east.

He looked at the advertisements for the films. There did seem to be a lot in which the novelty of their special effects was emphasised. There also appeared to be a disproportionate number of horror films.

Davenport got up and changed the channel. There were highlights of the previous day's cricket test between Australia and India playing. For a time, he had fancied himself as a spin bowler. He sat down to watch, as Chatwin, the finest left-handed wrist spinner of his generation set out to tantalise, trick, and inevitably dismiss the Indian tail-enders. But even that was insufficient distraction.

He tiptoed to his front door and slowly, and ever so carefully and slightly opened it. He would have to have one of those peepholes installed. There was no one outside. He closed and locked it immediately. The long night stretched ahead of him. He cleared away the few things that he had used for his meal, and bathed. That was another thing he would have to do, install a shower over the bath. As he toweled himself dry, he tried to recall something he had once heard Barry Humphries say about the English and baths, but apart from recalling that it was very offensive, he couldn't bring it to mind.

He stepped over to the small cabinet in the wall and took from it one of the three sleeping pills that his doctor had prescribed to help him sleep on the flight from Australia. He swallowed it and looked for a book in the pile that he had sent as unaccompanied baggage. The one that he selected was *Great Dealers* by a retired art critic from the *Times*.

He checked his bedroom window to make sure that there was no gap between the architrave and the blind. When he had satisfied himself about that he turned on his bedside light and began to read. The first essay, of course, was on the greatest dealer of all, Duveen. Davenport already knew the essentials of his life and career but it was interesting to read about them again, as well as the other less known incidents and people in his life. When he read for the third time a paragraph telling how Duveen insisted upon paying far above a vendor's asking price for a Gainsborough on the ground that it would be damaging to his reputation if it became known that he was dealing in slight works, he knew he was ready for sleep. He marked his page, put down the book, and turned off the bedside light. He closed his eyes.

He was jolted awake by the ringing of his phone. He picked it up.

"Davenport?"

"Yes."

"Rupert here. I'm sorry Olga was a bit rough with you today." He made no mention of his own conduct and waited for Davenport to respond. Davenport said nothing.

"I would hope that a mild disagreement about the Kruffinski wouldn't stop us from doing other business."

"What other business?"

"As you know, I do get some good work other than the Russians from time to time."

"I didn't notice any."

"I keep most of that sort of thing at home. We shouldn't have any hard feelings about Kruffinski. I told Olga none of it would have been of your making. I think she's coming round to a rational view."

A rational Olga sounded improbable to Davenport.

"Yes, there's no point in our arguing. You will find Oleg difficult to deal with, but then a hundred or so Kruffinskis on the block are worth a touch of trouble. I suppose your Gerald will be going to St Petersburg himself soon?"

"I tried to tell you, Gerald did the deal with Oleg. I've got no idea what his plans are."

"He sent you to the panel hearing."

Davenport was too weary to argue with Rupert. There was something likable about him however. The obviousness of his desire to find out Londys' plans for securing the Kruffinski was rather endearing. "Whatever you say Rupert. I'm going back to sleep now."

"Wait a minute. I just want to say that I won't hold it against you if you're prepared to deal with me in the future."

"Does that go for Olga too?"

"Perhaps not in the near future in her case."

As soon as Davenport arrived at work Gerald told him that he had arranged for Peter Lanson to call upon him at eleven o'clock.

"We've got a few balls in the air now Davenport. Don't fumble them. And just remember, a well known city accountant can put a lot of other useful work our way."

"Are you going to be present when he comes?"

"I can't do everything. You've got to learn to stand on your own two feet. By the way, I think you should make your debut on the podium on Friday. Early twentieth-century art. We're throwing in a few Aboriginal bark paintings of the period; right up your alley."

"I don't know anything about Aboriginal art."

"But the punters don't know that. Just as everyone thinks all Arabs know everything about making bombs, they think all Australians know about Aboriginal art. You can take the second fifty lots, nothing important in them. Think of yourself as a change bowler, giving the strike bowlers a spell."

"What about the Kruffinskis? Are you going to put in an appearance at the panel hearings?"

"Certainly not. Oleg's covering that. And I wouldn't want to be seen there anyway. The less the media and our competitors know about our interest at this stage the better. Shouldn't you be clearing your desk now? And make sure you're very appreciative of Peter remembering his old school friend as he has."

As Davenport was leaving, Gerald called out: "If he's not already engaged he'll expect you to take him to lunch. Likes a good Burgundy, Peter does."

As soon as he saw him, Davenport found it easy to believe that Peter was a man who enjoyed a good Burgundy. His round mottled face contrasted with his dark-blue, pin-striped city suit and sombre club tie. He had no brief case with him.

After they were introduced by Gerald, who then left them,

Davenport said, "I understood you were bringing full details of the pictures with you."

"Should be on the fax by now. I carry nothing and send nothing by email. Faxes aren't completely secure of course but they're better than anything else."

Davenport had the fax machine checked and soon had in front of him several pages of descriptions, artists, provenances, sizes, and some old condition reports. "I'll have to examine each picture carefully and have someone else, someone independent of the firm verify my assessments. To achieve the best prices we may have to do some conservation work and re-gilding of frames."

"You're the expert. That's for you to decide. Don't stress though. Gerald says you're Australian."

"Yes."

"You don't know a man called Cassius Morton do you?"

"Should I?"

"He was at school with me. I believe he's a very successful accountant in Adelaide now."

"Adelaide is at least six hundred kilometres from the nearest other state capital."

"I thought not many people live in Australia."

"About twenty million or so."

"You've never been in the Army, I take it?"

"No."

"I did three years. Good training for life."

"Do you mind if I skim these quickly? Then I'll need to ask you some questions."

"Not all that hard you know, to turn a young man into a trained killer."

Davenport looked up from the papers in puzzlement.

"Military training. You could say I was a trained killer," Lanson added.

Davenport doubted that. "I'll just finish these if you don't mind."

"It won't take too long I hope. Lunch time's not too far off."

Londys on the Move

"I'm sorry, I forgot. You might care to have lunch with me. We could talk about anything we have to there."

"Lunch. Now that's a thought. Let me see." Peter pulled out a small black diary and flicked to the present. "No, seems to be clear."

"There's a small Italian place in Mount Street that's supposed to be good."

"No doubt, but the Vine is better. Don't you ring, I'll do it. I'm known there."

Davenport didn't doubt that. He only hoped that he could put in a chit for the cost because he had no reason to believe that Lanson would be picking up the bill. The booking made, Lanson saw no reason to detain himself at Londys any longer. "Let's go then. They're very good to fit us in. They can't hold the table for too long."

"But what about the exhibition, and the sale?"

"That's why we've got Londys. Come along."

"But you haven't met Elena; she's helping me."

"Bring her along to lunch."

Uncertainty about who would be ultimately responsible for the cost of lunch was not the only deterrent: Davenport was not anxious to be alone with Elena after what he suspected would be a long and alcoholic meal.

The restaurant was already crowded when they arrived. The head waiter led them to a corner table. When they were seated, a long-haired thin man in early middle age who looked vaguely familiar to Davenport raised a hand to greet Peter. "That's Rocket Lynton Powers, a rap star whose tax affairs we manage. Not that many of our clients here in the old UK these days. One of the tax partners flies out to the Dutch Antilles four times a year. I should have chosen tax instead of insolvency. Still, having the shorts has its compensations. Auctioneers all over the country vie for our favours. I've a few Iranian, could be Caucasian, rugs in my house in the country. A Bond Street importer went belly up and I had to choose an auctioneer to sell the stock, bales of it. Most of the stuff went for a song."

"But wouldn't that be a conflict of interest?"

"Don't be naïve. You're an auctioneer yourself. Don't tell me you haven't given a few of your friends a quick hammer. Ah, the card. A glass of Krug to start." He signalled for the waiter whom he called by his Christian name and ordered a bottle. "A burgundy I think. You have no objection? Claret, not homosexuality, is the English vice. I'll order some when he comes back." He looked at his watch. "Fifteen minutes will do. That's another myth, breathing the wine."

Davenport couldn't imagine that Lanson had ever allowed any wine to breathe for long.

Tasting, interrogating the waiter, 'Giles' about the specials, ordering, retracting, ordering again, and insisting that Davenport track him through the courses were interminable. When it was all settled, Davenport tentatively raised the exhibition and sale again. Peter was too busy waving to another celebrity to pay attention to Davenport.

"What?"

"You and Gerald have set an impossibly short schedule."

"Let me tell you something, Jones. Paintings are like any other commodities, with the exception of branded items. And it's an exception that makes paintings easier to sell than most other commodities. Lamborghinis, Chanel gowns, grand houses – dare I say it, beautiful women. Hell, they're all trophies. Rich people, particularly people who only got rich yesterday, love to acquire trophies." Lanson paused to wave to Rocket who was leaving.

"Take Rocket there, he wanted some fellow called Christo to wrap one of his girlfriend's houses up in plastic for her birthday. Christo quoted a quarter of a million to do it. But he couldn't do it in time. Rocket offered him another fifty. Still couldn't do it. Can you believe that? I don't understand it. Christo, an artist? If we had the time I'd get you to explain it." The waiter arrived at their table. "The best Chevre cheese soufflé in London," Peter said, as the dish was placed in front of him. He drank the last drop of his champagne and turned his attention to the burgundy. "You haven't drunk all of your champagne. You have to cleanse the palate for the burgundy," he declared.

"I've got quite a lot to do this afternoon. I need a clear head."

"I thought Australians drank anything, beer, cask wine, rum. Speaking of commodities wasn't rum used as currency in your early days?"

"Yes, by the soldiers, English soldiers. They were called the Rum Corps."

They worked their way through the courses, the accountant swiftly and efficiently, Davenport laboriously. Pessimistically, Davenport asked Lanson whether he would like coffee.

"A cognac," Lanson answered, and called for the trolley. The waiter took up a bottle and poured two snifters without being asked, and handed one to each of them.

"Now where was I? Selling. I don't know much about art myself, but I understand that all of the Maltby pictures are brand names. Buying art is like buying one of those handbags with writing all over it that the Japanese like so much."

"You'd get a lot of them for the price of a Monet."

"I'm talking principle, not detail." Peter crooked a finger at a passing waiter for another cognac.

Davenport who had lagged as far behind Lanson as courtesy and male congeniality permitted, had a headache and mildly blurred vision. Apart from a heavily flushed complexion, the accountant seemed unaffected. "We'll stay in touch," he said as he got to his feet, much more athletically than Davenport. He made no mention of the bill. His exit was far grander and faster than Rocket's.

Davenport's hand trembled as he signed the bill under the watchful eye of Giles who made sure that he had included the full amount of the 'optional tip' which had already been included.

It was three-thirty in the afternoon. It took Davenport thirty minutes to find a vacant cab, and another half hour in crowded traffic to reach Londys. He went directly to Gerald's office.

"I can't work with your old school chum. My liver's not up to it."

"Davenport, we pay you a very large salary to do more than tell us whether a painting's any good or not. Anyway, some people would jump at the opportunity for long lunches and fine wine. Do you remember what burgundy Peter chose?"

"A very strong one."

"Is there anything else? I am rather busy."

"Yes. Even if I had the liver for it, I couldn't work with the man. I can't pin him down. I need cooperation, arrangements for access, insurance, condition reports, conservation; there's bound to be some of that necessary. You know yourself the sort of thing that's involved. He wouldn't even talk about it."

"He can be hard to pin down. But there's no such thing as a perfect client. He's also partial to a well turned ankle. Have Elena deal with him in matters of detail. Concentrate on the big picture yourself, Davenport. Start to act like a senior executive." Gerald pointedly looked down at the papers on his desk. Davenport could see that it would be fruitless to complain any more. He reached the door. He didn't raise the matter of the bill but he couldn't resist asking the question.

"Who's Rocket Powers?"

"Who's Rocket Powers? You might as well have asked who John Lennon was in 1968." That definitely was the end of the interview.

"How did it go?" Elena asked when Davenport returned to his room. "Are you feeling all right? Not coming down with anything?"

"Cirrhosis of the liver."

"Well, you men bring it on yourselves. How often do you see women executives gorging themselves at lunchtime?"

"I'd willingly change places. I fear that there'll be more of those lunches. You can deputise for me any time."

"See now, I haven't been idle. I've refined the memorandum of tasks still to be done, and the likely costs. First, we need to inspect the pictures with a good conservator. I've spoken to one, Frank Sklavas, an English-born Greek. He's one of the best. By day he works for the London Impressionist Museum; at night for private enterprise. He's got access to the museum and everything he needs at any time there. He seems to be able to get away during the day to make inspections. I've also engaged Fine Art Removers to collect and carry the pictures either to Frank at the museum, or here if they don't need work. Peter says he's insured them but to be on the safe side I've arranged for our own insurance to cover any liability if anyone tries to sue us. The other decisions you'll have to make, whether any work apart from repainting needs doing in Sale Room Number 1, and everything about their hanging and a catalogue. I've told our photographer he'll have to activate himself. Davenport, you're not dozing off are you?"

"Of course not. Go on."

"I think that's enough for one day. I did think we might have dinner together tonight but you don't look up to it."

"Afraid not. I couldn't eat another thing. What do they call those geese they make *pate de foie gras* out of?"

"Strasbourg, I think. I can see you're going to have to go into training. You won't be any use to anyone, yourself included, otherwise."

Elena closed the door behind her unnecessarily hard, and Davenport sighed in relief.

12

A Violent and a Gentle Confrontation

'Brawl at Hearing' the poster for the *Evening Star* proclaimed in heavy letters. A newspaper seller pressed a paper upon Davenport and held his hand out for the money. Davenport handed him a pound. Only when Davenport refused to move did the man give him his change. He paused to read the front page.

> There was a wild scene at Somerset House today during a public hearing by the Spoliation Panel presided over by High Court Justice Stedley. The purpose of the hearing was to establish the history of a painting by an obscure modern Russian master, Kruffinski, in the possession of the Deptford Institute in Liverpool.
> Oleg Kruffinski, 45, the painter's grandson and representative at the hearing alleges that the painting was looted from Leningrad during the siege of the city during WWII by Nazis acting on behalf of Herman Goering who assembled a massive collection of old and modern masters for his country hunting lodge, Karinhall. It was sumptuously decorated with valuable paintings, magnificent furniture, tapestries, sculpture, and oriental rugs. Goering, the bloated former WWI air ace, strode its halls in comic opera uniforms, pointing out his looted treasures to his psychopathic guests.

A Violent and a Gentle Confrontation

At the end of its deliberations the panel is expected to make a decision, either that the picture be returned to the artist, or that a payment of a fair sum in lieu be paid to him. The panel could also make a declaration that the institute's claim of title is untainted by any theft or extortion. In that case the panel would make no recommendation.

Also present at the hearing was the artist's granddaughter, Olga Kruffinski, who launched an outburst during some further evidence of the grandson. 'Liar, cheat, filthy communist pig,' she chanted.

This is the first time the panel has conducted its proceedings in public. One member of it was heard to whisper it will be the last.

Oleg Kruffinski told his cousin to sit down and shut up. He had just finished telling the panel that his grandfather had expelled Olga Kruffinski from his home in St Petersburg when he found her trying to remove some preparatory pencil sketches he had made for a larger work.

The artist was very briefly in vogue before WWII. He was accused of Western decadence and excluded from participation in the official art establishment of the communist party.

There has been renewed interest in his work in recent times. There is a rumour that he is sitting on a cache of his best work, which, if he is able to export it from Russia, would revive his reputation and make a fortune for him and his family.

The grandson and granddaughter obviously think there's a potential fortune at stake. After the outburst and its response, the chairman of the panel called for a security guard. Before the guard arrived, Ms Kruffinski attacked her cousin with an umbrella, landing one blow which drew blood from his forehead.

The chairman of the panel kept on calling for order. He could not be heard above the shouting.

Twice, Oleg Kruffinski tried to land a punch his cousin. She skipped and danced around him like a feather-weight boxer, prodding him as hard as she could in the stomach with the ferrule of her umbrella.

The story continued in the same vein, concluding with the statement that Olga had been arrested by the police and remained in custody, and that her cousin had been taken away in an ambulance.

At the top of the page there was a photograph of Olga with her umbrella levelled at Oleg's stomach and a highly agitated High Court judge in the background.

Davenport hastily telephoned Rupert. "Have you seen Olga in the last hour or so?"

"No. Why?"

Davenport saw no point in softening the blow. "Then she'll still be in the hands of the police."

"What for? Abusing a parking attendant?"

"Much worse than that: I should think causing grievous bodily harm to her cousin, Oleg."

"Little Olga! Don't be ridiculous."

"They were stitching Oleg's forehead when he was last seen."

"By whom?"

"The *Evening Star*. There's a photograph on the front page of them fighting. It's the lead story."

"She is inclined to be emotional that girl. I've warned her, we English prefer understatement. I suppose I'd better go and bail her out. Do you know where they've taken her?"

"How could I? I'm a stranger here."

"Look at the paper, man. It'll tell you."

Davenport did as instructed, but the paper didn't provide the information. "Why don't you ring the paper or the police yourself?"

Davenport's infatuation with Olga must have been obvious. "That's not a very helpful attitude, Davenport. Don't you care about Olga?"

"Of course I do. It's just that I don't know the ropes here."

"It's always the same. You have to do everything for yourself these days. Do you think the bail is likely to be very much?"

"Perhaps they won't grant her bail."

"She's a woman, an attractive one, who's being cheated out of her inheritance. They'd have to give her bail. Do you know whether you have to put up some actual cash?"

"That or title deeds, or a bond or bank guarantee, is what they ask for in Australia, I think."

"There is one painless way you could help out, Davenport. How much cash can you put your hands on at short notice?"

"Not nearly enough. It's just occurred to me though, has Olga been naturalized?"

"I don't think so. Why?"

"I think it's harder to get bail if they think you might abscond. From what I see over here, anybody who is not British who is in trouble is expected to abscond."

"Nothing wrong with that. That attitude gets rid of its foreign criminal classes very appropriately. Damn it, Davenport, you're no help at all."

Davenport would have liked to help free Olga but believed there was nothing he could do that Rupert, whose responsibility she was, could not. He also knew that Gerald would be angry if his name and connection with Londys were to be associated with the fracas at Somerset House, and with his defiance of Gerald's direction that contact with Olga and Rupert end. Still, he couldn't bear the thought of Olga in a cell surrounded by rough prostitutes, cocaine dealers, and Gypsy pickpockets. If he knew where Olga was being held, and there was no Rupert to take responsibility, he would have set aside his fears and sped to her side. "Well, Oleg's certainly got the publicity he wanted, compliments of Olga," he said.

"There's no middle ground with Russians. They're either gloomy or exuberant."

"I'd hardly describe assault and battery as mere exuberance."

"This is no time for semantics. You're sure you've got no cash on you."

"Not much. And I don't have a cheque book here yet. You'll have to use yours."

"Well, I have to say that I'm disappointed in you, Davenport. I thought you'd at least try to be helpful. Olga will be very disappointed too when I tell her."

"Perhaps there might be something I could do."

"I'll pick you up in ten minutes in front of your flat."

Twenty minutes later a battered, ancient, yellow, E-type Jaguar pulled up in front of Davenport's flat. The driver sounded the horn long and urgently. Davenport got in and the car took off with a shudder.

"You couldn't carry many pictures in this," Davenport observed.

"It's my Sunday car," Rupert said. "Almost a museum piece."

"You're right about that," Davenport agreed. "Where are we going?"

"They're holding her at Leicester Square Police Station. They're apparently still trying to make up their minds what to charge her with."

"Not whether to charge or not to charge?"

"That wasn't my impression."

The sergeant at the desk was a woman of about thirty-five. She must have just finished her beat because she was in the middle of taking off her torch, handcuffs, asp and various other paraphernalia that Davenport couldn't identify. She was a muscular woman with cropped pepper and salt hair, and the easy familiarity with which she handled these formidable means of restraint awed the two men.

"What do you two want?" She asked when she had finished.

Rupert explained their purpose.

A glint came into the eye of the sergeant. "That little minx, she's certainly a headache. I arrested her myself." There was admiration rather than animosity in the woman's voice.

"We were told that a decision was being made about whether she would be charged or not," Rupert asserted.

"Oh she'll be charged with something," the sergeant said.

"Does that depend upon Oleg?" Rupert asked.

"Who's Oleg?"

"The man she...as I understood it, the party who struck first."

"He tells a different story."

"Well does the charge depend upon what he wants?"

"No."

"Then who decides?"

"As the first officer on the scene, I do."

A Violent and a Gentle Confrontation

"I can see you're a busy officer. You wouldn't want to waste too much time on a bit of a scuffle," Rupert suggested.

"What's it matter to you? What have you got to do with her?" The sergeant asked the question that Davenport had wanted to ask from the time that he had first met Olga and Rupert.

"Master, servant. She works for me. I own an art gallery. She's a fine arts graduate. Very knowledgeable."

"And you?" The sergeant nodded at Davenport.

"Reinforcements. I'm in the art business myself. He asked me to come along."

"Serious charges could be open," the sergeant warned.

"There's always a discretion though, isn't there?" Rupert unconfidently suggested.

"Anything from breach of the peace to attempted murder."

"That's a wide range," Davenport said. "Surely not attempted murder."

"I've seen weaker ones succeed," the sergeant said with satisfaction. But she was tiring of the game. It would be a nuisance to prosecute a serious charge against the young woman. The man she hit looked as if he deserved it. And she is pretty – very pretty.

"I'll make it breach of the peace." She wrote something in a big book and then typed the same information on a computer. "Fifteen quid in bail and we'll let her go. She's obliged to front the magistrate in the morning. Tell her not to turn up. Bail will be forfeited. Fifteen quid's less than it would cost to get a lawyer to stuff it up for her."

Rupert turned out his pockets and wallet, and then turned to Davenport. "You wouldn't have fifteen on you would you?"

Davenport handed over three, five pound notes. The sergeant took the money and handed Rupert a form to sign while she went off to fetch Olga.

Five minutes later she returned with her. There was not the slightest hint of regret or contrition about Olga. There was a tear in the back of her dress and her hair was awry. The sergeant was holding her arm close to her own body as she looked down admiringly at the young Russian woman.

"You'd better take her before I decide to keep her," the sergeant said.

Olga ungratefully shook herself free. Davenport thought that the sergeant would have been unlikely to disapprove of much that Olga might do.

Out in the square, amid the milling tourists, Davenport mildly asked Olga why she had publicly assaulted her cousin.

"Stupid question," was her response. She glared at Davenport. "He try to punch me."

"Only after you hit him, as I understand it," Davenport said.

"You think that man can punch woman if it suit him?"

"Perhaps he was acting in self defence."

"That man coward. Nothing more to say." She clamped her mouth shut until she was perched uncomfortably behind Davenport in the Jaguar. "Straight home," she commanded Rupert. And that was her last word until they reached her flat which, Davenport was pleased to notice, was only four blocks from his. "I come to work tomorrow. I would not be dragged by vicious wolves to watch panel tomorrow."

"I think you mean wild horses," Rupert corrected her but she was not interested.

"Fancy a drink?" Rupert asked.

"I gave you the last of my money."

"You've got credit cards, surely."

"They're up to the limit," Davenport lied.

"We'll go to the Swinging Gate. They'll let me put it on tick there."

They had hardly settled at a table when Davenport noticed a dog, again in the shadows under another table at which two men were drinking, their backs to him. He walked over to the table.

"Goldilocks's owner?" He asked when he was a few paces away. He still could not distinguish the colour of the dog under the table. "And that must be Goldilocks."

One of the men was sitting on a swivel chair. He swung it around to face Davenport. "Wrong on both counts." The dog put its head out from under the table. Its hair was jet black.

"You know him then?"

"Everyone knows Jack and Goldilocks. Especially Goldilocks. Intelligent bitch. I swear she knows when she's expected to run dead and when they want her to win. You can make a lot of money with a dog like that. Saves you a great deal of trouble too. No need to glaze her eyes with Vaseline before the race. Dogs don't bet. Give me a reliable dog over a jockey any day. Are you looking for a dog yourself?"

"I'm looking for Goldilocks's owner."

"You're out of luck there. Owes you some money I daresay?"

"More than four hundred pounds."

"I haven't seen them for a few weeks. They had a big success recently."

"So did I. Or so I thought. Where are they?"

"That I couldn't swear to. But if you asked me to conjecture..." Davenport noticed a faint Irish intonation in the man's voice. "I'd say they're on a moor somewhere, somewhere quiet, where they like to hunt in the old way, strictly cash betting, the stakes pretty high."

"If you happen to see them, would you please tell them, Goldilocks's owner I mean, that I'm still looking for my winnings. My name is Davenport Jones."

The other man just smiled knowingly.

Rupert asked the waiter to put the drinks on his account. "Davenport, you'd better open an account here. I'll vouch for you."

"I prefer not to run up credit."

"You'd never make a gallery owner then."

"That's one thing I've no desire to do."

Rupert ordered a second drink for each of them. "Olga looked like a fury when she came out," Rupert said admiringly.

"That's probably how she looked to Oleg just before they joined in combat."

"I haven't given up on Londys you know," Rupert said.

"You're wasting your time."

"Perhaps I should turn Olga loose on de Pyne. Despite that

temper of hers, she seems to get the men in, and judging by that police officer, some women too. You're not immune to her yourself I've noticed."

"It's a clinical interest only," Davenport disingenuously claimed.

"How do you think de Pyne would react? I must say he seemed rather asexual as an adolescent."

"Self-defence perhaps. It was a great public school you went to wasn't it?" Davenport asked with a knowing expression.

"There wasn't much of that sort of thing around when we were there. I've always associated it with flogging. There wasn't much of that either by then. Still, he's never married and he's in the arts."

"Hardly. He runs a company that sells art. You're in the same line of business yourself."

Rupert changed the subject, but Davenport was not entirely satisfied that the man would not try to arrange for Gerald to be seduced by Olga.

Gloria came to work at Jeremy Baker's apartment. The author was seated, waiting for her in the living room with the two girls. He was dressed for the occasion as the successful author: velvet monogrammed slippers, corduroy trousers, an alpaca cardigan, and the eye-shade again. He waved Gloria to a chair without bothering to stand. He did nothing to conceal his brief examination of his Breitling watch. Gloria had left very early but delays on the tube had made her five minutes late.

She could see immediately that the girls were uncomfortable in their own clothes. They looked like children of well-to-do parents of the 1930s about to leave for a sitting with a society photographer. When they spoke to Gloria, they were polite but uninterested.

"Well, I'll leave you three to it," Baker said. "The girls will show you around. Nothing's sacred except my writing sanctuary, and nothing's more sacred than that. You know, good writing is nothing more than a collection of plausible emergencies bookended by felicitous aphorisms."

The girls looked as if they had heard that one before.

A Violent and a Gentle Confrontation

When Baker had gone, Cassandra spoke. "Father says you're Australian, is that right?"

"Yes."

"And you spent a lot of time in India."

"Yes."

"Father says that if there's the slightest hint of drugs, we're to tell him," Polly warned.

"Does your father drink alcohol?"

"Only champagne and cognac."

"Well, they're drugs."

The younger girl seemed to soften at this hint of insurrection. "Sometimes he drinks too much," she offered.

"You shouldn't talk about that Cassandra," Polly said.

"Well it's true. You know it is. You remember that time he drank a whole bottle and we found him on the floor behind the couch asking where Lady Clesham had gone."

"No more, Cassandra," Polly ended the discussion.

"Now girls, I've had a lot of experience with children. I understand them and I like them to understand me. That's not difficult. I'm not complicated. I expect obedience. I won't ask you to do anything to which you could rationally object. There are many things we can do together. Some we'll have to do because your parents expect me to make sure you do them, others because I say you should. Where's your mother? I would like to meet her."

Cassandra spoke before Polly could. "Travelling. She's on a cruise."

"Not a cruise ship though," Cassandra emphasised. "She's in the Mediterranean. It's a yacht. Mummy said it was once a corvette in the Italian Navy. It goes very fast."

"I'm sure Mrs Jones isn't interested in converted warships." Polly was anxious to end the conversation.

"Mummy says the crew are mainly young Greek fishermen. They wear a kind of a uniform..."

"Mrs Jones isn't interested in livery Cassandra," Polly snapped.

"But I am. Besides, if I'm to understand you girls, I have to know something about your family and their homes." Gloria decided it was time to begin imposing her will. "And if Cassandra is telling me something Polly, I don't expect you to interrupt."

Gloria could see that Polly was unaccustomed to being rebuked. "Daddy says that in households like ours, the staff should be called by their surnames. We'll call you Jones will we?"

"No, you'll call me Mrs Jones." India, travel, and disillusion had cured Gloria of progressive education and tolerance of bad manners in children. And closer acquaintance with the Baker family did nothing to reduce her certainty of the view she had formed, that she was, for them, the last hope. She decided to remain on the front foot. "Now, I want to see your report cards for this year."

"Why?" Polly demanded.

"To find out your weakest subjects so that we can work on them at home."

"You're not our teacher," Cassandra was shocked now too.

"No, fortunately. But nor am I your entertainer. You will do school work, not just your homework after school, as I direct. If you want help I will provide it. While you're getting the cards I'll check my room and unpack."

The two girls hesitated. Gloria ignored them as she gathered her bag, soon to be replaced, which still carried the dust of India.

When she returned the two girls were still looking a little bewildered. They were seated demurely on the sofa with their report cards on the low table in front of them. Gloria gave them a half-smile of approval and began to read the cards. Polly's results were satisfactory but the commentary on them disapproving.

"According to your form teacher, you should be doing much better."

"If I can continue to do as well as I am I will get my O-levels." Gloria was unsure of what that meant, but assumed it was a standard high enough for entry to a university.

"That may be so but while I'm here, you'll be expected to work to your ability." Gloria then read the other report. Cassandra's marks were average. Only then did it strike Gloria that the school the girls attended was of a kind at which she had never taught. Students were given real marks here, and a place in their class. Form teachers' remarks were honest and direct. Those in respect of Cassandra stated, 'This student has a refreshing ingenuousness but needs to learn tact and restraint. Her school marks can be improved by hard work. Much, but not everything, to achieve improvement, can be done by the school. The rest must be done at home by reinforcement of a strong work ethic and close supervision of homework. If that cannot be done then she should be placed in a different school having lower ideals and standards.'

"Do you ever ask your parents to help you with your school work?" Gloria inquired.

"I wouldn't do that. They're always too busy, father that is, and mother travels a lot," Cassandra answered.

"It surprises me that your father can write for so many hours a day. I thought writers dried up after a certain daily quota."

"There are many misconceptions, Mrs Jones, about the life and labours of authors." Baker had re-entered the room soundlessly in his padded velvet slippers. Gloria glanced up at him. "The process of creativity is not confined to the passage of the pen across paper," he continued. "I write by hand, never by typewriter." He flourished his thick, heavily gold banded Mont Blanc pen.

"But you don't always write by hand Daddy," Cassandra chortled. "What about Mrs Digit? You're dictating to her all the time."

Baker addressed Gloria. "Mrs Digit is not, definitely not the muse in this household. That is a position that is at present vacant." This was a statement upon which Gloria would need, she knew, to reflect before she could decide whether it was an observation, a reference to Mrs Baker, or an invitation to herself.

Redirecting his attention to his daughter, Baker said, "Correspondence, hundreds of pages of it, that's what Mrs Digit does." He then turned to Gloria. "You'd be astounded by the number of letters a successful author receives. I reply to every one of them."

"Daddy's got one of those machines like the Queen has. It writes your signature for you, thousands of times," Cassandra explained to

Gloria.

"The signatures may not be entirely personalised, but the letters are." Baker, who could not keep all of his limbs still at once, was moving around the room. "There's nothing you need Mrs Jones? I see you've moved your luggage in. Room comfortable?"

"It seems so. One never knows until one has spent a night in a new room." She wasn't going to allow Baker to forget that she wouldn't be taken for granted in any way.

He seemed reluctant to leave. He sat down on a chair opposite to Gloria. "I never quite know what to do with the girls on a holiday. There's a limit to the number of times you can visit the zoo, and there aren't many matinees that are suitable for children. And I can't watch the films they want to see. I long for the pantomime season." His tone was of a devoted father wearied by a never-ending search for diversion for his children.

"He's given us an account at the video store. That's how we spend the holidays, watching videos," Polly disclosed.

"An occasional video as a last resort," Baker claimed. "I'm desperate for inspiration. What do you think Mrs Jones?"

"The Tate Modern, but with your interest in art I suppose you've taken them there often enough." To make the point, Gloria waved at the valuable paintings on the walls.

"Daddy hardly even looks at them, unless visitors come. He shows them the pictures and tells them the prices, don't you Daddy?" Again it was Polly, growing in confidence and independence, who made the disclosure.

But Baker was insensitive to it. "I was saving the Tate Modern up for a rainy day," he said.

"Then that's what we'll do this afternoon," Gloria announced. "After the girls have done some homework. Have you read their report cards Mr Baker?"

"Yes, a little while ago." He waited for Gloria to tell him what was in them.

She did, and added, "Both girls should be doing much better, obviously. That will be my first project." She looked at each of the

A Violent and a Gentle Confrontation

girls in turn, daring them to protest.

Gloria almost felt sorry for Baker. Here he was, a man in the prime of life, rich and famous, with two comely young daughters, a fine and unique residence in the greatest city in the world, but anxious - like a puppy - for approval and, more pathetically, for company. At the same time, Baker was feeling sorry for Gloria. It was obvious that the woman had hardly a penny to her name. Yes, she had driven a hard bargain for her salary, but who wouldn't in the circumstances. There was disillusionment in her eyes. One could not ask why. Anyway, it was obvious without asking that her husband must have maltreated her. Australian men were rough and unruly. You only had to watch their footballers sledging and kicking heads. Baker wouldn't put it past the woman's former husband to have beaten her. Forgotten soon was the hard bargain she had driven over the terms of her employment. Also forgotten was the last affair he had had. Baker decided that this was a woman who needed support and kindness.

Gloria had no way of knowing of this decision, not yet, but she sensed a softening, a pliability in Baker's attitude to her. "Come girls, we'd better start your homework and leave your father to get on with his work." She made the work, agreeably to Baker, sound as if it were *War and Peace*.

13

Davenport Takes Off

There was a touch of hysteria in Gerald's voice when he summoned Davenport to his office.

"That Russian woman was right."

"What are you talking about?" Davenport asked.

"Rupert's friend, mistress, whatever she is."

"I don't think she's his mistress," Davenport optimistically replied.

"Doesn't matter what she is. She was right about that cousin of hers. He's betrayed us, done a deal with Athicas."

Everyone who dealt in major works of art knew of Athicas, dealers who had been in business for more than a hundred years at the same address in St James's. It was a firm that had been universally, justifiably, mistrusted by all other dealers for the same period.

"Well, they deserve each other," Davenport said. "We've still got the Maltby sale, and after that I can start putting together the Australian sale we talked about."

"Did you fail elementary arithmetic at school, Davenport? The Kruffinski deal would have been our biggest since the war. You're lucky to get something like that once a century." Gerald fell into a gloomy silence.

"What happened? How did you find out?"

"Our lawyers were slow in drawing up the contract. The usual things. Where was the power of attorney, or the authorisation? They needed to do a five-thousand pound check on Russian law first before they could do a draft. Questions about an inventory, and so on. You could almost see the time sheets being filled in. Finally, today, they sent the contract round." Gerald pointed to a thick bundle of papers prettily laced together with green ribbons and bearing the red wafers of a notary's seals.

"I immediately rang Kruffinski, asking him to come in to sign. I was prepared to let him take the contract away to show to his own lawyers if he wanted to, but I didn't think he would because ours have been in regular touch with his. As cool and slippery and dirty as a piece of thawing Russian gutter ice, he told me he wasn't prepared to deal with us. We were too slow. He had signed with Athicas."

"Have you paid him anything?"

Gerald looked sheepish. "Not much."

"Doesn't that mean you must have had an agreement? If he's taken money then surely he can be held to his agreement even without his signature."

"So now you're not just the Divera expert, you're a contract lawyer too," Gerald replied.

"I was just trying to be helpful."

"Yes, you were. Sorry. It's not as simple as that. He'll deny he was paid anything."

"Produce a bank statement, the cheque. The bank can provide all the details."

"It's a Swiss bank."

"It's still a bank."

"Davenport, because I'm not going to take this lying down, and because I'm expecting you to look after Londys interests in the Kruffinski affair, I'm going to tell you something on a need to know basis. I'll deny I ever told you if the occasion arises.

"As you are aware, Londys has antiquities sales from time to time. As you also know, countries tend to be touchy about antiquities. I believe that if they'd had a Spoliation Panel two hundred years ago,

The Russian Master

heaven forbid, the Elgin marbles would long since have been sent back to Greece. A fat lot of good that would have done. The Turks would have ground them down for cement or something. I like to think of the trade in antiquities as a granting of reprieves, reprieves of objects likely to be condemned to destruction in the countries from which they come. If I had been around and I'd been alive a hundred years ago, I would have reprieved the pyramids, and the sphinx, and bought them here. The Germans didn't mess about the way we did last century. Have you seen the antiquities museums in Berlin, Davenport?"

"No. Is that what you wanted to tell me in confidence."

"Sometimes the people who deal in antiquities like to remain anonymous. You can understand why. They like to be paid in cash, or in Switzerland, or the Bahamas. The last thing they want to leave is a money trail. In the end, we found it most convenient to have our own anonymous numbered account in Switzerland. We paid Kruffinski in cash out of that. We can't prove payment. And if we tried, we'd have the Inland Revenue, and God knows who else all over us."

Davenport had thought that by now there was nothing he didn't know about the art and antiquities business.

"I'm shocked Gerald, I really am."

"It's the competition. That's one of the ways we deal with it. How others do it I don't know. Put it out of your mind. We've got more important things to think about. You've never been to Russia, Davenport, have you?"

"No."

"Well you're going there now – in company, I hope, with the mercurial Olga. You're more than a little partial to her aren't you? There must be some reciprocal interest."

"If there were, you fixed that, signing with Oleg, being offensive to Rupert."

"I've always been offensive to Rupert, ever since our prep school days. I'm sure he's not very complimentary about me."

"What are you suggesting, that somehow I repair the damage

you've done, cultivate Olga, ask her to go to St Petersburg with me, take me to see her grandfather and persuade him, if he's capable, or Olga - assuming she can get an appropriate authority - to enter the agreement that Londys have already rejected, and which Rupert and Olga were prepared to sign a few weeks ago? That sounds like a pretty easy job."

"That's the sort of thing we pay you for, Davenport."

"It's a crackpot scheme." Davenport had long ago learnt that, in the art business, anger was fruitless. His outburst was one of frustration. "You can't be serious. I'm a curator, an art expert, not some latter day Duveen. Besides, Russia's full of gangsters these days. Look at me, I'm a pretty frail character. I'm sure Oleg has mafia connections. Can you imagine what they'd do to me in St Petersburg?"

Throughout all of this Gerald remained unbending. "Davenport, you mentioned Duveen. I can see you as the new Duveen. Better perhaps. You not only sound and look innocent, I think you are innocent, ingenuous, but clever. Look what you did with the fake Divera. That's what people like in this business. People who buy expensive paintings want paintings that come with a story. Art and entertainment go together these days. We want the new rich: bankers, internet players, popstars and centre forwards. Who's ever heard of anyone from any of the old families paying a million pounds for a picture? They've got all the million pound pictures they need, and anyway, why would they spend that sort of money on a painting when the roof needs replacing, or when they can buy the adjoining farm or the fishing rights over a good stream for the same amount of money. Everything has changed. Davenport, you won't remain as you are today. In the future, you'll become jaded and cynical; you might even have my job. I'm thinking of grooming you for it. It could be sooner than you think. This is hard and unrewarding work. I'm approaching burnout, Davenport."

"Why would I want your job if it's going to burn me out?"

"Davenport, just try to concentrate on the task in hand will you.

There's very little time. Now, I know these things can be costly, and you've had a lot of expense setting yourself up in London, although you did rather live it up before you went into that flat. But spend whatever you have to to lure Olga back. It'll all be on expenses."

"She was never with me."

"Well it's hardly my fault if you want to have it both ways – Elena one night and Olga the next. That's something you kept to yourself – that you were a great pants man – when you applied for your position here."

"I'm not, as you say, a pants man. And you headhunted me. I never wanted the job, and the more I find out what it involves, the more I think it was a mistake to take it."

Gerald ignored this. "There are plenty of flights to St Petersburg." Forgetting his promise of largesse, he added, "They tell me you can get cheapies from Stanstead twice a day on Econoair. How long will it take you to win the hussy back?"

Like anger, further protest would be unavailing. There was also the Hermitage. Its fabulous treasures beckoned.

"I could have a shot at it, I suppose."

"That's the spirit."

"What authority do I have to make an agreement, that is in the unlikely event that Olga's even prepared to talk to me?"

"You can agree to what they first proposed."

"No more? They might go elsewhere, to some other dealer, like Oleg has."

"No more without my prior approval. You're wasting time."

"There's just one thing...it's Elena..."

"You want me to bail you out of a sex entanglement now? You should have thought about Olga and all the others, whoever they are, before you entered into that one. I'm not a divorce lawyer, you know. I can't make any promises. All I can do is try to keep her fully occupied on the Maltby sale."

In the reflective atmosphere of his own room, Davenport asked himself how he could possibly have agreed to Gerald's plan. Had he agreed to it? Like so much that had happened to him since Gerald had flown out to Australia to speak to him, his agreement, if he had given it, seemed to have occurred independently of the exercise of his will.

It occurred to him that if the Spoliation Panel was still sitting on the case, he might have an opportunity to speak to Olga there. He had almost reached the back door when he was intercepted by Elena.

"You always seem to be sneaking out the back door, Davenport. What are you escaping from this time?"

"Escaping? I'm off on company business."

"There's something up. Gerald's just told me that he's taken you off the Maltby sale for a few days. He says it's about time I learnt something about the commodities we handle. I'm to have much more involvement. What's he up to?"

"How would I know? Gerald's so devious I don't think he knows what he's doing himself half the time."

"Well what are you doing, you must know that?"

"Some ground work on the Australian sale, as a matter of fact."

"That couldn't be as important as the Maltby sale."

"Well, I think Gerald believes he and you have got the Maltby in hand. 'Must look to the future, always to the future', that's what he said. Must fly."

Looking very dubious, Elena stood aside. "When are we going to be together again?" she asked.

"I can't say. I think there's going to be quite a bit of travel involved in getting the Australian stuff together." He patted Elena on the arm and scurried out the door as one porter held it open so that another could carry a large gilded frame inside.

It was a cool day but the sky was cloudless. Davenport's spirits lifted as he walked along the sunny side of the Strand. If he were going to remain in London he would need to buy a good overcoat. Then he remembered. He would need one, a heavy one for his trip to St Petersburg, if, that is, it happened. He saw himself walking down Moskovsky Parade with Olga beside him. She was dressed like a Russian countess in a Hollywood film, a sable coat down to the ankles of her polished high boots, and her soft curls fringing her high cheek boned face under a matching fur bonnet. It was snowing, lightly, in powdery flakes that dissolved without leaving any dampness. He was almost run over as he crossed the street. But he continued to fantasize. Suitably armed, and assisted by a team of fearless Cossacks, he might well save Olga from a pack of hungry wolves. He wondered, however, whether he would be able to save himself from the mafia of St Petersburg.

The Spoliation Panel was sitting, but on a different case. The chairman had acquired a taste for public hearings. The media rarely troubled to report the day-to-day fare of the Royal Courts of Justice.

Davenport left the building and walked out onto the middle of Waterloo Bridge. It didn't look much like the bridge in the film in which Robert Taylor and Vivien Leigh starred, and which his mother used to watch two or three times a year on her video player. He leant on the balustrade and looked down on the river below. He really must buy that coat. The wind off the water was as chill as the draught from a refrigerated cold room.

He didn't know Olga's telephone number. Gerald's intentions were typically cryptic. He had said nothing about Rupert but, nonetheless, Davenport assumed that he was expected to exclude him from the transaction. But even Gerald should have known there was little chance of that.

Davenport called Rupert's number. He thought he could detect suspicion in the man's voice but the heavy traffic on the bridge made it difficult to hear anything.

"You say you want to speak to Olga. Why?"

"I, well, I just thought explanations might be in order. I wanted to see how she was."

"She's still rather touchy. It might have been different if you hadn't been so reluctant to bail her out."

"I didn't have much money on me. And I did pay the bail in the end. You told me she would get over it. I thought you were encouraging me to make things up with her."

"Does de Pyne know you're calling?"

"Why should he? Anyway what's it got to do with you?"

"Olga's all alone here. She needs protection." He spoke as if he were a nobleman in a Walter Scott novel providing protection to his vulnerable ward. Davenport resolved not to explore the nature of the protection.

"Well I'd like to talk to her. Would you put her on please?"

"Can't do. She's not here."

Davenport didn't believe him. He hung up and hailed a taxi to take him straight out to Worlds End. The traffic was light and he reached the gallery in twenty minutes. The painting in the window had been replaced by one of Marshall Zhukov standing on a hill, more gloriously uniformed than a general of a people's socialist republic should be, watching hundreds of Soviet tanks rolling in pursuit of a fleeing German army.

Inside, Rupert and Olga were companionably drinking tea from a samovar.

"What are you doing here, Jones?" Rupert demanded.

"I've come to tell Olga that Londys is prepared to accept her offer."

"Steady on. You wouldn't have a bar of it before. And it's not just Olga's offer. It's a joint offer by her and me, and I'm not interested."

"It wasn't me who rejected it. You know that. It was Gerald."

"That's typical of him, sending an emissary out, not game to come near us himself."

Davenport turned to Olga. He held out his hands beseechingly. "It's your only chance. Without the backing of somebody like Londys, Oleg and Athicas will walk away with the estate."

"Why you not believe me when I tell you Oleg thief?"

"I believed everything you told me Olga," Davenport emphasised the 'I'.

"He is right Rupert. I prefer not to deal with anyone but have no choice."

"In view of what's happened, the offer will need to be

refined."

Davenport understood exactly what Rupert meant. "I've got no authority to agree to anything more. Look, we don't have time to waste. Oleg's got what he wants, publicity. Athicas will already be contacting their clients worldwide, offering the great museums first refusal on the best pieces. Gerald has given me a blank cheque – well, almost a blank cheque – for expenses. We should be on our way to St Petersburg by now."

"You understand that if we do this, I won't let Olga out of my sight for a second."

"From what I've heard about Oleg's associates I'd say that was a very good idea," Davenport agreed.

Olga immediately was a woman of resourcefulness. "I check on transport," she said, and picked up the phone.

They arranged to meet at Gerald's office two hours later. By then the contract would definitely be ready to sign and their airline bookings made. Davenport packed hurriedly and went directly to his own office. Elena was waiting for him there.

"So, you seem to have got your way, Davenport."

Davenport believed that he had been misrepresented. To be reproached by Elena was the last straw. He was uncharacteristically abrupt. "If you think I want to be given the impossible job of putting together the Maltby sale, taken off it, and sent to St Petersburg on a few hour's notice, pulling off the impossible, and then expected to resume working on the Maltby, is getting my way, you must be insane."

"Don't take your troubles out on me, Davenport."

"Look Elena, I'm leaving for St Petersburg in a few hours. I've got an enormous amount to do before then. Would you please leave me alone?"

"I had no idea you were so duplicitous."

"If you think so." He would have liked to add that, in the circumstances, they should confine their meetings to their work, but before he could say anything, Elena turned on her heel, flounced out, and slammed the door behind her.

After tidying his desk and making some telephone calls he made his way to Gerald's office where Gerald was waiting for Olga and Rupert.

"You know, I envy you Davenport: travel, exotic places, a beautiful woman, a meeting with a forgotten genius, an opportunity to become an acknowledged – probably the first – international expert on him, and all with the support of the premier auction house in the world."

"Why don't you go yourself then?"

"How I wish I could. But duty, a hundred duties here call."

Gerald's secretary knocked and showed Olga and Rupert into the room. They displayed no joy in being there. All unctuousness now, Gerald was on his feet and around his desk to shake their hands. To show that they had acquired the status of honoured clients, he took them over to the black leather couch at the end of the room and inquired whether they would like tea, water, coffee, a whisky perhaps. "Or should I say vodka?"

Rupert and Olga stonily refused all offers. "Why," Olga began, "you trust thief Oleg and ignore me?"

Rupert patted her on the arm. "Let bygones be bygones."

"This is the contract," Gerald said. "I can assure you it reflects the offer you made precisely."

"That's as may be." Rupert replied, "but you need us more than we need you now."

"Rupert," Gerald began his lecture, "Londys started in this business in 1832. It has survived and flourished through depressions, wars, strikes, the regimes of rapacious taxing governments, traditionalism, impressionism, post-impressionism, the Pre-Raphaelites, cubism, post modernism, vorticism, surrealism, modernity, the cyclical revivals of each of them, and God knows what else. It is the artists, the dealers and the parasites who need Londys, and not vice versa. Londys needs no one."

Olga did not like the sound of the word 'parasites'. She turned to Rupert. "Parasites? I hear that word before. What's he mean?"

As always, trying to be helpful, Davenport answered for Rupert.

"A creature that lives upon another, an unwilling host. A flea is a parasite on a dog."

Olga jumped to her feet. "He call us fleas. I do no business with this man."

"Gerald wasn't suggesting you and Rupert were parasites. He was talking about the fringe dwellers who prey on widows and people who don't know anything about art or values. He wasn't talking about really knowledgeable people like you."

"Do shut up," Gerald barked. "There isn't time for your solicitors to look over these papers. Just read them quickly yourself." He handed the contract to Rupert.

"I wouldn't trust you, Gerald, if you were selling me a postage stamp. Even this pretentiously traditional establishment must have a fax machine. I want this contract on it to my solicitors who have been waiting to hear from me for the last two hours. Here's their number."

"I'm disappointed in you Rupert, not least because we were at Brenton together."

"Being at Brenton was for most people merely a lesson in life. Being at Brenton with you, Gerald, was a lesson for eternity. I won't sign without my solicitor's approval."

Davenport reinforced his employer's concern about the time. "We can't do it. Our flight's due to leave in two and a quarter hours. Stanstead's forty minutes by train."

Gerald reached for the card that Rupert had produced with his solicitor's name and numbers on it. More in sadness than in anger, he said, as he took the contract to his secretary to fax to Rupert's solicitors, "This could take some time. You'd better see if there's a later flight to St Petersburg."

Davenport had no desire to stay in the room while they waited for Rupert's solicitor to approve the contract. "I'll check with the airline from my office." He hurried out of Gerald's room.

It took him a quarter of an hour to establish that the only remaining flight to St Petersburg that day was a BA plane at nine-thirty at night from Heathrow. He booked three seats on it, on

Londys account.

"Was that necessary?" Gerald asked when Davenport told him what he had done. "BA charge double what Econoair do."

"I didn't book business class," Davenport pointed out. "Even though my contract allows me to travel at that class."

"Not with a team of freeloaders." Gerald noticed a sudden restlessness on Olga's part. "What I mean is that the three of you should stick together, on the plane, on the ground, everywhere." He amended. "You might be able to get an Econoair flight home."

There was a knock on the door, and Gerald's secretary entered.

"Yes, what is it?" he asked with asperity.

"I didn't want to disturb you, but she was most insistent."

"Who was?"

"Mrs Jones. She wants to see Mr Jones."

A slightly malevolent grin appeared on Gerald's face. "You do have a current wife after all. Why did you deceive me and others?" He looked meaningfully at Davenport.

"I don't have a current wife."

"Current, past, future, what's the difference? Current, what are you, some kind of a serial groom? This isn't Hollywood, Davenport."

"What will I tell her?" the secretary asked.

"It's not my concern. You'd better tidy your life up, Davenport. But remember, you haven't long. You'll have to leave in an hour at the outside," Gerald pronounced.

Davenport, with a despairing look at Olga, hurried out. Gloria, finely manicured, pedicured and coiffured, was demurely seated, ankles and knees close together, in the foyer – under the perpetually suspicious eyes of the new receptionist. Gloria stood up as Davenport approached. He had to admit that there was now a maturity, and perhaps even a vulnerability about her that agreed with her. Then he recalled her implacable approach to the property settlement. Cautiously, he began. "I didn't expect to see you here."

"Nor I you," she countered.

"What do you want?"

"That's not a very civil question, Davenport. Couldn't you have asked me how I am, what I have been doing, what my plans are?"

"I know what you've been doing. What I don't know is what you're doing now."

"I read about you in *Jove*. You've become very famous. I have to say, I never expected you to end up in a place like this, though. You must have an office of your own. Can't we talk there?"

The woman at the desk had not missed a word of the conversation. She caught Davenport's eye just as he was about to deny that he had his own office.

"I haven't got long. I'm flying to the continent tonight." He pointed to the door to the corridor off which his office opened, and headed towards it, followed by Gloria. By the time she was seated in front of his desk, he was in an agony of uncertainty, whether to close the door against intrusion by Elena, or even Olga, or to leave it open to convey to Gloria that there was nothing personal to discuss. He shut the door.

"I really am pressed for time. What do you want?"

"To see you, Davenport. That is if you count our courtship, engagement, and marriage – we were together for a long time – as worth anything. You can't just brush those years aside."

"You did when you took up with your teacher friend. Where is he, by the way?"

"I don't think that's any concern of yours Davenport."

"I agree. Look, if it's money you need, I don't have it, to spare I mean, not at the moment. There's been a lot of expense just setting up here."

"How could you say such a thing. You make me sound like a gold digger. I have a very good job, interesting too, with the novelist, Jeremy Baker. I just thought I should look you up for old time's sake. You see, Davenport, unlike you, those years meant something to me."

Without knocking, Gerald threw open the door. "Davenport, we don't have time for old dalliances." He paused and took in Gloria. He saw an attractive woman who reminded him of a cousin to whom he had unconvincingly proposed marriage ten years before. "I'm sorry, Mrs Jones, you've arrived at a difficult time." He spoke in a somewhat softened tone. "Their solicitors want some changes to the contract. And Rupert's wife has rung to say that she saw Oleg on the news boarding an Aeroflot flight for St Petersburg. I really do have to drag your husband away..."

"Former husband," Davenport made clear.

"Why don't you call in tomorrow?" Gerald suggested. "I should be free at about ten thirty. I can fill you in on Davenport's movements then. Come on Davenport, quickly. I'll get my secretary to show you out, Mrs Jones." He tugged at Davenport's sleeve and drew him into the corridor.

"Gerald, I don't want that woman to know anything about my movements."

"How very ungracious you are, Davenport. Your wife comes all the way from Australia..."

"Former wife. Haven't I made myself clear? And not from Australia, but India. She's been in some Ashram with the fellow she ran away with."

"India, now I've often thought of going there myself. To learn Yogi."

"Yoga."

"Yes yoga. To learn to relax, pace myself, to learn how to deal with the recurrent stress that people like you create around here."

The travelling party was finally assembled at Heathrow. Olga and Rupert stood out from the chaos of the disoriented and the unaccomplished fliers. Davenport was struck by the difference between the scene before his eyes and one described by the author Anthony Powell, whom he had recently been rereading, of a pre-war French railway station, of opera cloaked officers, impressive black soldiers, and lounging matelots – all positioned as if for the rising of the curtain to a popular musical. Here, the preponderance of the travellers, in their jeans, anoraks, and discoloured backpacks, were as uniformed as the businessmen and women in their black suits clutching tightly their indispensable lap-tops.

"Lend me forty quid, Davenport," Rupert said.

"What for?"

"Vodka."

"Good heavens, Rupert, we're going to the land of vodka."

"That's the whole point. The export product is always the best. At least that's what any officials we might have to deal with will believe. Dollars and vodka are the currency franca as they say. You've got some dollars, haven't you?"

Davenport assured himself that the eight thousand dollars that Gerald had reluctantly allowed him was still in the cloth money belt awkwardly tied around his waist beneath his shirt and, with equal reluctance, handed Gerald forty pounds from his wallet.

He and Olga waited while Rupert went into the duty-free store to buy the spirit. They could see him slowly and meticulously making his choice as if he were selecting paintings for an artist's showing. Time was passing. Someone always seemed to interfere with the careful plans that Davenport made to arrive well ahead of scheduled times of departure. "They'll be calling the flight soon," he said to Olga.

"Hah," she replied. "They always say first and final call and then they say it three times. After third time is time to move to boarding gate."

Rupert returned with three bottles of vodka. He had made an extra special, sartorial effort for the journey, a thick chalk striped, double-breasted suit that any thirties gangster would've been proud to wear, a mauve tieless shirt, and a pair of white athletic shoes. It was just possible, Davenport thought, that he might also have had his hair trimmed.

From the back of the aircraft they had a good view of the other passengers.

"Former party officials, crooks then, crooks now," Olga made her judgment. "Look at them, designer shopping bags, vulgar show-offs, expensive cognac. Look at women, hookers all of them. Come to London to launder money." She was sitting between Davenport and Rupert, and made no attempt to lower her voice.

A tall, bulky Russian man in a suede coat with a fur collar turned and glared threateningly at Davenport who was in the aisle seat. For a moment he thought the man was going to come down to him, but he settled when the dyed blonde woman beside him with a coiffure six inches above her head pulled his arm.

"Got to be a bit careful from now on," Rupert tapped Olga's arm as he said it. "Some of these people can be pretty vindictive."

"All cowards!" Olga declared, making no concession to the relative quietness that had descended now that everyone was seated.

Fortunately the captain started the engines and began to taxi away from the terminal.

Rupert bent across Olga to address Davenport. "One doesn't want to overstate the position, but I have had the odd close shave over there." He nodded in the direction in which he thought Russia lay.

"Only in central Asian republics. You go there because pictures cheapest there. Must take risk to make profit. Only one bad thing result of collapse of communism, people there make trouble, start wars, bomb, take hostages." She turned on Davenport as if he had contradicted her. "You see. I know my country and neighbours better than you. Everyone east of Moscow is potential Genghis Khan."

"I like travel," Rupert said. "I'd like to go to Australia one day, but not until I've done the exotic places. I had a place in Montevideo once – took it in exchange for a small Botero bronze. Rather good if you go in for that sort of thing, breasts and bottoms like balloons, but not really my personal cup of tea."

"What happened to the house in Montevideo?"

"Not a house actually, a kind of *hacienda* I suppose you'd call it, with a few acres around it, on the outskirts of the city. I had to sell it. Cecelia said Spain was far enough. Ever danced the tango?" Rupert's spirits seemed to be rising with the ascent of their aircraft. "I spent a few days in Buenos Aires when I was out there. Now there's a city: beautiful black-haired girls dancing the tango. The men are Latin spivs, though. I took some lessons: would've become proficient if Cecelia hadn't called me home. Ever been to BA Davenport?"

"No." The answer was emphatic.

"You should."

"I have reason to believe that the fake Divera was painted there."

"All the more reason for you to go. Anyway, why should you complain, that fake made your reputation."

For a moment, Olga, ear phones clamped to her ears, went out of Davenport's consciousness to be replaced by the elusive and beautiful Jocelyn August, who with her aunt had deceived him into recommending the purchase by the museum of the forged Divera – a recommendation subsequently retracted but overlooked by the director and the trustees who had already paid for it. Happily for Davenport, the press and the art world were prepared to forget his earlier verification, and focus on his unheeded denunciation of the picture. He was as certain as he could be, that if he were to visit Buenos Aires, he would find Jocelyn and her aunt living there a life of measured and private luxury, just as they had appeared to be doing at the Gold Coast in Australia when they first crossed Davenport's path.

"No, I am never going to Buenos Aires," he repeated as Olga removed the earphones and shook her shiny hair.

"You told whoever is looking after your grandfather to expect us I take it?" he said to Olga.

"I tell no one anything. Everyone in Russia spy or informer. Habit of lifetime, habit of three lifetimes."

"Don't worry old boy," Rupert said. "Despite what Olga says, they're a lot of very warm hearted people, the Russians. Quite different from us, of course. Who was it said the Orient begins at Calais?" He ordered a small bottle of red wine for each of them from a passing stewardess. By the time that he had drunk all three bottles, they were about half way across the North Sea and he was blissfully asleep.

"It is true," Olga said fondly (too fondly in Davenport's opinion), "Rupert has done dangerous things in many places in Russia. The people he deal with, the cash he carry... Then the guards at frontier – there will always be frontier between Russia and West – he have to bribe; always dangerous. Sometimes he travel in old Russian truck, or worse, Trabant from East Germany across Asian Republics where warlords take place of leaders of old party factions."

Rupert was not a topic he wished to pursue with Olga. "Tell me about your grandfather. Do you remember him from when you were young?"

"He always very serious man. How it can be otherwise? Have very hard, sad life."

"Did he draw for you, talk to you, try to teach you to draw and paint?"

"No. Very busy with his own work. Understandable. Many years when he was not permitted to paint. All work institutional: schools, universities, public buildings. Paintings of great leaders, victories, happy miners, dancing, fruitpickers, tractor makers. All must be realistic, more realistic than photo realism but not real because workers always smiling. Party graffiti he call it. But always kind man, gentle to children."

"Who looks after him now? Why didn't he get himself an agent after the iron curtain collapsed? Has he travelled? I know that if you go to the Hermitage you will see examples of all the great masters, but I would have thought once he could travel anywhere, he would have wanted to visit Paris and London, New York, to see the great works there?"

"So many questions. You sound like KGB. Next you pull out my fingernail unless I give you right answer. Do Australians ask questions all the time?"

"I can't help being curious. To you, he may be a grandfather. To me, he is a great modern master, a survivor, an exotic genius from a country that turned its back on the West for seventy years. Anyone interested in art or history would be curious. Besides, I don't want to put my foot in it when I meet him, assuming of course that I do, in regard to his current infirmity."

Davenport was unable to decide whether Olga had fallen asleep or chose to ignore him. Her eyes were closed but she had replaced the earphones on her ears. He took a small notebook and pen out of his pocket. Gerald had told him he would be required to account for every pound spent. He entered the expenses so far incurred, including the wine that Rupert had ordered, drunk, and left Davenport to pay for. Then he flicked over a few pages and began to make a list of questions he needed answered. One of the most important was whether Rothko's shimmering panels and bars of colour preceded those of the old man. If not, was the latter aware of Rothko's work? Were Kruffinski's works derivations or pastiches of Rothko's art? It might be that they were caricatures of it. He sounded as if he was quite capable of deriding artists whom he did not respect. It was clear enough that the old man was very versatile, like Picasso. That was the problem with geniuses. They could do the lot. Facility, technical skill, became boring. What was left? The truth, often enough, was excess, seeing how far they could go, *epater les bourgeois*. Davenport recalled a remark that one of Picasso's biographers had attributed to him, that there was no end to the contempt in which he held the public who invariably accepted as serious and valuable his repeated artistic insults to them.

On the whole though, Kruffinski didn't sound like that. It did seem likely that his almost monochromatic panels with their luminous borders were adopted as a means of concealing, or at least making ambiguous, the beautiful, usually anti-communist, drawing and painting beneath them.

Davenport put away his pen and notebook. Rupert's snoring made it impossible for him to concentrate. He reached for, and with difficulty turned off his reading light, and Olga's too, and tried to compose himself for sleep.

Davenport Takes Off

Davenport was an enthusiastic man and not a vain one. Gloria used to reproach him for being an unambitious one as well. She was right, of course. It was a lucky accident that his name had leapt to international prominence, not just in the art world but also in the popular press, over the Divera affair. His last conscious thought before falling asleep was that surely he was not going to be so lucky twice.

St Petersburg may be much closer to the West than Moscow, but still there was about it, even at the airport, a sense that one had left the West even if one had not quite arrived in the East. And as with the peoples of other countries who had escaped from communism, overnight, the people here were divided as to the virtues of the new and old regimes. The job of the man who presided over the luggage carousel had ceased to be a party sinecure: now he worked ten hours a day and had to pay a proper rent for the flat that had formerly been included with the position. His current contribution largely consisted of his kicking fragile looking luggage into the centre of the conveyor while he smoked a malodorous cigarette of black smouldering tobacco and grumbled loudly and continuously.

Rupert's luggage consisted of an elegant valise with the famous logo of Valerie Stampel on it. It had been made in Ho Chi Minh City and bought by Rupert in the souk at Casablanca for the equivalent of ten pounds. He had become very attached to it.

Rupert approached the carousel supervisor angrily. He stood in front of him, the top of his head about six inches below the man's chin, and admonished him in a mixture of English and rudimentary Russian. The man prodded Rupert in the chest. "He say he hand Rupert over to airport police," Olga translated.

She gave Davenport her hand luggage to hold and dashed over to Rupert. She prodded the official in his chest, not with a finger but a clenched fist. The man moved backwards in surprise. Olga's voice was high and emphatic. Even without understanding a word of Russian it was possible for Davenport to know what she was saying: that the man was some low, probably the lowest, specimen of animal life on the planet, that he should be in a gulag to which he had no doubt consigned people by informing on them when the murderers were in power, and that if he put a hand on Rupert or his filthy foot near his luggage again, she would have one of her friends in the local mafia take care of him.

How, Davenport asked himself, had he, a gentle person who had preferred tennis and cricket to rugby at school, and who had never lifted a hand in anger, or raised his voice in violent argument since the kindergarten playground, become entwined with these people? But as that thought passed through his mind, he admired Olga's dashing fearlessness, and the fire of her beautiful flashing eyes.

14

A Day in the Country

When Gloria was shown into Gerald's room he was standing looking out the window. He turned as she entered.

"I have just sent your husband to Russia Mrs Jones."

"But not to Siberia I trust. Call me Gloria."

"I'm sorry, I should have said your ex-husband. Please sit down. Would you care for some tea?"

"Thank you."

Gerald went over to a silver tray on a console. On it were a Dr Wall teapot, sugar bowl, two cups and saucers, a milk jug, a bowl, a tortoiseshell tea caddy, and an electric jug. In the way of people who have lived alone for a long time, he carefully adhered to a well established order: turn jug on; when boiled, pour a small quantity of boiling water into the teapot; empty into bowl; spoon three level spoons of tea into the pot; turn jug on again very briefly; turn off and pour water into the teapot until three quarters full; pick up tea pot and gently swirl contents.

"I'm sorry, I should have asked. Is China all right?"

"Don't apologise. China tea sounds divine. I don't think I want to eat or drink another Indian thing in my life."

"Weak or strong?"

"Middling."

Gerald poured her a cup of tea and brought it and the sugar bowl and milk over to her.

"I never take milk or sugar," she said. "Although I have to say that I'm not as particular about what I eat or drink as I used to be in Australia. Food, that was a point of contention between Davenport and me. I tried so hard to look after him, vegetables, practically no alcohol, vitamins, organic food. If I turned my back for a moment, he lapsed."

Gerald sat down with his tea beside Gloria in front of his desk. "I've never spent much time in India, a few nights once in New Delhi and a day excursion by train to Agra. You must know the place pretty well after the time you spent there."

"Too well."

"I'm an Atlantic man myself. If the country doesn't face that ocean, it's not for me. Sorry again. I mean no offence to Australia."

Gloria ignored the last. "Does the English Channel count as the Atlantic?"

"Definitely not. I don't regard the French as qualified."

"But the Americans, they qualify?"

"Only those on the East Coast. The Californians and Texans are as bad as the French. Now, how can I help you?"

"It's kind of you to ask, but I think it's too late. There's nothing, well nothing remotely physical, between Davenport and me these days. There never really was much in that way between us. Davenport, well, Davenport...no, I shouldn't talk about it. But if you've been married to someone, cared for him, tried to advance his career, you get into a habit that's hard to break, of always worrying about him. It was only because I read in a magazine, *Jove*, I think, that I found out he was in London. I really just wanted to make sure he was settled and well. Not that I would want to renew anything. Still, if I could have helped him I would. But there are some people, you know, you just can't help."

"He sounds rather ungrateful."

"I've said too much. I'm not one of those women who spend the rest of their lives criticising their exes. It's just so demeaning." What could have been a tear appeared at the corner of Gloria's left eye. On the other hand it could have been a discharge from a mild but persistent Indian eye infection from which she was still recovering. Regardless, its appearance was fortuitous.

Gerald put his cup and saucer on the desk. He touched Gloria lightly on her left hand. She clasped his hand briefly before releasing it. "So kind," she said.

"Well, I can tell you he seems to have done rather well for himself here. He's got a good flat. I think I should also tell you that one of the women here – a financial controller – seems to have take him under her wing. There was a time when a firm like ours would never tolerate in-house relationships. Nowadays anything goes."

"It seems the case, doesn't it. Well, she'll learn."

"How long will you be staying in London?"

"I've no fixed plans. I do have a job, though." She told Gerald something of her interview with Jeremy Baker, omitting, among other things, the financial details.

"He buys here occasionally. Some successful authors like to be seen as arts all rounders." Gerald repeated the Maugham story. "Somerset Maugham had a valuable art collection. I can't recall who said that he knew the price of everything but the value of nothing. I suspect your employer is the same."

"I may be able to help his children. One gets one's rewards in helping children. But tell me about your work. When Davenport and I were together, he was with a public museum. It surprises me that he's been able to adapt to private enterprise."

"Well, I'm teaching him. I've been doing this for a long time myself."

"It must be fascinating. But how can you bear to sell the wonderful things that you keep on seeing?"

"You have to be strong, disciplined actually. Sometimes you succumb, of course. We have strict rules about personal acquisitions. Any interest must be disclosed in advance to the vendor. We can't hammer an item to ourselves. If I'm interested, I stand down from the podium and let my relief take over. I would never bid myself. I get one of our trainees to do it."

"That's very ethical. Tell me about some of your things."

"I've had a particular interest in the Austrian Secession. I suppose my most valuable article is a pencil by Klimt." He could not refrain from telling her its value. "On a good day it might be worth forty thousand pounds."

"For a drawing?"

"Klimt and Schiele are like money in the bank. Do you know Klimt's work? He painted beautiful women in an elongated way, in dresses of gold and other vivid colours."

"I think I may have seen reproductions of them. All the women seem to be very beautiful but very thin."

"True. He obviously agonised over the dresses they wore. There's an interesting story about that. It caused a scandal in its day. I'm not boring you?"

"I'm intrigued."

"There was a break-in at his studio. The press came and saw the unfinished works. He painted the women in the nude first and then laboriously painted their dresses on them. If that's what he liked, who are we to criticise."

Gerald's phone rang. He picked it up. "No, don't put any calls through. Tell him I'll ring back." Gerald settled down for a long conversation with this sympathetic woman.

As they came out of Pulkovo Airport, Davenport asked Olga where the taxi rank was. The question immediately provoked an argument between Rupert and her.

"No," Rupert said, "we'll take the bus to the metro at Moskovskaya station, then the metro to the city, Sennaya Place in the city centre."

"Do not be silly, Rupert; all those changes. Better to catch car."

Davenport looked in bewilderment at Rupert. "What's she mean?"

"You hail a passing car by holding your arm out, palm turned down and some passerby in a clapped out Zhiguli, or worse, a Lada, will stop to pick you up."

"Nice Russian hospitality."

"Nice Russian opportunism you mean. Everybody who isn't a member of the mafia or a politician moonlights here. The driver will ask twice what a registered taxi – if you could find one – would cost. By the time we negotiate a fair rate, we could be in our hotel if we used the metro," Rupert explained.

"Gerald might be mean about expenses but he wouldn't begrudge us a proper taxi from the airport."

But Rupert had turned his attention back to his argument with Olga. The wine and his long sleep on the plane had energised him. It had been a long day for Davenport. All he wanted was to reach their hotel and go to bed. "What's the quickest?" he asked. The combatants ignored his question.

Finally, there was a resolution. Rupert walked to the kerb and stood dangerously close to the passing traffic. He held out one arm while clasping his precious counterfeit Valery Stampel bag in the other. Within a minute, a car like a box on wheels clattered to a stop. Rupert stepped back to allow Olga to undertake the negotiations. The driver had assumed Rupert to be an inexperienced foreign visitor. A look of surprised irritation crossed his face when Olga engaged him in her St Petersburg Russian. Contrary to Rupert's prediction she completed the negotiations quickly. The driver had soon realised that he had met his match. Olga told them to hold on to their bags and to get into the back seat.

"I sit in front. Make sure we get to hotel and not be raped and murdered in broken down old factory."

The seat in the back of the car was a wooden bench with plastic covered cushions stretched across it. Davenport was too tired to complain, and knew that it would be useless anyway. All that he wanted was for the bone shaking journey to end; remaining oblivious to the sights that Rupert pointed out to him, subject to regular spirited correction by Olga.

An hour later the car stopped in front of a masonry building with tall Corinthian pilasters not quite in proportion with the grey walls into which they were set.

" 'The Great Western', formerly the 'Lenin People's Place No. 2'," Rupert announced. "A fine example of totalitarian architecture. Its bite is not nearly as bad as its bark. They've modernised most of the rooms. The dining room's a bit rough. Still, it's very central and close to the metro."

"So long as it has a comfortable bed, I don't care," Davenport said.

There had been no modernisation of public relations at the hotel. It took them half an hour to convince the receptionist that they had confirmed bookings for their rooms. They agreed to meet in the dining room at nine o'clock in the morning. Davenport was pleased to find out that his and Olga's rooms were on the same floor and Rupert's three below.

Davenport wearily unpacked and undressed. He was about to go into the bathroom when his phone rang. He picked it up.

"Is that you, Davenport? Thank God. It would have been quicker to use Morse code. I've rung five times. I got either a recorded message that they were too busy to answer the phone, or told that there was no guest of your name booked or staying in the hotel. You can't really blame them for that I suppose. You've got to admit that you do have an improbable name."

"Gerald, I'm very tired. What do you want?"

"A progress report."

"Progress? I've just spent hours in economy on a BA hell plane, sat on a wooden bench in the back of a car driven by a freelance thug doubling as a taxi driver, been interrogated by a former attendant from the Lubyanka masquerading as a hotel receptionist, refereed three arguments between my travelling companions, and find myself booked into a hotel built for provincial party officials on rare visits to the city – and you want to know what progress I've made?"

Gerald didn't really want to know what progress Davenport had made. "Your wife called in today, Davenport." He said it reproachfully.

"Former wife, Gerald."

"Aren't you interested in why she came?"

"I know why. She wanted to complain about me."

"With cause, perhaps, Davenport."

"Gerald, I don't intend to have an argument with her again, and I certainly don't intend to have an argument with anyone else about her. As I told you, I've had more than enough arguments for one day."

"They're your friends, Davenport."

"They're not my friends. They're clients."

"Much to your regret. You can't fool me. I know what you'd like to be up to with that bad-tempered little Russian fox. Not very loyal to Gloria that, Davenport."

"Don't you ever listen, Gerald?" Davenport shocked himself by the asperity of his retort. As an antidote to it, instead of slamming the handpiece down, he replaced it with a gentle click.

Within ten minutes, he was in bed. But despite the hardships of his day he could not sleep. It seemed to him that the mattress must have borne the weight of thousands of party officials. He estimated its compressed thickness to be no more than two inches. Down in the street some prostitutes noisily solicited passing drivers and pedestrians. The television in the room next door was playing at full volume. Davenport only fell asleep when they turned it off at 3.30 am.

In the morning, both Rupert and Olga gave every appearance of having slept well. Davenport's envy was tempered by his assumption that they had, therefore, in all likelihood, slept separately.

The topic for discussion, and accordingly for their usual amiable disputation, was their means of travel to Kruffinski's dacha. Olga wanted to catch a car again. Rupert had immersed himself in maps and guide books.

"I estimate he's about 8 kilometres from Tsarskoe Selo which is only about an hour or so away by bus. Or we can go by train from Viltelosk."

"And after that?" Olga demanded.

Davenport had had enough. "After breakfast I'm going to talk to the concierge, or if there isn't one, to the manager of the hotel, and I'm going to get him to engage a car and driver to take me to your grandfather's house, wait for me there, and bring me back when I'm ready. You're both welcome to come with me if you want to." For emphasis he stabbed the cold grey piece of pickled fish on his plate.

"Well all I can say is that Londys must give you a hell of an expense account," Rupert said.

"Better I talk to manager," Olga said.

"No, not this time. You couldn't help yourself. You'd end up arguing with him, and to get square he'd give us a villainous driver on probation for some vile crime."

Olga fell into a rare silence. It was even possible that for a moment her face wore an expression of respect for Davenport's unexpected masterliness.

The rest of the breakfast proceeded calmly. Olga suggested that they might have an opportunity of visiting Tsarskoe Selo if there were not too many tourists. "We show you park anyway," she said. "Tsasrkoe Selo most beautiful summer palace in Russia. Built by wife of Peter the Great, Catherine. Extended later in Baroque style. Everyone who come to St Petersburg must see it."

"We'll have to see how much time we have. Now, have you telephoned ahead to let the old man, or rather, whoever is looking after him, know we're coming?"

"No notice. I told you, cousin might have told him about us, told them not to let us see or talk to grandfather."

"I'm not too comfortable about just turning up there," Davenport said.

"It's obvious you know nothing about Russians, old boy," Rupert said. "They're different from us; very informal people the Russians. The only ceremony they stand on is the ceremony of toasting one another, repeatedly, with vodka."

"I still think we should call ahead."

As only Olga knew the number, and as she was adamant she would not call, Davenport had to let the matter go. He departed to

A Day in the Country

speak to the manager.

Davenport had already decided to pay the asking price, for the car and driver without haggling. Accordingly, his discussion with the manager – whose English was adequate – was friendly and fruitful.

"You like Mercedes Benz, red one? Black one?"

"The colour doesn't matter. I just want to be certain that the car and its driver are reliable."

The manger was confident about the former although he didn't disclose the reason why: that the car, then only two months old had, some fifteen months earlier, been stolen from a car park near St Stephen's Cathedral in Vienna, driven non-stop, except for fuel refills, to a workshop on Petrograd Side, and there rebirthed after filing off its engine and other numbers – which were then replaced by a specially made stamp, and repainting.

"I want a driver who can speak English." Davenport had made up his mind that Olga would not be in sole control of this expedition.

"People who speak English are educated people. Educated people are expensive."

Davenport doubted that, but he had resolved to pay the price and was not prepared to quibble, although, inclusive of everything, it did amount to what seemed to be a very large number of roubles. He merely nodded.

"I pay you?"

"That would be satisfactory."

"I'll pay half now and half when we return."

"That too is satisfactory. I will telephone. Your driver's name is Peter. The car will be at the front in half an hour."

Davenport returned to the dining room. It was clear to him that both Olga and Rupert had not believed that he would be able to arrange transport on his own. It took him three attempts to convince them that a suitable car and driver would be ready in half an hour.

When the car arrived, both Olga and Rupert moved towards the front passenger seat. Davenport had anticipated that. He pulled open the passenger side back door leaning against the front as he did.

"You don't think Olga should sit in the front, to navigate, that is?" Rupert suggested.

"The driver knows where to go. The manager has given him the address. And in any event, if Olga has to navigate she can do it equally well from the back."

"Well, he who pays the piper calls the tune I suppose. As I said before Davenport, I wouldn't mind your expense account."

As they drove out of the city, Davenport noticed the contrast between beautiful churches – restored and in the course of restoration, and decaying apartment blocks with columns supporting porticos that threatened to fall to the ground at any moment. He had not expected to see as many new cars as were on the road, or for the traffic to be as heavy as it was.

At the fourth amber light, their driver decided it was time to obey a signal. He brought the car to a sudden stop. Immediately, a man in a wheelchair rolled across to them from the footpath. He stopped beside Davenport's door, tapped on the window and held out his hands in a begging motion.

"Don't pull down window," Olga said. "Give him nothing. Half go to them," she pointed to two men in a car parked in a side street across the intersection.

"It's true," Rupert confirmed. "The mafia take a commission on everything, even begging."

"Probably not cripple anyway," Olga said, before engaging the driver in conversation in Russian. Davenport thought he heard the words, "Tsarskoe Selo."

He was, however, not disposed to argue. If Olga wished to travel past the palace, why should he complain. He had had his way about the car. And the fact was, he wished that there were more time, and that he could explore all of the magnificent palaces and art collections of the fabulous city. He must have heard the name correctly, because Rupert who had visited Tsarskoe Selo twice before told him that much of it was reproduction because there had been fierce fighting around it in the war, and that the bulk of the original had been destroyed.

A Day in the Country

"You wouldn't know it though. The restoration is superb. You wonder where they get those craftsmen from, given how many they lost in their great patriotic war, and the communists' aversion to wealth, other peoples' that is. They must have intended to move in themselves, the leaders I mean, when the work was finished and decent heating installed."

"Vandals. They burnt Amber Room from Catherine Palace."

"What's she talking about?" Davenport asked.

"There was a beautiful room made of real amber in the Catherine Palace. The Nazis looted it and took it to Kalingrad but they didn't destroy it. It was burnt when the Soviets reoccupied the city. They blamed the Nazis. Everyone was terrified of Stalin. It's supposed to be restored now. Who knows?" Rupert said.

After about an hour they reached the park in which Tsarskoe was built. Olga told the driver to slow down. It was possible to glimpse beautiful arbours, terraces, streams, ornamental lakes, statuary, temples, and follies from the road.

"You should stay on here, Davenport," Rupert said. "For a month. It's unthinkable that you might come here and not see the palaces and parks. You need a fortnight for the Hermitage alone."

"I'm under a lot of pressure from Gerald."

"Pressure, he wouldn't know what it meant."

After a time the driver turned away from the park and drove on to a narrow road of broken bitumen. The white birches were losing their foliage, and the surface was centimetres deep in leaves as bronze as recently minted coins. Above the road there were still enough leaves upon the branches to provide a light dappled canopy. Between the trees, bracken and blackberry bushes fought for space and sunshine. It was easy to imagine bears and deer in the forest beyond the first line of trees.

The driver made another turn. This time the road consisted of two rutted, unsealed tracks. On their left, through the undergrowth, Davenport could see a wide stream, its waters rippling across and around heavy black boulders every few metres along its course.

Suddenly, the stream made a sharp turn left, and the countryside opened up into a water meadow, and beyond, a field rising to a small plateau on which stood a large imposing timber house of two storeys.

"Grandfather's dacha," Olga announced.

"Does he own it?" Davenport asked.

"God knows who owns what in this kleptocracy," Rupert answered.

There was an old, gravelled drive up to the front door, where Peter stopped the Mercedes. Davenport, with Olga's assistance, told him to wait. Rupert and Davenport walked up on to a verandah which ran along the front of the house, and stood aside to let Olga ring the door bell. They could not hear it ringing. The only sound was of birds in the forest. Olga knocked loudly. Two minutes passed... Then, suddenly, the door was thrown open. A statuesque woman in her early forties surveyed them with distaste.

Olga said what Davenport assumed to be, "I have come to see my grandfather."

The woman responded at length but in obviously negative terms. "Translation Olga please," Rupert demanded.

"She say grandfather too ill and old to see anyone. He sleep all day, practically in coma. Too many people pester him. Everyone want something from him, paintings or money."

"Who's she, anyway?" Rupert asked.

"She say she his nurse."

"That's a likely story. Does she look like nursing material to you, Davenport?" Before Davenport could reply, he continued. "Tell her as a non-relative she has no authority to stop you from seeing him."

"I've done that."

"Tell her again. Tell her we'll get a court order if she won't let you in."

"Court order in Russia; no one believe that."

"Tell her you've got friends in the mafia, anything."

For once Olga was nonplussed. "This very strong woman. I think it better we not make threats." Olga then spoke to the woman in a conciliatory tone. She pointed to Davenport, and then to Rupert.

A Day in the Country

"Translation, Olga."

"I told her Davenport my fiancé and you his brother. I said I wanted Davenport to meet or at least see my famous grandfather, and that we want nothing from him."

The woman continued to look at them impassively. Olga told the men that she would repeat that all they wanted to do was look at her grandfather, that they wouldn't even try to speak to him.

By now, Davenport's eyes had further adjusted to the dull light. Behind the woman he could see a long hall with a stained glass window at the end of it. There were three long Caucasian rugs on the floor, and armchairs covered in rich Khelims. He could see paintings on the wall but could not make out whose they were. There was fretwork above each of the doors. The house, unlike the grounds in which it stood, was well maintained.

Olga tried again. The woman listened, and finally, to their surprise, nodded. She put a finger to her lips and beckoned them to follow.

The artist's bedroom was the last room on the right of the hall. The door to it was tinted blue by the stained glass window just beyond. The woman had moved so quickly that Davenport had no opportunity to take in the window or any of the paintings.

She put a finger to her lips again and silently opened the door. The light from two large open windows flooded the room and dazzled them after the dim hall. Against the far wall, dwarfed by the high ceiling, standing on a rich blue rug, was an old iron bed in which a slight figure – with only his white haired head exposed – appeared to be sleeping. Above the bed was the most beautiful gilded and enamelled ikon that Davenport had ever seen.

It was possible to see that the old man was breathing easily, his frail body gently raising and lowering the light blanket covering him. He appeared utterly composed. Olga started to speak in a normal tone. The woman pointed threateningly at the door. Rupert could be silent no longer. In more than a whisper, he said, "If he's in a coma he can't hear what we're saying anyway. Tell her that."

Olga did, and the woman shook her head violently. Only then

did Rupert notice the ikon. "My God, look at that."

Olga said, "Very beautiful. Even in time of Soviets, grandfather collected ikons. Many lost in time of Stalin."

"They are not my field. You know anything about them, Davenport?"

"Not especially. But anyone can see how beautiful that one is."

"I'd like to get my hands on it," Rupert said. "There's a dealer in Brook Street who'd pay a fortune for it."

Davenport was shocked by the turn the conversation was taking. "I think we should leave. That ikon must be the old man's favourite, and his consolation. We're intruders. Let's leave Mr Kruffinski in peace," Davenport moved towards the door.

The woman was ushering the others out by now. She stood by the entrance waiting for them to pass but Davenport was the last to leave. For a moment he looked around at the old man. His eyes were open, and Davenport was sure that he was looking approvingly at him before they closed again.

They walked along the hall to the front door where they were swiftly shown on to the verandah. The woman closed and bolted the door behind them.

They wandered down from the verandah on to the drive out of ear shot of the artist's keeper. "What do we do now?" Rupert, who was usually so inventive, asked.

"We must come again. But first we make inquiries about that woman. We find out more about who else sees grandfather. We must find lawyer in city to help us. Perhaps one lawyer know if grandfather have own lawyer. Lawyers great gossips. Grandfather's estate so valuable, someone know," Olga answered.

"The house appeared to be in good condition. I can't imagine that dragon on her hands and knees scrubbing and polishing," Rupert said.

"Woman must eat, buy food. We go to nearest village and inquire there. If they not know, we go to all other nearby villages and towns. Get information who go there. Find out where nearest doctor lives. Old man must see doctor sometime."

A Day in the Country

Davenport listened to their plans with only half an ear. He could still see the old man's eyes, his amused, aware expression. He felt that it offered something more to him. Encouragement perhaps.

"Have you got any ideas, Davenport?" Rupert asked.

"No, no, what Olga suggests seems pretty sensible. But I don't know what we're going to do when we do find out who looks after him, and who else goes there."

"The doctor is the important one. Even in this barbaric country, a man would need to be of sound mind and understanding before he could validly part with his possessions. And if he isn't, then surely Olga has rights."

They had to wait some time for their driver to wake up. When he did, Davenport allowed Olga to explain to him in Russian what they wanted even though his English was adequate. Rupert, despite his best intentions had forgotten to bring a map of the district. The driver told Olga that he had memorised the route to the dacha, but knew nothing otherwise of the district: there were many roads and cross-roads and tiny hamlets that wouldn't even be marked on any map.

When this was translated, Davenport suggested, "A well-to-do man like your grandfather would probably have a physician from the city, and not a general practitioner from a village."

"Perhaps," Olga rejoined, "But in Russia there is no shortage of good doctors. To survive, they have to go into countryside."

For once, neither Rupert nor Olga had any firm, let alone competing, view about what they should do. Peter the driver spoke again, this time in English. He was unwilling to explore the district without maps.

"We'd better head back to the city," Rupert acknowledged. "Olga, you can make inquiries there first. There are some dealers I want to talk to about other painters. They may know something. Yes, back to the city I think, to regroup. We can return in a couple of days, with maps and whatever we've been able to find out. Your Gerald won't like the delay though."

"There's no choice. If he thinks he can do better he can come

The Russian Master

out here himself." Davenport recalled a comment Gerald had made back in London: 'It's a blessing for you Davenport, you can have a couple of days in the Hermitage. You look as if you need a holiday.'

Davenport would have liked a holiday. As much as he was attracted to Olga, her company was fatiguing. And as amiable as Rupert usually was, his impulsiveness made Davenport dread what he might do or say next.

They re-entered the car, Olga too quiet for Davenport's liking. She secured the seat beside the driver. About five hundred metres beyond the end of the track through the woods, she spied a side road with some houses on it – unnoticed on their outbound journey. She ordered the driver to turn into it. After a couple of kilometres they came to a village with a post office, a few stores, a hall of the Soviets – the blade of its sickle on the façade long gone, and a church. She told the driver to stop and opened her door. Rupert got out with her. Davenport waited in the car and began to doze. They seemed to be gone for a long time.

"Any luck?" Davenport asked when he was awakened by their return.

"Only the priest knew anything, and that wasn't much," Rupert replied. "He knows the house and who lives in it. He knows nothing of the woman except that she claims to have been the old man's model. He doesn't come to church, or not at least to this church. The storekeepers know nothing."

"They *say* they know nothing," ever suspicious Olga interpolated.

"No, I really don't think they do. And his mail doesn't come through the post office."

"How did the priest know about him?"

"He said everyone knows that a famous painter lives there, a man who suffered during the war and afterwards. 'The painter must be wealthy', he added, 'because the dacha is a very fine one'. It was apparently an official country residence for the party secretary in Leningrad for many years."

"Only way to find out more, will be to travel whole district."

A Day in the Country

"Yes, yes Olga, but let's see what turns up in St Petersburg first."

They returned by the same route, skirting the park of the Palace, before heading into the chaos of old cars and the fumes of leaded petrol. Olga and Rupert could make their inquiries in St Petersburg. Davenport had other plans.

15

A Secret Visit

For Davenport it was a luxury to be alone, to take off his shoes and clothes, have a leisurely shower, and stretch out on his bed. He did not intend to fall asleep, however, because, after Olga and Rupert left the hotel, he had business to transact with the manager.

But he did fall asleep, and had been in that state for an hour, when the phone rang. Even not yet fully awake as he reached for the handpiece, he knew that it had to be Gerald.

"I didn't expect you to be in, Davenport."

"Well, why did you ring?" Davenport could sense Gerald's surprise at this newfound assertiveness.

"I thought I could leave a message. Why are you back at the hotel, anyway?"

Davenport gave a full account of the morning, omitting only his distinct impression of the old man's still-bright, blue eyes, open and fixed, as he believed, not disapprovingly upon him.

"So you're idle for a couple of days?"

"No. I'm going to talk to the director of the Hermitage to see whether he might let Londys flog one of their Rembrandts or a couple of Renoirs."

"This is no time for flippancy, Davenport."

"What was the message you were going to leave, Gerald?"

"The Spoliation Panel had handed down its decision. It's already been on the radio. It'll be a big story on the television evening news. They've held that there should be mediation to have the painting restored to the artist."

"Well that means Kruffinski's going to be a household name."

"All the more reason for urgency."

"I'm, we're, doing what we can."

"Do you think I should come over?"

"No. If the word got out that you were snooping around, your competitors would be on your track in a flash."

"I can be very discreet, you know."

Davenport didn't think that worth a reply. "Is there anything else?"

"I've agreed to talk to your ex-wife again." He emphasised the 'ex'.

"Please don't talk about me."

"You may not be my favourite topic, Davenport, but you're hardly one I can avoid in a conversation with your ex-wife."

"There's nothing else then? No? I'll keep you informed." Davenport replaced the handpiece and returned to his bed.

Two hours later, much refreshed, he rose and went downstairs to talk to the manager. "I would like to hire that car and driver again tomorrow, from say, eleven o'clock."

"That should be possible. The price will be the same."

"I will be travelling on my own. It is a personal matter. I do not want my companions to know anything about it."

"You wish me to give Peter instructions?"

"No. I will do that myself."

"The matter will remain between us. The young woman you are travelling with will never know."

"Nor the middle-aged man."

"It is our secret. But there are many, very attractive and lonely Russian women. It is not necessary to venture out of the city to find them. I myself know several such women, blondes, redheads, brunettes, blue-eyed women from the north, and black haired Orientals from east of the Urals. They all find their way to Moscow or St Petersburg." The manager assumed the Australian was headed for an assignation that he was keeping from Olga, who was surely his mistress.

Davenport returned to his room. It was not until seven o'clock that his phone rang again.

"Davenport, what have you done this afternoon?" Olga asked.

"Rested. And you?"

"Rupert and I talked to dealers. I tell you over dinner."

"Where's Rupert?"

"He is having dinner with dealer who has works from 1930s. They discuss exhibition in London. I see you downstairs in half hour."

Davenport dashed into the bathroom and quickly showered and shaved for the second time that day. He selected a clean shirt and polished his shoes with paper tissues he found in the bottom of his suitcase.

Olga was waiting in the foyer when he came downstairs. She seemed more relaxed in the absence of Rupert. "Where are we going?" Davenport asked.

"Food can be good in St Petersburg. Most visitors eat at grand hotels or new fashionable restaurants. Good, traditional Russian food hard to find. There is place ten blocks away, the 'Czar's Kitchen', quite good and not used only by criminals. All right last time. We try again. We walk so you see city."

Outside, she linked her arm, continental style, in Davenport's. She was wearing a fur coat but he could still feel her warmth through it. "You warm enough?" she asked. This was a different Olga from the disputatious version he had come to know.

She found the restaurant without any difficulty. They walked down a staircase to a large, crowded basement. But there were still vacant tables. Olga studied the menu. "As this your first visit to Russia, you must drink vodka like all other tourists." Davenport agreed. "We also eat Russian food." Olga ordered caviar, borscht, and venison. Davenport did not doubt that he would be paying.

A Secret Visit

When they had finished their vodkas, Olga called the waiter over and gave him another order. "I order French champagne, but not expensive brand. Russian wine too sweet."

While they waited for their meal, Davenport told Olga of the decision of the Spoliation Panel. The food was better than Davenport expected. The champagne, non-vintage, at the equivalent of fifty pounds a bottle, could have been Krug so far as Davenport was concerned as he hung on Olga's every word and watched her heartily eat every morsel on every plate that was put before her. She was, Davenport noted, equally enthusiastic about the champagne.

She told him that she and Rupert had spoken to three dealers. None of them knew anything about Kruffinski except that there was not a work by the artist for sale anywhere in St Petersburg. Tomorrow, Olga and Rupert had arranged to see a lawyer. Olga had learnt from one of the dealers that this particular lawyer advised writers, painters, ballet dancers and opera singers. "Is possible he is lawyer for grandfather. He can advise me, anyway, about my rights."

For once, Olga seemed to be in a gentle mood, not challenging or contradicting the waiters or anyone else – including Davenport. Her eyes glowed softly in the dimmed lights of the restaurant. She was wearing a white blouse, low in the neckline with puffed peasant sleeves, but it was not at her arms that Davenport was looking. He drank only one glass of the champagne. She leaned against him and hummed as they walked back to the hotel. He asked her what the time was. A Russian nursery song she replied. He was oblivious to the drunks lying in doorways and the rich, promenading in their clothes from Paris and Rome. Nor, with Olga's fur coat and her warm body within it – pressed against him, was he aware of the cold wind that blew from the northern tundra.

At the hotel, Davenport pressed the lift button for their floor. When they reached it she pushed his hand away as he searched for the key to his door. She fell into his arms. She led him to her door and gave him her key. Inside, casually and naturally and not deliberately tantalizingly, she began to undress. She was as unselfconscious fully naked as she was fully clothed. She told Davenport, who had been as watchful as he was speechless, to undress as she slipped under the bed clothes. In his haste, Davenport almost tore his shirt. After he managed to convert a bow on one of his shoes into an untieable knot he pulled both of them off.

Just as he climbed into bed there was a loud knock on the door.

"Ignore it," Olga commanded.

But the knocking persisted. "Go away," Olga called out. Her call was ignored. "Who is it?" She finally demanded.

"Let me in, I've got to talk to you." The voice was very slurred. It was Rupert's.

Olga threw the blankets aside and jumped out of bed.

"Make him go away," Davenport said.

By now Olga was getting dressed. She pointed to Davenport's clothes.

"Please, please tell him to go away. He sounds drunk."

"He may have information from dealer."

"Can't it wait until tomorrow?"

"We have little time. Now that, English panel give decision, Oleg will do anything to stop me getting inheritance." The gentler Olga had entirely disappeared.

Davenport hurriedly dressed and, as he did, Olga tucked in the bed and pulled the covers up. When Davenport was ready, she opened the door. Rupert who had been leaning against it, almost fell inside. He was wearing a traditional Russian fur cap at a lopsided angle, and a silly grin. When he entered the room, he made no comment on Davenport's presence. It cheered Davenport to see that Rupert was unfamiliar with Olga's room. He had to look for a chair to fall into. But then, perhaps, in his drunkenness he had forgotten the geography.

"Heavy drinker that Petrov," Rupert ultimately managed. His eyes closed and then re-opened. "'Lo Davenport."

"What did Petrov say?" Olga asked.

Rupert's eyes shut, this time firmly and for a long time. "Too drunk even to talk," Davenport unnecessarily commented.

"Stupid man think he can drink vodka like Russian. He will be useless in morning. Take him to his room."

Davenport feared that his evening of promised delights was over. He found Rupert's key in his pocket and lifted him out of the chair. Olga held the door open as Davenport half carried and half dragged his companion to the lift and then into his room. He pulled off Rupert's shoes and coat, and put him on his bed. The fur cap had been lost somewhere, but Davenport was unconcerned about that. He turned off the light and shut the door. For a moment he contemplated knocking on Olga's door, but somehow he knew that he would be unwelcome now.

Gloria had almost finished checking the girls' homework when Baker came home. He was wearing another of his author's suits of a dark, but nonetheless electric blue soft velvet, and a large floppy yellow bow tie. He sat down on the sofa. "Carry on," he said.

"I'm not accustomed to personal supervision when I'm teaching children," Gloria said. "However, we have just finished. Off you go girls. Don't forget, violin lessons tomorrow. It's an early start."

"They're doing well, Mrs Jones. You've done well."

"I think so." She got up to go.

"Don't go. Would you like a drink?" As he spoke he went into the living room and opened a cabinet which contained a small refrigerator. All that was in it were six bottles of Louis Roderer Cristal. He took one of them out and picked up two flutes.

"I don't drink, not alcohol, that is."

"I suppose you're a vegetarian as well?"

"I was, still am most of the time. Although in India..." She left the sentence unfinished. "I might have a mineral water, though; natural that is, without gas."

"Afraid not. This is Cristal, you know. For my money better than Krug or Dom. Why don't you try a drop?"

"I'll have a glass of water."

Baker left the room and came back with a glass of water with an ice cube in it. "I usually don't have ice." Gloria said.

"This is England, you know. Not India."

The Russian Master

Baker was at a loose end. Gloria considered leaving him to it but could think of no way to do it politely yet. She made a perfunctory offer to get him some food.

"No, I've eaten. I've been to a book launch. I did it as a favour for my publisher. I certainly didn't do it as a tribute to the author. Robert Caswellton, read any of his books?"

"I've heard the name."

"Airport scribbler, that's what he is."

"But aren't your books on sale at airports?"

"Of course. Not all people who travel are intellectual lightweights. The media were there, more interested in the celebrity guests than the book. God, publishers are becoming stingy. They were serving a sparkling Spanish wine. The only people drinking it were the journalists."

"It's still quite early. Where did you eat?"

"I went to the Vine. I had to table hop because I didn't have a booking, although they offered, as always, to fit me in. Still, being alone I preferred to share a chair brought up to a table, or tables I should say."

Once, in a glossy magazine, Gloria had read about the Vine, with its elaborate stained glass windows and cellar of thousand-pounds-a-bottle vintage wines. It and Indulgence, another restaurant in the same ownership, were the Mecca of actors, authors, pop stars, footballers, successful models, and anyone else with at least ten million pounds, or a title, or the foresight to make a booking three months in advance – as Davenport had learned from Lanson.

"Do you know the Vine?" Simon asked.

"I'm a working girl. Of course I don't, not personally, although I've read about it." It would have infuriated her if she had known that Davenport had lunched there.

He poured himself another glass of the Cristal. "You're sure you won't have a taste? Would you like to go to the Vine sometime?"

"If that's an invitation, perhaps for lunch sometime."

"It's better at night, although there was rather a dull crowd there this evening. I left when Caswellton's bunch turned up and, I might say, with Lacey."

"Who's Lacey?"

"Our, that's Caswellton's, and my publisher. He's never dined me at the Vine even though my sales would be twenty times Caswellton's."

"He probably thinks he doesn't need to buy you dinner then."

"That's hardly the point. Publishers are expected to take successful authors to dinner. I think Lacey's been conned. Because his books are full of classical allusions, he thinks Caswellton is a scholar and an intellectual. If I went to his home, I bet I'd find a one volume dictionary of quotes, translated – of course – from ancient Greek and Roman authors. Do you know what Caswellton had on? A battered tweed sports coat with leather patches on the elbows. And he had a pipe in the top pocket. Straight out of central casting, exactly what a Hollywood producer of the forties thought a writer should look like." He fell silent as he finished his second glass of wine. But then he continued.

"Tell me to mind my own business if you like, but your former husband, what does he really do at Londys? I only ask, because the girls say you don't talk about him."

"He's an expert. I thought I'd told you that. I'll repeat it. They apparently headhunted him. He had a great piece of luck in Australia. He denounced, correctly if belatedly, a forgery of a Divera that the museum where he worked insisted on buying. He's a world expert on Divera. When we were married he was always going on about him, trying to make some obscure connection between him and some Australian artists."

"I never cared for Divera." Baker dismissed the artist of whom he had only become aware when Gloria had mentioned him earlier.

"Well you and Davenport wouldn't have much in common then."

"No, I shouldn't think so." Baker poured himself a third glass. Gloria reminded him of a younger version of his wife – attractive, alert, firm in her opinions and lacking in introspection. The fact that, like his wife, she did not seem to be impressed by him, made her no less attractive. He adopted what he believed to be his most charming manner. "I hope you're settled here. Is there anything I can do for you?"

"There is, as a matter of fact. The curtains in my bedroom need replacing. They're a bit skimpy. They let in the light where they should meet."

"Soft furnishings are not my field. Everything else, the pictures, the furniture are mine. You'll have to talk to my wife I'm afraid."

"That's rather difficult when she's not here. Will she be back soon?"

"Her travel plans are always flexible. One simply never knows. Sometimes when she comes back to England she heads straight for our house in the Cotswolds. She'll often spend a week or two there before coming home. She says she needs to re-acclimatise to England, not literally, although once she did take a tour across the Sahara in summer. She means socially and culturally."

Gloria concluded that Baker hadn't the slightest idea where his wife was, or when she would be returning. "Well, none of that is going to fix my curtains. Do you think you could buy a blind? Mrs Baker could change it when she finally does come back."

Baker remembered how long it had taken him to find someone reliable to care for the girls. He was also anxious that Gloria, an unattached, attractive woman who so far seemed uninterested in him, his possessions and, worse, his achievements as a best selling author, stay. "I could, yes I will do that, first thing in the morning."

"Thank you," Gloria rose to leave.

"Don't go. Sorry. I suppose it's boring sitting here while I drink champagne. Why don't you let me get you a cup of tea. Chamomile?" He guessed correctly. She nodded acceptance.

Gloria's wits as well as her personality had become much sharper than they were when she was Davenport's wife and a school teacher in Australia. She readily summed up Baker as a vain, rich, and successful man, but a lonely one. 'Table hopping at the Vine,' she thought to herself. 'All those people being nice to his face and damning his success, his vanity, and his prose when he hopped to the next table,' she could easily guess.

He brushed her shoulder with his spare hand as he passed the tea cup and saucer to her: Versace china of course; nothing subtle about Baker. She tasted the tea and sipped from the cup.

"It's not hemlock you know," was his attempt at humour. The remark momentarily converted Gloria's indifference to revulsion. She stood up and put the cup and saucer down.

"It's not only the girls who have an early morning. Goodnight." She was out of the room and behind her locked door before he had finished pouring his fourth glass of champagne.

In bed, Gloria reflected on the period since her divorce, and on the end of her relationship with Walter. Out of Australia, he had turned out to be, not to put too fine a point on it, a sponger and a bore. The money and property that Davenport had transferred to her, after putting up little more than token resistance to her lawyer, was gone. She had only her apartment, now mortgaged, in Australia. The encounter with the American in India had come to nothing. Baker may well have been the sort of person other Englishmen would call a bounder, a word not prominent in her vocabulary, but uniquely appropriate to him. No, Baker would not do. That left only Gerald or... She was not ready to acknowledge the other possibility, indeed target, yet. Now Gerald, there was a man who had achieved a great deal; but what, forty, forty-five or so, not ever married and apparently not attached to any woman. Obviously, he had been educated at an English public school. That always raised a question, she thought. Still, there was no evidence of a male lover either. Gerald, however, like some wines and, so she had been informed, the Indian cricket team, did not travel well, certainly not to Australia anyway.

Davenport and Olga had almost finished their breakfast when Rupert appeared. His eyes were glazed and he had not shaved. He sat down and said nothing until his coffee was poured and he had drunk half of it.

"Has either of you seen my hat? I don't want to lose it. It's Arctic Fox, you know."

Neither responded. "What did you two do last night?" he asked. Clearly, he had not the slightest recollection of anything that happened after he had returned to the hotel. "Let me give you a tip. Never go head to head with a Russian with vodka. Even I had no idea there were so many varieties."

"What time do you think you got in?" Davenport asked.

"I haven't the foggiest. In fact the whole evening's a bit on the foggy side. Still, I managed to make it to my room and bed. Davenport, would you mind putting that plate with the fish skeleton on it downwind of me?" He finished his coffee and looked around for another one. "You two are pretty quiet this morning."

"We have serious business, Rupert. You must sober up quickly," Olga said. "And Davenport have other serious but pleasant business. He will spend day at Hermitage. Now, what did dealer tell you at dinner?"

"I think he said he'd make some inquiries." Rupert waved aside the waiter who approached him to take an order for food. Otherwise he hardly moved.

It was already nine o'clock. Davenport was becoming anxious. "Shouldn't you be leaving now?" he said to Olga.

"It not necessary for you to wait. Rupert like zombie this morning. Rupert, wake up. Go upstairs, tidy yourself."

"Well, I think I'll go up stairs and get ready myself. Will we meet here for dinner?" Davenport asked.

At the mention of dinner, Rupert groaned. "Good idea, but we won't eat here." He looked at Davenport's plate and shuddered. "Seven o'clock should be just about right." He stood up, swayed, held on to a chair to right himself, and headed for the door like a remote controlled robot.

"Rupert not much use today," Olga said.

"Olga, do you, do you think you and I could have dinner together, tonight, alone, without Rupert that is? Perhaps we could have room service in your or my room." Olga made no reference to the intimacies that Rupert had interrupted, indeed stopped, last night.

"Room service here?" Olga was shocked. "Food from kitchen reach room colder than food cooked and brought overland from Omsk in winter." Davenport's only consolation was that Rupert, despite his recuperative powers, would be in no condition to offer any serious rivalry to him.

"Till seven o'clock here then," Davenport rose to leave. As he did Olga put her hand on his.

"We get together sometime soon, Davenport," she said.

Davenport waited in his room for a short time and then headed down to the foyer. Hesitantly, when the lift door opened, he put his head out first. Olga and Rupert were not in the immediate area. Nor were they in the dining room. Peter, his driver, was waiting at the front door. Davenport went over to him. "How long have you been here?" He asked.

"Ten, fifteen minutes." He answered.

"You didn't see Olga and Rupert, the people I was with yesterday?"

"I did, as I was parking the car."

"Did they see you?"

"I do not think so. The man looked sick and they seemed to be having an argument."

"Good. Now I want to go to exactly the same place as yesterday. You can do that?"

"Of course."

The weather had turned cold and there was a threat of rain in the northern sky. Davenport wished that he was here as a tourist, free to spend the day at the Hermitage and see the other sights of the city. This reminded him that he had better rehearse an account to Olga of what he was supposed to have seen and the pictures that he liked the best. Fortunately, he had some knowledge of the most famous of these, sufficient, he believed, to convince her that he had spent time in front of them.

The driver, now acquainted with the route, made good time. As Davenport stepped out of the car in front of the dacha, it began to sleet. He hurried to the verandah and knocked on the door. It was as if the woman had been waiting for him. She opened it before he could knock a second time. She stepped across the threshold to check that he was alone. Then, without speaking, she gestured for him to follow her down the hall. This time the lights were turned on, and he could see the paintings on the walls. They were all by Kruffinski, some of them very large. The woman gave him no time to examine them. She opened a door about half way along the hall. The room was a sitting room with a studio built on to it. Half of the ceiling of the latter was of sloping glass. Kruffinski was seated in an armchair from which he could see out into the fields and forests in the distance. He turned his head as the woman closed the door behind Davenport and, in heavily accented but good English, said, "Ah, you came back. I thought you would. Sit down." Davenport took a seat opposite to him.

"You are well today I see."

"As well as can be expected for a man of my age. My granddaughter and that other fellow, where are they?"

"Trying to get information about you, and the lady who is looking after you."

"Catherine, she was my last model. What information do they want about me?"

"I should disclose that I work for Londys, the English..."

"I know who Londys are. Why are you in St Petersburg, with my granddaughter?"

"Can't you guess? Olga believes you to be terminally ill, or incapable of looking after your own affairs. She thinks her cousin has overborne you, or cheated you. She thinks that as your granddaughter, she has an entitlement. Rupert, the man with us, is a London dealer. He has travelled extensively in Russia, the Ukraine, and the new central Asian republics. He has bought and sold many paintings from all of those countries; none by well known artists. Olga works for him. They have agreed that such of your paintings as she can get will be auctioned by Londys under a special arrangement. Londys has subsidised their trip here. I represent Londys."

"You are frank," Kruffinski said nothing more as he weighed up what Davenport had told him. He stood up and walked stiffly to the glass wall of the studio. "Your accent is not English."

"I'm an Australian. I was a curator at an art museum."

"What brought you to England?"

"I left the museum to take a job in the private sector. You know what I mean by that?"

"You ask a Russian that. Once everything here was public. Now everything is, as you say, in the private sector. Were you dismissed?"

"No. It's a long story. There was a scandal over a forgery. I got the credit for exposing it. I did not want to stay there after that."

"You liked my ikon?"

"Yes."

"You thought it should remain with me. You were sympathetic."

"Is that why you have not turned me away?"

"Yes. And I was curious. The other man seemed close to Olga, her lover I suppose."

"I hope not."

"Ah. You are attracted to Olga?" He sighed. "She is like her grandmother; impulsive. What can I say? She would be a handful. Catherine never argues, not with me. You need much energy for a woman like Olga. But yes, I was curious about you, who you were, and what you were doing with them. I have no knowledge of Australia. Do you have to be an expert to be a curator there?"

"A degree in fine arts is usually necessary. I have that degree."

"You know of my work?"

"Yes, but not very well."

"Whose art do you know well?"

"The Spanish artist, Divera. The forgery I spoke about was supposed to be by him."

"Do you know anything of Russian art?"

"Only the obvious, the works of people like Malevich and Kandisky."

"Well, we shall see what you know about painting." Davenport started as the artist picked up a bell that stood beside his feet, and rang it loudly. Catherine must have been listening for it – she was in the room in seconds. After a few words with Kruffinski she left and returned with a tray with cups and saucers. She went to a table in the corner on which there was a tall silver samovar and poured tea from it. "You have not asked me why I would not speak to Olga yesterday?"

"That is your business."

"I have not made up my mind yet about what I shall do for her and her cousin. Both of them need to learn some lessons."

"Do you know about the Spoliation Panel's proceedings in London?" Davenport asked. The old man shook his head, so Davenport explained what had happened.

"It is possible. The war years were very confused. And afterwards I forgot much of what had happened."

"Deliberately perhaps. I understand it was very unpleasant for you."

"You cannot know how unpleasant." Abruptly, he changed the subject. "Some say I copied Rothko."

"Not me."

"I painted the way I did to obscure the drawings and the stories they told. I had never seen a Rothko or a reproduction of his before I painted my pictures. What he did is not hard to do, colours and tones with shifting edges. The edges, and sometimes the bars of colour, are the only interesting parts. There is no draughtsmanship in his work. A great artist needs more than inspiration and novelty. He also has to have the ability to see and to be able to draw, craft that is. What do you say." Kruffinski looked appraisingly at Davenport.

"Many of the great abstractionists were very good draughtsmen. Perhaps they became tired of making the effort."

"Your national museum bought a Jackson Pollock for a very large sum of money. Even *Pravda* reported it. There was a reproduction of the picture, in black and white of course. He dripped paint on the canvas." The artist shook his head. "American counter-culture. It is difficult to imagine anything more different from Bolshevik art with its heroic miners and farmers in idyllic landscapes."

"Did you ever paint pictures like that?"

"Never. They tried to make me. I could have had a life of ease painting portraits of Lenin and Stalin from photographs. Every school and every town hall has such pictures."

"Life has improved for you now?"

"You like my dacha?"

"It is large and in good condition."

"I bought it with the proceeds of the sale of two pictures to a Danish businessman not long after the communist state collapsed. I have sold only three other pictures since. I have enough for myself and for Catherine when I am gone. Come, we will look at some pictures." He put down his cup and got to his feet.

For the next two hours Davenport looked at the artist's paintings and drawings. Those that were not hanging in the house were carefully stored in racks and drawers built in a large room opposite the artist's bedroom. Some of the works were very early. Davenport marvelled at the ingenuity that had gone into the paintings and the obscuring of the elegantly inscribed narratives in them. Some of the drawings were no more than a few lines of pencil or charcoal, and, in a few instances, of Conte. He was transfixed by the last of these. The subject was an older version of Olga. It was more detailed than any of the other drawings. Much love and pain had gone into every feature of the sitter.

"You can guess who it is?" Kruffinski asked.

"Olga's mother or grandmother."

"Her mother. She died of tuberculosis. Olga is very like her."

"May I ask what happened to your wife?"

"When I come back from the gulag she had disappeared. They had told her I had died. Much later, I found out that she had moved to Moscow and remarried, a soldier I think. When she went to Moscow she left Olga's mother with a neighbour. I had no wish then to look for my former wife." He emphasised the 'former'. "I will not offer you food. I do not take lunch. Instead, I sleep because I cannot sleep at night. Now, what am I to do with Olga and her dealer friend?"

"I can't advise you about that."

"You are all in a hotel in St Petersburg? What is the number?"

Davenport did not know the number but told him the name of the hotel. "They don't know that I was coming here."

"If I decide to call her, I will not tell her of your visit. I don't have to tell her anything if I don't want to."

"She'll wonder how you found out where she is staying."

"Let her wonder."

For the next hour Kruffinski and Davenport discussed art. Much of their conversation consisted of the artist interrogating him about the last forty or so years of art history in the West. Kruffinski was especially intrigued by Davenport's account of the rumour that the CIA had promoted Jackson Pollock and his colleagues because their work was so far removed from contemporary Russian realism, and was therefore an antidote to it. He laughed at Davenport's story of how, as a gesture of contempt to the art experts, Picasso had made a point of buying a work by Bongo the chimp painted under the supervision of a famous zoologist, Desmond Morris, in the 1950s.

"It does not matter to me what people say about Rothko and me. Unlike him I am not vain. Ah, the vanity of that man. And so many other artists. To draw and paint is the thing, not to be acclaimed."

Davenport would have been content to continue their discussion for days but he could see that the old man was tiring.

"Now, my Australian friend, it is time for you to go. I have enjoyed your visit. I believe that you truly love art."

"I only wish I could make it, but I cannot."

"It is important that there are some who truly appreciate it. You are obviously a man who would respect it and see that it is preserved."

They shook hands. Catherine reappeared and led Davenport to the front door. When he had reached it, he heard the artist's voice. "Your name, what is it again?"

"Davenport Jones."

It was still raining. Davenport had to knock on the driver's window to wake him. "Back to the hotel."

On the return journey, Davenport was preoccupied with what

he had seen and learnt that day. It was rapidly becoming a matter of little or no concern to him whether Olga got the paintings and Londys auctioned them. He reflected on the suffering that the old man had endured, and the indomitable spirit that had inspired him to continue painting and not to bend to the demands of the regime. He did not want the artist to be harassed. He wished that he had asked him his telephone number so that he could warn him if Olga or Rupert had been able to find anything out about him, and when they next intended to drive to the dacha to see him. But then he recalled that the painter had hinted that he and Davenport might speak again. Perhaps he would relent and talk to Olga after all.

16

Rendezvous in St Petersburg

There had been some harsh words said to Gerald at the board meeting. The chairman, a former Minister for the Army, usually so urbane, had positively barked at him. "We're being outgunned every day. What are you going to do about it?"

"Well, there's a good chance we'll get the Kruffinski sale."

"I'm not interested in chance." The chairman had glared at Gerald. The other directors had nodded their assent. "There'll be changes unless you deliver, Gerald."

Gerald had immediately phoned Davenport's mobile after the meeting. It enraged him that not only did the call ring out, but also that Davenport had not activated the message facility. "Find out," he demanded of his secretary, "what flights there are to St Petersburg tomorrow; BA, not Aeroflot."

He remembered then that he had told Gloria that he would ring her the next day. He called Baker's residence. For a time, Barnes the butler, who answered the telephone, pretended that he had no knowledge of Gloria whom he regarded, as he did all other employees of Baker, as a rival. But Gerald was not to be denied.

"Gloria, I may not be able to ring you tomorrow. I think I'll have to go to Russia. I might say that I'm not too pleased with your Davenport. God knows what he's up to there."

"Davenport is a person who needs a great deal of guidance."

"I'll certainly give him that when I get there. I think I know what's in his mind: getting into the pants of that young Russian woman."

There was a pause in the conversation. "Are you still there, Gloria?"

"Yes. What time do you think you'll be leaving?"

"I'm finding out flight times now."

"I wonder whether I might be able to help you. I've got a knack of bringing Davenport to heel when he misbehaves."

"He can't be contacted on his mobile."

"I wasn't thinking of telephoning. I had in mind meeting him face to face."

"In St Petersburg?"

"There's no other way."

"I'm afraid Londys couldn't pay your fare. I could possibly cover your accommodation though, as a consultant's fee." Gerald was rather pleased by the thought of Gloria as a travelling companion.

"The only problem for me is getting the time off. Would it be possible for you to make a booking for me, economy naturally, on your flight? I'll reimburse you, or cancel if I can't get away."

"I don't see why not."

"I'll let you know later how I get on. Goodbye Gerald."

Gloria knocked on the door of Baker's forbidden study. "Yes." The tone was one of irritation. Gloria entered. Before she could say anything, Baker spoke. "I could hardly have made it clearer. My hours between 9:00 am and midday are sacred. They are the hours when I write." He was seated on a reproduction Empire chair with gilded caryatids on the arms, and faux leopard-skin upholstery on the seat. The computer and word processor on his desk would not have looked out of place in the control room of the latest nuclear submarine. There were no paintings on the one wall not covered by bookshelves, only photographs, and none in which Baker did not appear: with Spielberg at Cannes, the Prime Minister at Downing Street, the English centre-forward at Wembley, on stage at a charity concert shaking hands with Jimmy Doolan who was still sweating and holding his electric guitar, and last – enlarged and in colour – of the Queen presenting him with his MBE. He pointed to a ladder chair beside his desk. Gloria sat down on it. "Well, you're here now. What is it?"

"I'm afraid I have to go to Russia tomorrow."

"You! Russia! What are you talking about?"

"I know it's sudden. But it's very important for me. If you tell me not to bother coming back, I'll understand."

"Whereabouts in Russia?"

"St Petersburg."

"A long journey."

"Have you been there?"

"No, but I've always wanted to, to see the Hermitage and the palaces. Is it permitted to ask why?"

"To bail my ex-husband out of trouble."

"Has he been kidnapped by the local mafia or something?"

"No. He was sent there to do a job. He's allowed himself to be, well, distracted. If he doesn't do the job quickly and properly he will be sacked."

"He's your ex-husband, what's it to you?"

"I can't help feeling responsible for him. In many ways he's a hopeless character, always has been. My friends say that I worry too much about everybody I'm close to, or, as with him, have been close to."

"What's he doing in Russia anyway?"

"His job was to track down an old painter, Kruffinski or some name like that, and to get him to do whatever needed to be done to enable Londys to auction whatever of his works Davenport can get his hands on."

"And the distraction?"

"A pert little Russian blonde."

"It's very inconvenient and very short notice. However, as it turns out my wife has just telephoned me to say she is coming home tonight. She may be prepared to forego re-acclimitisation to spend a few days with the girls. If she is prepared to do that tomorrow, I'm inclined, against my better judgment, to say you can go. But for three days only."

"That'll be enough." There was determination in Gloria's voice.

Baker appeared to be in deep thought. Gloria waited for his next pronouncement. "I could go to Russia myself tomorrow. An author must experience the places he writes about."

"Do you intend to set a book in Russia?"

"Inevitably. How could any writer in Europe fail to do that? The enigma of Russia. That's what Churchill called it." Baker said, not quite accurately. "A country in transition, grist to a novelist's mill. Yes, I might join you on your trip." Baker's books had bought him a great deal, including an incurable arrogance. It never occurred to him that his presence might be unwelcome.

Gloria could see no particular way in which she might be able to turn his visit to her advantage, but who knew what might happen. She did not think that he would seriously interfere with her activities, and, it might be that he could turn out to be useful to her even though he clearly wasn't interested in her on any long-, or even medium-term basis. He was just one of those men who regarded any moderately attractive woman who crossed his path as his *droit de seigneur*.

"You're not doing it for me, are you?" Gloria asked and, when she did, implanted in his mind the notion that he was.

"Well, perhaps. Gathering material was only a secondary purpose."

"You needn't, although I appreciate the thought. I am an experienced traveller."

"I've decided." Now he was a man of decision. "If I can get a flight I'm going to St Petersburg."

"When will you know if Mrs Baker can look after the children?"

"I'll try to get her now."

"I've taken up too much of your time, your most valuable time too." Gloria pushed back her chair, marvelling again at Baker's infinite capacity to absorb flattery. "I'll make sure of my booking then, tentative-only at this stage."

"Do that. I'll have Barnes make mine. Please keep him informed."

"Is he coming too?"

"No. He may be required to do some driving here. Damn it. I do like to travel with him. He usually looks after the minor things while I concentrate on the majors."

In the event, Baker travelled to St Petersburg on the same aeroplane as Gerald and Gloria, in seats 1A, 2A and 29C respectively. Baker and Gerald knew each other slightly from the former's forays in the sale room, and occasional other encounters in the circles in which they both moved. They had both gone straight to the first-class lounge and entered the plane by the separate entrance provided for business-class passengers. Neither of them had spoken to Gloria at the airport. They had exchanged a few words with each other in the lounge but Baker had volunteered nothing of his reason for travelling to Russia to Gerald, who, although curious why Gloria's employer would do so, could think of no reason to ask why.

On arrival, Gerald told Gloria that they would be staying at the same hotel as Davenport. Baker, who had hand luggage only and had hurried ahead, was booked into the Grand Hotel. It was almost midday when Gerald and Gloria reached theirs and Davenport's. He had given no notice of his journey to Davenport. Once he had booked in, he had immediately called Davenport's room. He was surprised when his employee answered the phone. "What are you doing at the hotel again? Why aren't you talking to Kruffinski?"

Davenport repeated his account of his visit to the painter with Rupert and Olga. He said nothing of his own trip there the day before. He explained that Rupert and Olga were still trying to obtain information about the painter's condition.

"I'm beginning to wonder," Gerald mused, "whether we shouldn't be going it alone with Kruffinski. That woman you've got the hots for is very argumentative. It wouldn't surprise me if she's completely alienated the old boy."

"But Gerald, you signed a contract with Olga and Rupert."

"Not worth the paper it's written on, full of loopholes."

"What about Londys's reputation?"

"These are hard times, Davenport. I think you're letting your emotions get in the way of Londys's best interests."

"Well, I don't see how you can deal directly with a comatose person." Davenport consoled himself for his lie with the thought that he had not actually said that Kruffinski was comatose.

"I wish I understood Russian law, assuming there is any. You're probably right. At present anyway, we'd better continue to deal with that odd couple. That reminds me, Gloria came over with me on the same flight."

"What! You're here!...She's here! What on earth for?"

"You can ask her yourself. We've both just booked into this hotel."

The astonishment in Davenport's voice was obvious. "We're divorced. We've got nothing to say to each other."

"Not according to her. She still feels responsible for you."

"I don't want Gloria being responsible for me."

"Anyway, enough of your personal affairs. I'm here because I think you need help. What's the next move?"

Despite his dismay that Gerald – and Gloria – were now in St Petersburg, Davenport tried to sound businesslike. "Olga and Rupert are also trying to find out more about the woman who's, as they put it, guarding the old man. I don't think they're going to get much useful information. I think we'll just have to go out to his dacha again. Knowing Olga there'll be a major confrontation between her and the woman."

"I'll go out with you."

"Do you think that's wise. If there are too many people there the woman looking after him will almost certainly be even more obstructive."

"Well, *you* haven't achieved anything have you?"

"With a little more time and patience on your part I might have."

"We haven't got time. Our competitors are at our heels. The

board's on my back. Heaven only knows whether the Russian authorities, another contradiction in terms, will step in to prevent the pictures leaving the country. And then you've got the grandson claiming the lot. And don't forget that the decision of the Spoliation Panel has stirred up the media. It wouldn't surprise me if they didn't urge the Russians to keep the stuff. Look at how the Gypos are performing about the Rosetta Stone. Next they'll want Cleopatra's needle back."

"Do you want me to tell Olga you're here?"

"She's not there with you is she by any chance, Davenport?"

"Of course not. She's out inquiring."

"Naturally she should be told, and Rupert too. There's another thing, Baker, your wife's employer was on our flight."

"I don't know anything about him and I don't want to. Now, what do you want me to do?"

"Make sure there's a car and driver available for me tomorrow, and have dinner with me tonight." As if he was passing on a great state secret, he confided, "We'll go to the Czar's Kitchen. It's very good I'm told, not a place for the ordinary tourist."

"What are you going to do until then?"

"See some of the Hermitage. You don't mind if I take your wife..."

"Ex-wife."

"She'll be joining us for dinner, naturally. Just try to be rational and civil."

Gerald hung up before Davenport could protest. Davenport was about to call Gerald back to tell him that he would not dine with Gloria but he was still in no mood for the long argument he knew would follow. A better idea occurred to him. He rang both Olga's and Rupert's rooms to leave a message that Gerald was in St Petersburg, and that he wanted the three of them to have dinner with him at the Czar's Kitchen at seven thirty. "I'll meet you in the foyer here at seven so we can travel together. I'll arrange a car. By the way, my ex-wife may be there too."

Davenport felt that he had been oppressed ever since he had left

Australia. He was entitled to some relaxation. But first there was an important call that he needed to make. He checked the time. It was almost one o'clock. 1:00 pm was 7:00 pm Australian time. Beverley would be having her evening meal right now – but she might not even be at home. He would wait until two o'clock St Petersburg time. In the meantime, he poured himself a vodka from the refrigerator, added some tonic, and stretched out on the bed. To keep himself awake until two o'clock he turned on the television. The only news was in Russian. There were no programs in English.

Olga and Rupert were in the foyer when Davenport came down. They were impressed by Gerald's invitation to dine at the Czar's Kitchen. Rupert had ironed, not very expertly, his second shirt and had put on a pair of leather shoes. "You don't happen to have a spare tie do you?" he asked Davenport. "Just in case they won't let me in without one; although no doubt the mafia in their leather jackets will be swigging their champagne and devouring caviar at the best tables."

Davenport went back to his room to find Rupert a tie. He chose the brightest that he had with him. Rupert's response, as he tied it, was, "A bit sombre".

While they waited for the car and driver, not Peter this time, because Davenport did not want to risk any indiscretions by him, he asked Olga whether they had found out anything more.

"Nothing," Rupert answered for her. "We've tried other dealers, and the lawyer we saw was of no use. No one knows anything. Tomorrow we'll go back to the dacha and camp on the doorstep until the doctor comes, or until that woman tells us what's wrong with him, and who his attorney or lawyer is. I don't know whether there's such a thing as an enduring power of attorney in this country." He explained to Olga that in the United Kingdom, an old or infirm person concerned that he might soon become incompetent, could appoint an attorney to attend to all of his affairs if that eventuality occurred.

Davenport suggested that Rupert and Olga go ahead. It had

begun to rain. Surprisingly, they agreed to take a cab.

"Just remember," Davenport said, as they got into it, "that Gerald is bringing that woman with him. Our parting was not amicable."

Olga who had either not received or had forgotten Davenport's message heard only that Gerald might be bringing a woman with him. "He only arrive today and already he picked up by prostitute?" Olga said.

"They're like bees around a honey pot in front of the hotels," Rupert who also had forgotten what Davenport had told him, said.

"It's my ex-wife, actually."

"Sorry old boy, I'd forgotten." In puzzlement, Rupert asked, "But what is she doing here, and why with Gerald?"

"You'll have to ask them," Davenport replied. He had decided that the only way to approach the evening was fatalistically. He decided at the last moment that he would leave Gerald a message and travel with Olga and Rupert.

When Gloria arrived with Gerald she looked different from the way she had looked when she and Davenport had last met a few days ago. The difference was in her expression, now neither aggressive nor discontented. For a moment Davenport was reminded of the young, vibrant woman he had courted and married. He was not, however, deluded. This was not a woman with whom he wished to have any further connection.

Gerald looked dismayed when he noticed Olga and Rupert. He demanded in a stage whisper, "What are they doing here?"

"I had to bring them. We're staying at the same hotel, and, in case you've forgotten, we're all engaged in a joint venture."

Rupert treated the exchange, of which he had heard every word, as being beneath him. "Evening Gerald," he said. No one had yet spoken to Gloria. Davenport moved too late to avoid her kiss on his cheek. She barely nodded at Olga and Rupert.

"I haven't booked a table for five," Gerald grumbled. At this early hour for fashionable Russians, dozens of empty tables, like an archipelago of starched white islands greeted them in the dining room.

"Russians late eaters," Olga said.

The head waiter gave them a choice of four tables. Gloria moved quietly to seat herself between Gerald and Davenport. "Jeremy Baker came over on the same flight." She said brightly.

"I've worked out what he's after," Gerald said, "a few cheap Kruffinskis."

"Aren't we all?" Davenport said.

Gloria turned earnestly to Davenport. "Isn't it marvellous, to think that here we are, together again after so long, in Russia of all places. We have so much to tell each other."

The acrimony of their parting still stung Davenport. "I don't want to be rude, Gloria, but I've got nothing to say to you and there's nothing that you can tell me that would be of any interest to me."

"Please don't be like that," she said. What had been a possible target had now become a firm objective. Davenport had his faults but nonetheless he always seemed to be able to snatch success from impending failure. Nor had he let himself go to seed. Success had not turned his head. He remained quietly spoken, modest and well-mannered. Someone was teaching him how to dress properly, probably that accountant woman, she decided. How short-sighted she had been, taking off to India with that parasitic weakling, and worse, careless in wasting so much of her own money on him. Gerald, she there and then decided, could never be a serious prospect, although he was magnetically rich. Like so many Englishmen of his class, he had spent too long at his boarding school, and at Cambridge which was little more than a licensed version of his school. He had been a bachelor too long. He was too settled in his ways. Gloria finally resolved that, with all of his faults, she wanted Davenport back.

By now, however, he had turned his attention to Olga on his right, and was making animated conversation with her.

Rupert was at the same time studying the wine list. "Fiendishly expensive, any drinkable imported wine," he noted. "But you can't drink the local stuff. Georgian mainly. They say they put all sorts of chemicals in it, anti-coolants, anti-rust, colouring, God knows what else. Worse than the Italians. I'll have a glass of the Montrachet. You

The Russian Master

too, Olga? Well, we'd better get a bottle then," he advised Gerald when Olga said yes.

In bad grace Gerald ordered the wine and proposed that they all have the set menu. "To save time," He disingenuously suggested.

"Can't old boy," Rupert said. The main course is probably cooked with oyster sauce. I'm allergic to oysters."

When they had ordered, Rupert electing to have a starter, soup, a salad, a main course and three varieties of vegetables, and adding that he was looking forward to seeing the pudding menu, Gerald inquired whether he and Olga had achieved anything at all since they had arrived.

"We've located the old man," Rupert said.

"A lot of good that's done. He's comatose."

"A bit sleepy perhaps. We've only got his keeper's word for it that he's comatose. What do you think Olga?"

"I think she drugged him."

Davenport thought that he should make a contribution, "For what it's worth, I suspect that he's not comatose all the time."

"Some sort of sleeping sickness perhaps. I read a most interesting article about that some years ago. It affected a tribe somewhere, Africa or New Guinea I think. I know it was a tropical illness; wouldn't expect to see it here," Rupert said.

"Would you please keep your mind on here and now," Gerald said. "We haven't got unlimited time, or money," he added, as Rupert signalled the waiter to bring another bottle of Montrachet.

"No, I wasn't thinking of a particular illness. He's a very old man. My grandfather had trouble sleeping when he was very old, but when he did sleep it was for a long time, and deeply," Davenport offered.

"That woman in pay of Oleg," Olga said. "She drug grandfather for him."

"There's no evidence of that," Davenport risked Olga's wrath.

"Evidence, bah. You sound like English judge, that judge who interrupted me."

"Well, that's my opinion," Davenport offered.

The arrival of food at the table brought a lull in the conversation.

After Gerald had eaten his course; he resumed.

"I'm right aren't I, we're no closer to getting the pictures now than when we were in London. And what about Oleg? Where's he?"

Olga answered, "No one here in St Petersburg know. I ask dealers and lawyer about him. I even go to newspapers, Russian, and English language one to ask if journalists know anything about him."

"That was my idea," Rupert putting his glass down for a moment, boasted. "Both of them carried brief stories about the Spoliation Panel's proceedings this morning. I thought they might have tried to interview him."

"He's probably still in England, and with all of the paintings. I'm going to have to give you an ultimatum. Either we get the pictures, or a pretty clear indication that we can get them within the next seventy two hours or our arrangement is at an end."

"I don't remember that in the contract," Rupert said.

"I'm not going to get into a legal argument with you here. That's my last word on the matter," Gerald sensed a presence behind him. He turned around. It was Baker.

"May I join you?" Before Gerald could demur, Baker, the experienced table hopper, beckoned to a waiter to draw up a chair. "Just for a drink. I rarely eat dinner."

"We're having a business discussion," Gerald said.

Baker sat down. "Don't worry about me, I'm not in the art business, just a collector."

"These are confidential matters," Gerald insisted.

"I can guess why you're here. No, Mrs Jones didn't tell me. I read about Kruffinski and the Spoliation Panel's investigation. That's the real reason why you're in St Petersburg."

Gerald looked reproachfully at Gloria.

"I told you, she said nothing," Baker defended her. "You forget, I'm an accomplished novelist. I've got imagination and the ability to reason, to put clues together. Go on, deny that you're in St Petersburg to get your hands on the Kruffinskis."

Gerald pulled out his chair. "I've had enough. I'm going back to the hotel. Davenport, have a car and driver at nine o'clock in the morning. I'm sorry Gloria. You stay if you want to."

Gloria did not know whether to stay or go. It was difficult to regard Gerald's words and swift departure from the table without looking back, as any form of invitation, even if she were minded to accept one. If, however, she stayed and flirted with Baker, perhaps Davenport might become jealous.

"What upset him?" Rupert asked. He looked at Baker. "We were discussing business but nothing very confidential. I suppose he thought you might use it in a novel. Talking to a novelist is like talking to a psychiatrist. They're both weighing you up all the time. Anyway, now he's gone there's no need to be stingy with the wine. If you can catch the waiter's eye ask him to bring the wine list over again will you, Davenport?" Rupert was not in the slightest disconcerted by Gerald's departure. Steadily and determinedly, he ate his way through the rest of the menu and added a generous tip to the bill before passing it to Davenport for payment as if it were a hand grenade with a defective pin.

"Quite a coincidence, you and Gerald getting together," Rupert observed to Gloria. His assumption that she and Gerald were sleeping together capped off a bad evening for Gloria. She had attempted to flirt with Baker for a time, but he was too intent on trying to find out about Kruffinski to respond, and had left after about half an hour. Davenport had pointedly, almost completely ignored her, speaking to her only when he could not avoid it. Rupert, insensitive to the frosty distance between the former husband and wife, his mouth usually full of food or wine, had conversed freely and unconcernedly.

Davenport could feel a headache coming on but Rupert would not hurry as he called for a last cognac. Gloria decided to keep her options open for tomorrow. She stood up, and between gritted teeth said goodnight to Rupert and Olga, even adding that it was nice to meet some of Davenport's London friends. Then she turned to Davenport, her eyes full. "Davenport," she said, "I came so far just to see you. Perhaps tomorrow..." She broke off and hurried from the dining room.

"Did you say something to upset her?" Rupert asked Davenport.

When Davenport shook his head, Rupert said, "It must have been you, Olga. Misunderstandings are always on the cards between people without a common language."

That remark led to an enthusiastic disagreement about the quality of Olga's English that continued in the cab and into the foyer of their hotel. It only ended when Rupert asked Davenport whether he had made any arrangements for their return tomorrow to the artist's dacha.

"You heard what Gerald said. He wants me to go with him."

"He didn't actually say that we couldn't go with you."

"I don't think he had that in mind."

"Well, he can't stop a man's granddaughter visiting her grandfather, and we do have our deal. Anyway, Londys needs us."

"That's not how Gerald is thinking now. You heard him. I think he wants to make his own reconnaissance."

"Well, Olga and I are going there tomorrow, no matter what. We'll no doubt meet there. By the way, what did you think of that Baker fellow? Odd person for your ex-wife to be knocking around with."

Old habits die hard. Davenport tried to defend her. "She's working for him, I understand."

Olga had been silent during this conversation, and all that she said as she stepped into the lift ahead of both of the men was, "We get our own car tomorrow, Rupert."

In his room, on the phone, Davenport arranged for a car and driver, English speaking but not Peter, for the next morning.

He also had two messages left for him. The first was to call the Australian number that he had rung earlier in the day. The second was to call an unfamiliar local number. He rang the Australian number first and, despite it being the early hours of the morning there, had a brief but satisfactory conversation with Beverley.

And even though it was late, Davenport decided to also ring the local number. In some puzzlement he dialled it. A woman's voice that he thought he recognised, answered in Russian.

"My name is Davenport Jones. I have a message to call this

The Russian Master

number."

The woman said something which Davenport took to be, "Hold on."

He waited. Kruffinski came on to the line. "Mr Jones. You have been out?"

"To dinner, with my boss and some others."

"Your boss is in St Petersburg?"

"Yes."

"Are you prepared to tell me why, and whether Olga and that dealer intend to come back here?"

"Yes I am. My boss thinks that I have not done enough to get hold of your work. He thinks he can do better. He and Olga and Rupert are going out to your place again tomorrow. I will be travelling with my boss. My former wife may also come."

"Your former wife, is she a dealer?"

"Not in art. It's a long story. She has no genuine interest in art."

"What do they hope to do?"

"Bully you or your housekeeper, or whoever else has access to your collection, to have you part with it."

"You are an honest man, Mr Jones. I wonder why you stay with those people? To be near my granddaughter perhaps?"

Davenport ignored the question and told the artist about his earlier phone calls to Australia.

"You will definitely come tomorrow?"

"Yes, once more."

"Good. By then I will have come out of my coma. I look forward to talking to these people. Please confirm your room number."

Davenport, in puzzlement, did as he was asked, and then went to bed. The sleep that he slept was, at last, a contented one.

17

The Rivals Meet

Davenport, as did Gerald, steered clear of the dining room the next morning. They went straight to the car which was already in front of the hotel. It was a disappointment, but not a big surprise for Davenport, to find Gloria close on the heels of Gerald.

"Gerald, I don't really think it's sensible for too many of us to descend on the old man."

"What do you mean too many?"

"Well," Davenport looked at Gloria but decided to take the plunge. "Gloria doesn't have any interest in what we are doing."

Gloria pouted, "Davenport, you know I'm always interested in what you're doing."

Davenport ignored this flagrant piece of hypocrisy and appealed to Gerald.

"What's it matter? I thought you told us the man was comatose. He wouldn't know who was there?"

"His housekeeper, whom we ought not to offend, will though."

"Davenport, that's another of your weaknesses. You lose sight of the big picture. Nobody's concerned with what she thinks."

"I think she might have been more than a housekeeper once."

"We're wasting time. The granddaughter and Rupert are probably there by now." Gesturing for Gloria to follow, Gerald ended the

The Russian Master

discussion by getting into the car. Outside, once again, Davenport manoeuvred, this time unsuccessfully, to occupy the front seat. Before getting into the back, he protested that he might need to navigate.

"Do it from the back. I get travel nausea if I don't sit in the front," Gerald said. "I hope you've got a driver who knows where we're going."

Davenport sat as far from Gloria as he could. Her face wore the same expression of deep but regretful offence as he had seen so often in Australia. After a few minutes he thought he saw out of the corner of his eye, her hand, her nails still carefully manicured, slowly creeping along the space between them towards him. He folded his arms tightly, hunched further into the upholstery, and stared straight ahead.

After a time the silence was broken by the driver. "I think we are being followed."

They all turned. There was in fact a large, black car with dark glass windows close behind them. It was impossible to see who the occupants were. The driver accelerated.

"What are you doing?" Gerald asked.

"Don't like being tailgated," the driver, proud of his command of American, answered.

Gloria said she was frightened. She looked beseechingly at Davenport.

Davenport looked out the rear window. The black car was keeping up with them. He turned back and could see beads of perspiration on the back of their driver's neck. Suddenly the driver swung the car into a side street, almost colliding with a smoke-belching truck labouring towards them. The black car, waiting only for the passage of the truck, followed.

Gloria remained concerned. "Is it the local mafia?" she asked. "They kidnap people, don't they? It must be you, Gerald. They'll take you, and us with you, and demand a ransom from Londys."

Davenport was unable to resist observing, "From what you've been telling me, Gerald, I don't think the board's likely to come to

The Rivals Meet

the party."

"That's in very poor taste. Can't you go faster?" Gerald inquired of the driver.

Gloria had now thrown herself against Davenport. There was nothing he could do to escape her. For half a second, her once familiar contours reminded him of brief, rare, and happier times. But these were soon displaced by the bitter memories of how she had treated him. He sat up as straight as he could and told the driver, "There's no point in killing ourselves. They haven't tried to drive in front of us or anything. Just drive normally. It can't be far now." Davenport sounded calmer than he felt.

The driver slowed down. The black car stayed behind them, closely following them along the rough track to the dacha. When their car stopped on the drive in front of it, the black car also stopped.

The driver of the black car threw open his door and opened the rear door as Gerald and Gloria cowered below the window of their vehicle, and Davenport tried to sink further into the corner.

Baker slowly alighted from the black car and looked around. Seeing who it was, Gerald opened his door and ran over to the author. "What the hell do you think you're doing?" he shouted.

"Visiting a distinguished Russian artist. It's now a free, well, almost a free country isn't it?"

"If you think you're going to get a painting on the cheap then you're very much mistaken. Following us! You wouldn't have an original thought. I bet your novels are the same."

"Three hundred thousand readers of translated versions, and nine hundred thousand in English last year seem to think differently," the author imperturbably said. He surveyed the dacha. "Not bad for Russia, although the road needs grading." He began to walk towards the front door.

"Hold on," Gerald shouted. "Davenport, where are you, come on." He overtook Baker as they both moved towards the door.

"Gerald, don't you think we should look out for, wait for that is, Olga?" Davenport called as he stepped out of the car.

"To the contrary," Gerald – Baker standing beside him – knocked

The Russian Master

on the door.

This time it was not opened immediately. Davenport had time to reach the verandah, Gloria trailing behind him, before it did. Kruffinski himself, freshly shaved, his hair neatly done, and wearing an old but well-cut corduroy coat, stood on the threshold. Gerald realised that the old man could only be the artist himself. "But you're, you're supposed to be in a coma," he stuttered.

"I'm a heavy sleeper," the artist said, leaving Gerald speechless.

"Let me introduce myself," Baker pressed forward. "I'm Jeremy Baker, a connoisseur and a great admirer of your work."

"And where have you seen my work?"

"In the Tate, or, no, the Museum of Modern Art, New York."

"You must be confusing me with someone else. There is nothing of mine there."

"Well, I've definitely seen it somewhere."

"Forgeries I would think. I'm surprised that a man of your discrimination wouldn't recognise a forgery. Who are *you*?" he asked Gerald.

Gerald handed him his engraved calling card. "I'm the managing director of Londys, London. This is Davenport Jones and...and Mrs Jones who's assisting us." Kruffinski included Davenport in his suspicious appraisal.

"Londys London. It is not difficult to know why you are here. You want me to hand over my paintings for you to sell so that they can hang in fashionable Fifth Avenue apartments and on the walls of Japanese industrialists' houses."

"I wouldn't put it quite like that," Gerald said.

Baker interrupted. "I've a home in the country, in the Cotswolds actually. A couple of your works would be perfect for it. Not like those Americans or Japanese. They're trophy collectors, not art lovers. Where I am, your paintings would really be appreciated."

"You think so, Mr..." Kruffinski had forgotten his name.

They were still standing at the front door when Olga's and Rupert's car arrived.

"My granddaughter has come to see me. She was apparently here before, not long ago, with two men I was told. I was asleep at the time."

"I was one of them," Davenport said.

Again the artist gave no hint of recognition of Davenport as Olga and Rupert walked across to the verandah. "So, you have come to see your old grandfather. How lucky I am to have two caring grandchildren. And your name sir?" He asked Rupert. Rupert told him and explained that Olga worked for him and that he was cooperating with Londys.

"A dealer in partnership with an auctioneer. It is not an unusual thing but is it not usually a secret kept from the public?" Kruffinski innocently asked. "But I am being rude. Come in, all of you." He walked slowly down the hall to the studio in which he and Davenport had talked on Davenport's visit. This time, however, the chair that Davenport had occupied was turned towards the door and Oleg was seated in it. But even more distracting were the eight large canvases leaning against the walls. They were signature works of the artist, the morning light from the great eastern window revealing the subtleties and the complexities of the Russian master's work. Later, Davenport wondered whether he had placed them there to torment them.

"What have you done to grandfather?" Olga shouted as soon as she saw Oleg.

Oleg jumped up at the same time and yelled a long reply in Russian.

"Children, children, we have visitors. Speak in English please."

"Do not trust him grandfather. He is liar and thief."

"And you, why are you here? To steal all of your grandfather's work of course," Oleg responded.

Kruffinski addressed his words to Davenport. "For decades I painted in secret. I could not sell my work in Russia. It was not well known in the West: there may be a few pieces in the Baltic States, Sweden perhaps, in Madrid, four in Paris and one in England. I know of no others. And then, suddenly, everyone wants my work to go west."

"I am a fellow artist, an author, a novelist. I understand how you feel," Baker said.

"A novelist, the English Tolstoy perhaps?"

"Not quite, but my works are very popular. They sell worldwide, like your paintings will when they're on the market. I've been translated into Russian. You Russians aren't too reliable about royalties though."

"I apologise for Russia," the old man's attention focused on his grandchildren.

Davenport sensed that Kruffinski was enjoying himself.

"Now, Oleg and Olga, you should be friends with each other. Instead you make an old man sad by fighting, squabbling like old hens on a midden. Surely it cannot be that you are more interested in what you can get out of your grandfather than coming to see him to lighten his old age."

"It is you I really wanted to see," Olga protested.

"Have I not visited you much more than she has?" Oleg asked.

"No more arguing. Mr de Pyne has, I think, a business proposition to put to me."

Rupert intervened. "He has a contract with Olga and me. We are the ones to put the proposition."

"Look, before you do that," Baker said, "Could I suggest, Mr Kruffinski, that you give me the opportunity of buying two or three of your works. I'd be happy to take any of these off your hands. There would be certain advantages in selling to me."

"And what would they be?"

"No commission for starters. That's a two way saving you know. Because the auctioneers charge a buyer's commission as well as a seller's; buyers know they're going to have to pay seventeen and a half percent more than the hammer price, and lower their bids accordingly. You'd save thirty-five percent by selling to me, and that's not all. I've bought from all of the big auction houses in London. I know them all. I could start off a bidding war between them to reduce their seller's commission to you. There's more. The gossip columnists would write about what I'd bought. That would be priceless publicity for your work."

"You are a connoisseur, and yet an altruist as well as a famous novelist." Kruffinski said.

Baker was impervious to irony – and sarcasm, "I have given quite a lot to charity."

Gerald was losing his self-control. "You surely wouldn't deal with a man like Jeremy Baker. You're a great artist. He writes pot-boilers, and now he's trying to be an art entrepreneur. You can't go past us. We've put a lot of money into tracking you down and coming here. Londys is the most reputable art auctioneer in the world."

Barely audibly, Davenport whispered to the old man. "That is to say very little."

"Perhaps you could advise me, Mr Jones," Kruffinski said.

"I would be very careful about dealing with anyone in this room."

"How dare you, Davenport," Gerald expostulated.

"You traitor," Olga lamented.

Davenport well understood that Kruffinski intended to entertain himself by provoking and tantalizing each of the suitors for his work for as long as it amused him to do so. He winked at the old man and apologised fulsomely to Gerald, Rupert, and Olga. "I don't know what came over me. If you don't mind I'll just get a little air." He hurried to the hall and quickly walked along to the front door and out to Olga's and Rupert's driver who was standing beside his car smoking a vile smelling Russian cigarette.

"Driver, I'm not well. It's agreed you are to take me back to the hotel and return for the others." Davenport got into the back seat and subsided deep into its upholstery. "Just be careful, and quiet, driving away. I don't want any noise or jolting," he said. "When we're back on the main road go very fast though, because I may need to see a doctor urgently."

When Davenport reached the hotel there were three cardboard cylinders in his room and a letter in an envelope addressed to him. He read the letter and then examined the contents of the cylinders. The largest of them just fitted lengthwise and the others comfortably into his suitcase. He called the manager with whom by now he was on good terms. "I need to get back to London urgently. Can you tell me when the next flight to the UK leaves?"

He replied that if Davenport held on, he would check the timetables. "There is no BA flight until seven o'clock tonight. There is a Finnair flight to Helsinki leaving at five with a connection to London an hour after it reaches there."

"Nothing earlier?" Davenport asked.

Experience had taught the manager that most non-Russians were unwilling to fly on Aeroflot. "Just Aeroflot in two hours."

"Please get me a seat on that. And get me a car and driver immediately. See if Peter is available. And please have my bill made up."

Davenport packed in ten minutes, making sure that the cylinders were carefully padded by clothing. He hurried downstairs, tipped the manager generously, and paid his bill with his personal credit card. Peter was waiting in front of the hotel. He told him to go as quickly as he could to the airport.

At the Aeroflot ticketing desk he inquired of the clerk whether he was able to check upon flights from London to Australia that evening. "We are agents," the woman said, "for Constellation Airlines. I believe they fly to Australia as well as many Asian ports."

"Would you check? I would like to go as soon as possible."

The woman made a telephone call. She held the receiver. "There is a flight out of London to Sydney via Bangkok leaving at eleven o'clock tonight."

"Please book me a seat on it and find out whether I can pay here and can you ticket me all the way through."

She checked and confirmed that it all could be done as he wanted. Again, Davenport paid on his personal credit card. All that he had to do was check his suitcase through, to Australia, and clear customs and immigration. He watched anxiously as the suitcase was X-rayed. The attendants and the customs officers, who were smoking and animatedly discussing the football, paid no attention to it as it tumbled off the counter at the end of the X-ray machine.

Seven hours later, for the first time since he had walked out of

The Rivals Meet

Kruffinski's dacha, Davenport stopped feeling like a fugitive. The truth was, that apart from not giving Gerald notice, he had done nothing very discreditable. Perhaps he may have disappointed some people, Elena for instance. Still, she would now have an excellent flat of her own in London, nicely furnished with the sorts of pieces she liked. She might not be too keen on packing up and sending his personal items and clothing on, but he could live without them if he had to. As for Gloria, well, frankly, as Clark Gable said at the end of 'Gone with the Wind', he couldn't give a damn. Olga now; he did have more than a regret there, but he was accustomed to mixed fortunes in love. He felt a little sorry for Rupert. He rather hoped that the man might salvage something out of it all.

He looked out of the window. There were only a few faint lights below as the aircraft approached the French Alps on its way to Bangkok. He caught the eye of a steward and asked if he could have a glass of champagne. After it arrived, he took the envelope from his pocket and spread the enclosed letter on the tray in front of him. He sipped the champagne as he re-read the writing of the assured calligraphic hand that had penned it.

> To my recent, but good Australian friend Davenport Jones,
>
> As soon as you told me of my granddaughter's and her and your employer's intention to come to my dacha tomorrow, and of your own plans, I decided that I would entrust you with the three pictures that I will have couriered to you tomorrow with this letter. The courier is my neighbour, a reliable man, but I would like you to write to me to tell me that you have received them.
>
> Do not worry about Olga. Eventually she will settle down with a Russian. With her it could not be otherwise. In the meantime, she will break some hearts and cause many arguments, I make allowances for both Oleg and her. Russia was an unhappy, grey place when they were children. They both hardly knew their parents. I will make proper provision for them when they have learnt to be less grasping, or, if that does not happen very soon, when I die, which cannot be too far off. I hope I still have time to teach them some lessons.
>
> The idea that I would disperse my work by auction in London is preposterous. I will send some selected pieces to museums and

The Russian Master

people I respect – you are the first. The bulk of my work I will leave to mother Russia, with all her faults.

I selected you because you were refreshingly frank for someone from the world of art dealing, and because I saw that you were a true art lover, and sincere. This was confirmed by your decision to return to the Antipodean Museum where you worked as a curator before you were seduced by the art trade. I understood from what you told me that you have good relations with the director, Beverly Leer, who was a senior curator herself before she was promoted. She certainly seems to have made a swift decision to re-employ you after you telephoned her from your hotel. I think somehow you are better fitted for research and curatorship than business. Your Beverly will be even more pleased to see you when you tell her what you have brought.

I am giving you three of my works. The largest, painted in the early days of Perestroika, was an optimistic work, full of colour and enthusiasm. You will see that the drawing is more proud than it is in earlier work, and the overpainting lighter. I used a special glaze to create more light. I trust you to present this to your Antipodean Museum. But you may present it as your gift. I have read that in the West, gifts of this kind can be offset against personal income tax. If curators are paid as little in Australia as Russia, you might never have to pay income tax again.

The smaller oil is for you personally. I painted it in 1952, in secret. It is a hard, uncompromising picture. Every brush stroke was made with the finest sable brush I could find. I went without food and wine to buy that brush. I had my own visions of Hell at the time. Hell was all around us. It is a typical work of my best period.

The third is a charcoal likeness of you on paper. It is the only sort of work I do these days; quick, and I hope, a spontaneous likeness. I did it from memory.

To avoid doubts and any disputes, I have inscribed each work with my signature and a date, repeated on the back with the words, 'This is my gift to my Australian friend Davenport Jones'.

I know of no law yet that says that living artists' work may not be exported. But who knows what the law in this country is anyway? I recommend that you pack the tubes holding the pictures in your suitcase and not declare them. If you do, a venal customs officer will

The Rivals Meet

assume them to be valuable and steal them, or extort every dollar you have.

Perhaps you will become an expert on me, as you did with Divera, and write a learned monograph about the old man of St Petersburg. I am sure that you will be very famous again, anyway, when you present 'Perestroika' to the Antipodean Museum.

Travel well and safely my friend. We will not meet again but I would hope that you will always remember me with good thoughts.

The letter was signed in English and Cyrillic. Davenport refolded it and restored it to the envelope which he put in his pocket. He gave his empty glass to the steward, turned off his reading light and composed himself for sleep.

THE END